"Are you sure this is what you want?" Lynn asked quietly.

"No, I'm not," Ward said. "But if it's the only way I can get out of this . . . this prison . . . then I'll take it. I just hope we don't kill each other in the process."

"That will be entirely up to you, Commander." She pursed her lips and looked down at him. "I should warn you, if you don't behave, I'll bring you right back here to the hospital."

"Then you'll be bringing back a dead body."

"That," Lynn said carefully, "is something I'll be sure to consider."

She felt a small stab of satisfaction when she saw his start of surprise. She had no illusions about the situation. But one thing was clear. He'd been right when he said she owed him.

She'd made him a promise. Whatever it took, she would be there for him—and she could only hope they would both survive the experience.

Dear Reader,

When two people fall in love, the world is suddenly new and exciting, and it's that same excitement we bring to you in Silhouette Intimate Moments. These are stories with scope and grandeur. The characters lead lives we all dream of, and everything they do reflects the wonder of being in love.

Longer and more sensuous than most romances, Silhouette Intimate Moments novels take you away from everyday life and let you share the magic of love. Adventure, glamour, drama, even suspense—these are the passwords that let you into a world where love has a power beyond the ordinary, where the best authors in the field today create stories of love and commitment that will stay with you always.

In coming months, look for novels by your favorite authors: Kathleen Eagle, Marilyn Pappano, Emilie Richards, Kathleen Korbel and Justine Davis, to name only a few. And whenever—and wherever—you buy books, look for all the Silhouette Intimate Moments, love stories with that extra something, books written especially for you by today's top authors.

Leslie J. Wainger
Senior Editor and Editorial Coordinator

DOREEN ROBERTS

Broken Wings

SILHOUETTE·INTIMATE·MOMENTS®

Published by Silhouette Books New York

America's Publisher of Contemporary Romance

SILHOUETTE BOOKS
300 East 42nd St., New York, N.Y. 10017

BROKEN WINGS

Copyright © 1992 by Doreen Roberts

ISBN: 0-373-07422-0

First Silhouette Books printing March 1992

Printed in the U.S.A.

Books by Doreen Roberts

Silhouette Intimate Moments

Gambler's Gold #215
Willing Accomplice #239
Forbidden Jade #266
Threat of Exposure #295
Desert Heat #319
In the Line of Duty #379
Broken Wings #422

Silhouette Romance

Home for the Holidays #765

DOREEN ROBERTS

was hooked from the moment she read the first page of a Mary Stewart novel. It took her twenty years to write her own romantic suspense novel, which was subsequently published, much to her surprise. She and her husband left their native England more than twenty years ago and have since lived in Oregon, where their son was born. Doreen hopes to go on mixing romance and danger in her novels for at least another two decades.

This book is dedicated to Commander Charles T. Ryan, United States Navy pilot and former trainer of the Blue Angels Flight Demonstration Squadron. My deepest thanks for the inspiration and advice for this story, and especially for the information penned at thirty-seven thousand feet, somewhere over the Pacific.

Chapter 1

"Angels...left echelon...now." Commander Edward Sullivan of the United States Navy, leader of the Flight Demonstration Squadron, issued the order into the radio of his F-18 in the calm, efficient tone that was essential for the safety of the team.

Each member of the elite group known as the Blue Angels had been handpicked. Ward knew that every man's concentration was as acute as his own. It had to be, if they were to execute the maneuvers with no more than thirty-six inches separating each plane.

"Angels...diamond left...now." With thirty-two thousand pounds of thrust from the turbofan engines, one second of error meant a move off center by one-eighth of a mile, bringing certain disaster. It was an awesome responsibility, and one Ward never took lightly. His concentration was razor sharp, consuming his entire mind.

He narrowed his eyes while each jet edged into position. Satisfied, he gave the order, and the four jets swooped low

over the Oregon countryside, then soared back up into the
face of the sun. Mentally visualizing the next sequence,
Ward rounded out the orders to complete this one. One step
ahead. It was where he had to be—always one step ahead.
The second he started acting automatically, the danger increased a thousandfold.

It was an exercise in total control of every atom of his
mind and body. And he'd spent many hard years learning
how to accomplish that. Ward issued the next order and put
the jet into a slow roll, counting off the seconds in his head.

Far below the Blue Angels, heat shimmered off the runway as Lynn Barclay squinted behind her sunglasses and
tried to calm the ripples of apprehension invading her
stomach.

Seconds ago she'd watched the six pilots march down the
flight line toward the waiting aircraft. At least two of the
pilots had dark hair, but they had been too far away for her
to distinguish their features. It was unlikely that she'd recognize Ward Sullivan right away, she told herself. It had
been a long time.

It was even more unlikely that he'd remember her. She
hoped he wouldn't. The memory of that terrible summer
would be better left buried in the past.

She'd given her professional name when she'd made the
appointment for the interview. She'd been afraid Ward
might be reluctant to talk to her if he recognized the name
she'd taken back after her divorce. The name he'd known
her by all those years ago.

Lynn winced as two of the aircraft hurtled toward each
other, seemingly destined for a head-on collision, before
flashing safely past. She wasn't sure how she felt about seeing Ward again. If he recognized her, it was likely to be
awkward for both of them.

She heard the murmur of excitement from the crowd as the dark blue Hornets soared in the sky. The two solo planes began a series of rolls that drew cries and applause from the thousands of people watching from below.

Hemmed in on either side by the enthusiastic crowd, Lynn hardly noticed the antics of the solo planes. She kept her eyes glued on the lead jet in the diamond formation.

It had been eighteen years since she'd last seen Ward Sullivan. She found it difficult to imagine him up there, in control of a fighter jet screaming through the sky. The planes on either side of him looked close enough for him to reach out and touch. It was an incredible display of teamwork, coordination and control.

The Ward she knew had never been in control. He'd been a rebellious loner, constantly frustrated and angry at the world. In spite of that, she'd always admired him. No, she amended silently, it was more than that. As an awkward, spindly twelve-year-old, she'd adored him.

He'd been her hero—a breathtaking, awesome god, giving her a glimpse of a grown-up world full of promises and excitement, filling her with a longing to be part of it—until the unforgettable day that idyllic future she'd believed in had been shattered, never to be the same again.

Lynn shaded her eyes, her breath catching as she watched the four jets streaking straight up, looking as if they were joined together in one inseparable unit. Together they reached the top of the loop, and the sun glinted off their wings, turning them to gold as they swung over in a long, lazy arc. It seemed as if they hung there for a heart-stopping second or two before hurtling back to earth within a hair's breadth of touching each other.

All four planes completed the graceful maneuver, and Lynn felt a sense of awe as she watched the sun illuminate the bright yellow markings painted on the jets. Ward Sullivan had come a long way. She wondered if his dark good looks had changed.

His eyes, at least, would still be the same silvery gray. She could still remember the shiver that she, a shy schoolgirl at the time, had felt every time those eyes had rested on her face. And the dreadful ache of longing she hadn't understood when she'd wished he would look at her the way he'd looked at Sarah.

The pain of nostalgia knifed through her, and she closed her eyes in a brief reaction, opening them again as a roar from the crowd signaled the end of the demonstration.

The planes glided in one behind the other, touching down as lightly as a leaf floating to the ground. The excited spectators surged forward, anxious for a closer glimpse of the daring young men who had flirted successfully with death.

Inside the lead jet, Ward issued the final order. "Angels...canopies...now." He listened as the wingmen called off the numbers, then removed his helmet. He sat for several seconds in his seat, letting the tension seep out of his body.

This was the toughest part—coming back to earth. Up there, with nothing but air between him and the rest of the world, his body and soul soared, free and at peace. Up there he held his life literally in his hands—the ultimate control.

He seemed to lose that control on the ground. His dark moments would return to haunt him, tormenting his soul with the endless guilt that never went away. Here he fought his hardest battles, facing the challenge of making something of his life in spite of the scars that had never healed— the scars of his mind and his heart.

At times he felt as if he were in a vacuum that he couldn't escape, an evil presence that would one day overpower and destroy him. He wrestled with the foreboding, trying to erase it as he touched the control panel to release the canopy.

Tumultuous cheers from the crowd greeted him when he climbed out of the cockpit and dropped lightly to the ground. He acknowledged them with a brief salute and waited for his men to join him before marching back to the clubhouse.

Lynn edged her way through the crowd in the opposite direction. She didn't want to see him now. Not until she had to face him in the bar at the Royal King, where she'd arranged to meet him—she glanced at her watch—in less than three hours.

She wanted to be sitting there when he walked in, she decided. She wanted time to look at him, time to prepare herself before he saw her.

Would he recognize her right away? she wondered. If so, would he turn around and leave, or had he matured enough to face her and try to ignore the past?

She still wrestled with that question when she pushed through the swinging doors of the bar that evening. She found a seat at a corner table by the window and ordered a wine cooler. From there she would be able to see everyone entering the bar.

Staring out of the window, she paid no attention to the myriad of boats vying for space on the river across from the hotel. She was twelve years old again and was seeing Ward as he'd looked that last time. Just before he'd twisted on his heel and marched away from her, leaving her heart in shattered pieces.

He'd been eighteen years old then. Tall, breathtakingly handsome, he'd looked at her with such pain in his gray eyes that she'd wanted to die.

She'd spent many nights awake, struggling with her battling emotions. She'd told him she hated him—that she wished he were dead. Part of her had meant it, while another part of her, the part she didn't understand, had known she could never hate him.

Disillusioned and bewildered, she'd tried to understand how she could still care what happened to him, when he'd destroyed her childhood, her security, thrusting her into the cold, hard world of reality.

Those had been the worst weeks of her life. Nothing that had happened to her since had come close to the agony she'd felt then. A month later, she'd learned that he'd joined the Navy and hadn't died, after all. Relieved that her last words had not been prophetic, she'd tried to put him out of her mind.

A murmur from the customers in the bar caused her to lift her head. The pilots came in together, still in uniform, laughing, joking and looking much too young to be entrusted with such power and responsibility. All but for the last man to enter.

Lynn's hand tightened on the stem of her glass. Her heart accelerated, just as it had eighteen years ago. She would have known him anywhere.

She waited for the bitterness; the remembered agony of a child on the brink of womanhood. She wasn't really surprised when she felt nothing. She had long outgrown the shock of discovering that the real world was vastly different from those childhood dreams.

In his U.S. Navy uniform, he looked tall and imposing. He wore his dark hair shorter and neater, but it remained just as thick and wavy as she remembered. His shoulders seemed broader, and the lines etched in his face betrayed his age. In spite of that, or maybe because of it, he looked even more attractive than her memory provided.

Lynn tensed as his glance swept the room with a bored indifference. She felt the chill of his gray eyes flick over her without recognition and tried to relax. After all, this was the way she'd wanted it.

She could conduct the interview in peace, and he need never know who she really was. It was a relief to know that she wouldn't have to face the sight of that agony in his eyes again.

She finished her drink and reached for her purse. She'd chosen the peach-striped dress with care, confident that it suited her tall figure. She needed the security of a sophisticated and efficient image if she was going to carry this off.

Pushing her chair back, she stood and had to pause until the quiver of nerves in her stomach settled. Then, arranging a pleasant smile on her face, she made her way to the bar.

The noise level had risen, especially among the pilots jostling each other with an exuberance that came from released tension. Lynn edged past them, collecting appreciative smiles before coming to an abrupt halt in front of Ward Sullivan.

She had rehearsed her opening statement over and over again, but every word of it faded from her mind as he looked down at her, his gaze inquiring and somewhat distant.

His eyes, she noticed, were even more penetrating than she remembered. And she could see no sign of recognition in them. She ran a mental picture through her mind, comparing herself with the young adolescent he had known.

She'd been painfully thin then. The years had given her a few curves and filled out her face. The braces were gone and her hair, once straw-colored, had darkened to a light brown. The long braids had been cut off when she'd turned twenty-one, and her hair now swung just above her shoulders, smooth and straight. The contact lenses in her blue eyes had replaced her glasses long ago.

It was unlikely he would know her. She held out her hand and smiled. "Commander Sullivan? I'm Carolyn West with the *Columbia*. We have an appointment for an interview."

His murmured greeting went over her head. She was too busy dealing with the sensations his warm grasp had caused.

Aware that he'd asked her a question, she forced herself to concentrate.

"I'm sorry," she said quickly, "I didn't hear you. It's a little noisy here, perhaps we could find somewhere quieter?" She was dismayed to see an instant wariness in his eyes.

"What did you have in mind?" His voice, deep and vibrant, held a definite note of suspicion.

With a shock she realized he was wondering if she was on the make. It probably happened a lot, she thought wryly. With those looks and that uniform he was quite devastating. She hurried to reassure him.

"Perhaps that table by the window? If that's all right with you?"

He nodded. "Fine. Can I get you a drink first?"

She took more care with her smile this time. "Thank you. We can get one at the table." She moved away from him and led the way back to the window, where her table was still vacant.

Seating herself, she was relieved to find herself relaxing. She'd made it over the worst hurdle. She could conduct the interview without any awkwardness between them. She watched Ward Sullivan lower himself into the chair opposite her and give her the semblance of a smile.

"All right, Miss West, fire away. Or is it Mrs.?" His gaze slid to her bare left hand and back to her face.

"Carolyn will do just fine." She paused, and when no answer appeared to be forthcoming, dug into her sizable handbag for her notebook. Uncapping her pen, she settled back.

"First of all, what is the average age of the pilots," she began, "and how does one become a Blue Angel?"

His smile widened, revealing the dimple in his left cheek, and she wondered how she could have forgotten that endearing feature.

"That's an easy question," he said. "The average age is thirty-three. Any Navy or Marine Corps pilot can apply for assignment to the Blue Angels if he is career oriented, as long as he had accumulated fifteen hundred flight hours in tactical jet aircraft."

Lynn nodded, scribbling furiously. "Do they have to have any special abilities, other than being an excellent pilot?"

"They have to be comfortable with the speaking engagements—we visit a lot of schools and hospitals. And then there are the recruiting appearances for the Navy and Marine Corps, in addition to our flying performances."

"Is there a limit to the time they can be a Blue Angel?"

"Two years, then they go back to an operational assignment in the fleet." He changed his voice then, dropping the official tone he'd assumed. "However, once a Blue, always a Blue. They never lose that distinction—they are very special men."

Lynn looked up, warmed by the fleeting expression of pride that crossed his face. "And what about you? Where do you fit in to all this?"

"I'm their leader and sometimes their sounding board." He looked away from her, raising his hand at the waitress across the room. In profile, his features looked hard and uncompromising.

It showed, Lynn thought. The bitterness—it showed in the hard line of his mouth and the tense set of his jaw. Had he carried it with him all these years, or had he buried it under an avalanche of repressed memories?

What would he do if he knew who she was? she wondered, feeling sick at the thought. A wave of panic swept over her. She couldn't deal with it, she realized now. She should never have taken this chance.

He turned back to her, taking her by surprise. Caught staring at him, she dropped her gaze at once and made a big display of turning the page of her notebook.

Her pulse stilled, then rocketed when he said in a puzzled voice, "Have we met before somewhere?"

Somehow she found the strength to force a laugh through her dry lips. "I'm sure, Commander Sullivan, that if we had, I would have remembered it."

She made herself look at him. His gray eyes studied her, and her pulse raced as she read the uncertainty in his gaze.

"You remind me of someone," he murmured, half to himself. "I just can't think who."

To her immense relief, Lynn saw the waitress heading for their table. She ordered a wine cooler and tried to remember the rest of the questions she'd planned to ask.

By the time the drinks arrived, she'd managed to steer the conversation back to the interview, and soon, before she was ready, it was all over.

Lynn raised her glass, aware of a sharp flutter of regret. "Thank you, Commander," she said, her voice deliberately bright. "I appreciate your time and I've enjoyed talking to you."

"And I appreciate you not asking me a bunch of personal questions." He lifted his glass in a salute and drained his martini.

She'd had the personal questions on her list, she just hadn't been able to ask them. She was afraid to know too much about him, and afraid, now, to touch on anything that might bring it all back.

It didn't mean she didn't want to know. She longed to know if he was married. He hadn't mentioned a wife. Did he have children, to replace the one he'd lost? Can you ever replace a lost child?

Maybe you can, she thought, if you'd never seen it. Her mind slipped back to that awful day when her whole world had been destroyed in a few brief hours. Sarah, her older sister, had been found in bed that morning, silent and still, and gone from them forever.

Lynn's fingers clenched her glass. She could still remember her mother's face when she'd gently broken the news that Sarah was dead.

Lynn had thought that nothing could hurt more; but worse was to come. Ward came to the house and Lynn saw him when her father opened the door. The look on Ward's face terrified her.

Her mother sent her to her room. Desperate to understand everything that had happened, she crouched at the top of the stairs. In a haze of shock she heard her parents blame Ward for Sarah's death. Apparently Sarah had overdosed herself on gin and sleeping pills. It was only after she'd killed herself that her parents had learned she'd also killed the baby growing inside her. They knew it had to be Ward's baby.

Lynn heard Ward swear that he knew nothing about the baby. Her parents wouldn't listen. "You're a damn liar," Lynn's father had shouted. "You'll be telling us next it's not your child. Is that what you told Sarah? You walked out on her, didn't you, rather than face your responsibilities? Street bastards like you are incapable of facing the consequences of their actions."

"Sarah would never have done this terrible thing if you hadn't broken her heart," Lynn's mother had cried, her voice raw with pain.

Lynn's father kept yelling as Ward turned without a word and stumbled down the driveway. Yelling that Sarah would still be alive if she'd never met him.

It had taken days for Lynn to realize that she would never see her sister again. Sarah—so alive, so beautiful—would never laugh with her again, or huddle for hours on the phone giggling with her friends, or come home late at night with that secret, dreamy expression that Lynn had envied so much.

Lynn's childhood dreams vanished with her sister's death. Santa Claus no longer existed—no tooth fairy, no end of the rainbow. And the wonderful life that she'd envisioned had turned bitter and cruel.

Lynn saw Ward only once after that. Shortly after the funeral she came down the steps of the library and saw him walking toward her.

He paused in front of her, his face a mask of pain. She never knew what it was he wanted to say. She'd yelled at him, as her father had yelled at him. "You killed Sarah. I hate you. I wish you were dead."

Lynn came back to the present with a start, aware that Ward had spoken. "I'm sorry?"

Ward shook his head, amusement flickering in his eyes. "You must have a lot on your mind," he said, his voice almost teasing. "That's the second time I've offered."

She tried to calm the sudden leap of her pulse. "Offered what?"

"To walk you to your car."

Put off balance, she found herself stuttering. "Oh, really—that's very kind...that's not necessary, really... I...I..."

His smile widened. "Is it me or the uniform that's making you nervous?"

She stared at him, searching for something to say. With a sense of impending doom she saw his eyes narrow, his smile disappear.

Leaning forward, he said slowly, "We *have* met before, haven't we?"

Swallowing, she nodded. After everything that she'd done, she couldn't go on lying to him. She had to go through with it now. "Yes. A long time ago." She watched the recognition dawn on his face, her heart sinking as his expression hardened.

"Charlie," he said sharply.

The childhood name gouged her memory like a dull knife. "I . . . I wanted to tell you, but . . ." She gestured helplessly, willing him to understand.

"But you figured I'd tell you to forget the interview if I knew who you were? You don't give me much credit."

His frozen smile dismayed her. "Ward—" She broke off as he pushed his chair back.

"The offer is still open," he said, his voice cool. "It's not safe for a young lady to walk around a parking lot at night. Or perhaps you'd prefer to be alone?"

"Of course not." Lynn snatched up her purse and stood. Now that he knew, she wanted time to explain. Time to tell him what she should have told him long ago. Time to tell him the truth.

He gave her a long, searching look before getting slowly to his feet. Without speaking, he pulled a couple of bills from his wallet and dropped them on the table.

She followed him out of the door, conscious of the curious glances from the young pilots as she passed them. Conjecture would be rife at the bar, she guessed, and wondered again if Ward was married.

He stood silently by her side in the elevator, and though she searched her mind for something to say, nothing seemed appropriate. Desperation gave her courage as he accompanied her through the underground parking lot, their footsteps echoing eerily behind them.

"I appreciate this," she said, as casually as her jumpy pulse would allow. "I'm always nervous in these places at night."

She saw him give her a sideways glance, as if he were afraid to look at her. "You've changed, Charlie," he said quietly.

She smiled. "I grew up."

This time he did look at her. "That, too. I meant you being nervous. The Charlie I remember wasn't afraid of anything."

Her laugh sounded forced, and louder than she'd meant it to be in the hollow expanse of the parking lot. "That was mostly bravado. I was terrified of boys. I thought that if I behaved like one, they wouldn't expect me to do all those girl things I'd been hearing about."

"You really worked at it. Not many boys could pitch a fast ball or climb a tree better than you did."

She'd wanted the opening. Now that she had it, she didn't want to talk about the past. She would have liked nothing better than to put it all behind them and make a fresh start. There was so much she wanted to know about Ward Sullivan, and so many questions she couldn't ask.

She paused by her car and looked up at him. "Thank you, Ward. I meant what I said. I have enjoyed talking to you."

He gave her a speculative look that made her nervous. "*Is* West your real name?"

"My married name. I use it professionally, though I took my maiden name back after the divorce."

"I never knew your name was Carolyn."

"I don't use it much. Most people call me Lynn."

"I think I prefer Charlie."

They were avoiding the topic, treading around Sarah, she thought, like children afraid to wake a sleeping monster. Throwing caution to the wind, she blurted out, "Ward—about what happened. I—"

"Forget it. There's nothing either of us can say that will change things." His gaze met hers, cool and expressionless. "I hope the interview came up to your expectations. I guess it must be important to you."

She flushed. "It is. But it isn't the only reason I'm here. I wanted to see you."

He shook his head, and his expression made her feel like crying. "Nice try. But we both know better. I can't change the past, no matter how much I'd like to."

"Ward..." She searched for the right words, knowing that whatever she said would bring back the hurt. "Sarah loved you so much..."

She ached with sympathy as his face creased in pain. He thrust his hands deep in his pockets, and she couldn't stop herself from touching him. Laying her hand on his arm, she said softly, "Please listen to me—"

"Let it go, Charlie!" His harsh voice unnerved her and she dropped her hand. "Sarah is dead and I can't bring her back. I've paid enough for my mistakes, and I don't want to talk about it, especially to you. I'm sure you can understand that. So, let's say goodbye now and try to forget we ever saw each other."

Lynn's cry of dismay echoed down the parking lot. "You don't mean that."

He stepped back, away from her, putting more than mere distance between them. "Yes, I do. For your sake as well as mine."

"Please, Ward—"

"Do your parents know you're here?"

The abrupt question took her by surprise, and she knew he could read the truth in her face.

"That's what I thought. Given the way you all feel about me, they'd be shocked to know you were even talking to me."

I hate you. I wish you were dead. The words echoed down the years to haunt her. Unable to take any more, she fumbled in her purse for her keys. She managed to fit one in the lock and opened the car door. She made herself look at him. "I meant what I said. It was nice to see you again. And thanks for the interview."

He nodded, though the cool glint in his eyes remained. "So long, Charlie. Take care of yourself."

The dismissal chilled her. She climbed into the car and closed the door. The engine coughed, then roared to life when she turned the key in the ignition. She didn't look at him again. She didn't know if he watched her leave, her eyes were too misted with tears.

She wasn't sure if she was crying for Sarah or for herself. Or maybe for the tall, silent man who still carried the pain of a mistake that should have been forgotten long ago.

Sorting through her notes later that night, Lynn tried to read them with detachment, but the vision of sleet-gray eyes in a tanned face kept intruding.

She finally gave up and watched an old movie instead. It didn't help much, so she switched off the television, knowing she wouldn't be able to sleep. She should have told him. She should have made him listen.

Her restless steps took her back to her desk, where she pulled open a drawer. Her fingers shook as she withdrew a worn leather notebook. Opening the cover, she stared down at the words scrawled across the first page. "Sarah's Diary."

Several days after the funeral, her father had handed her a small wooden chest. It had contained Sarah's personal things, he'd told Lynn. Things he thought she might like to have. Her mother wanted to destroy everything, unable to bear any reminders of the daughter they had lost. Her father couldn't bring himself to do that, so he was offering the few possessions to his younger daughter.

"Sarah's diary is in there," he'd said, his voice trembling with grief. "We couldn't bring ourselves to read it. Knowing the torment that must have been in Sarah's mind would only add to the pain. Maybe later, when we've had time to heal, we can read it together."

It was the first time Lynn had ever seen her father cry. She'd put the box away, and neither she nor her parents had ever mentioned it again. It wasn't until her seventeenth birthday that she had opened the diary.

It seemed so long ago. She'd had another of her frequent arguments with her parents, who'd refused to allow her to go out and celebrate with her friends. Lynn had sat in her bedroom, seething with resentment. It was all Sarah's fault. Sarah was responsible for the stranglehold her parents had on their remaining daughter.

She wasn't allowed anywhere without her mother's permission, let alone go on a date. She had to be the only one in her class not allowed to date. What were they afraid of, for heaven's sake? Didn't they know that she would never make the mistakes that Sarah had made?

Burning with frustration, she'd snatched the box from her closet shelf, intending to throw it out. Instead she'd dropped it, and the contents had spilled across the floor. She hadn't meant to read the diary. But it had opened at the last page, that last day...

Tears blurred her eyes, and Lynn dropped the notebook on her desk. She pushed back her chair and walked to the kitchen. Automatically going through the motions of making coffee, she remembered the lines scribbled in Sarah's impatient hand.

How can I tell them? They will never forgive me. They don't like Ward, and if they found out about the baby they'd hate him. They'd say terrible things and make him hate me. I can't lose Ward, I love him too much. I must get rid of the baby. Paula says it's easy. They'll never know, and I won't have to tell Ward anything. Then we can be happy again. I love you, Ward.

Sarah had been afraid of her parents, not Ward. And she hadn't meant to kill herself. Lynn had realized then that

Ward had told the truth. She'd thought about contacting him, but the memory of his face the last time she'd seen him haunted her, and she hadn't had the nerve to go through with it. She'd kept the diary a secret from her parents, afraid to disturb their peace of mind and resurrect an agony they seemed to have overcome.

She was right to have left well enough alone, Lynn thought as she climbed into bed. It had all happened so long ago, and whatever she said now wouldn't change things. Ward's bitterness was too formidable to break through; he wouldn't even listen to her. How could she bear it if she asked for forgiveness and he refused? How could she make him understand why she hadn't let him know the truth, when she wasn't sure she understood it herself?

Sarah was dead, and the past should remain buried with her. Lynn reached over and switched out the light. She wished now she hadn't arranged that meeting. She had been selfish, wanting to ease her own conscience instead of considering the consequences.

She'd wanted the interview, true. It had seemed like fate when the Blue Angels had arrived in town and she'd seen Ward's picture in the advance publicity.

She had worked part-time for the *Columbia* for almost a year now, supplementing her salary with free-lance work. The local newspaper had gained some recognition, and the article was a chance to show what she could do. If she did a good job, she might finally get her own byline on a feature story.

Though it was just as well, Lynn thought soberly, that this particular piece wouldn't carry her name. If her parents knew she'd interviewed Ward Sullivan, they'd probably disown her.

Especially if they'd known her main reason for seeing him. She'd wanted to find out what kind of a man he'd become. She'd wanted to reassure herself that he was happy and content with his life. Maybe then, she'd thought, she could let her guilt rest in peace. This was her chance to wipe the slate clean.

She had to admit that even now, after meeting Ward and talking to him, she knew very little about the man behind the uniform. "Ward Sullivan," she'd written, "is a dedicated, fearless leader, whose pride and belief in his chosen profession shines through every statement he makes." Beyond that, she could only guess.

She fell asleep wondering if it was the man or the uniform that gave him the same powerful aura of a hero that had overwhelmed her eighteen years ago.

She made the deadline by a narrow margin, delivering the article to the editor's desk just short of noon the next day.

Marjorie Tyler looked it over, nodding her approval. "Looks good." She peered over the top of her glasses as Lynn. "Not much personal stuff. Wouldn't he talk?"

Lynn shrugged. "Commander Sullivan isn't a personal man. I got the impression the military is his life, and nothing exists beyond that."

"No wife, huh?" Marjorie said, picking up the publicity photo of Ward.

"He didn't mention one."

"Interesting. I wouldn't mind meeting a man who looks like this." The editor's dark eyes examined her own with a shrewd gleam. "What did you think of him—off the record?"

Lynn shifted uncomfortably. She didn't know how to handle Marjorie's sudden personal interest. Lynn hadn't mentioned her past connection to Ward, and if she mentioned it now she knew Marjorie's natural curiosity would result in awkward questions. "He seems to be very dedicated," she said, hoping that would satisfy her editor.

Marjorie nodded. "Well, you did a good job on this. Thanks, Lynn."

She escaped from the office and tried to tell herself she was glad it was all over. Time would soon smooth out the ripples made by Ward passing through.

Only time wasn't being too cooperative. She found herself thinking about his hard smile, the dimple in his left cheek and the way he'd looked at her when he'd realized who she was.

Images floated in and out of her mind, mixed with the past at first, then taking on the solidarity of the present, until it was difficult for her to remember what he had looked like eighteen years ago.

Just over a month later, news of Commander Edward Sullivan surfaced again. And this time Lynn was totally unprepared.

Hurrying down the corridor to Marjorie's office, Lynn hoped that her editor's summons meant an interesting assignment. She needed something to get her mind off her preoccupation with Ward Sullivan.

When Marjorie saw her, she waved her elegant red fingernails at the chair opposite her desk. "Sit down. I've got something here that might interest you."

Lynn sat, hoping it was something that would take her out of town.

Marjorie picked up a sheet of paper and studied it. "Remember that article you did on that Blue Angel pilot, Commander Sullivan?"

Thankful that the editor's gaze was still on the release in her hand, Lynn managed a fast recovery from her start of surprise. "Of course," she said, her voice deliberately casual.

Marjorie looked up, and the expression in her dark eyes started a small niggle of uneasiness in the pit of Lynn's stomach.

"I just got this in ten minutes ago. There was an accident involving the Blue Angels, at the air show yesterday in Seattle. They're not sure what happened yet, but apparently it involved only one plane. The lead plane."

Lynn bit back the cry or horror. She stared at Marjorie, rigid with shock, too afraid to form the question screaming in her head.

"I guess there was some kind of explosion," Marjorie went on, obviously unaware that every word she said burned into Lynn's frozen mind. "Commander Sullivan bailed out. He's in intensive care in a military hospital in Seattle."

Chapter 2

Lynn pressed shaking fingers against her lips and made a small, helpless sound in her throat. She didn't know if it was the shock, or the relief that at least Ward was alive, that made her feel so disoriented. At this point she wasn't sure of anything at all.

Marjorie apparently noticed that the news had produced a stronger reaction than she'd expected, and her gaze sharpened as she stared at Lynn across the desk.

"Is there something I should know about you and the commander?" she asked quietly.

Lynn lowered her hands and wished she could stop trembling. She could actually see her knees vibrating beneath her gray skirt. "I...didn't mention this before, but I knew Commander Sullivan when...a long time ago. I wasn't sure if he'd recognize me, so I didn't want to say anything before."

"And did he?"

Lynn looked into Marjorie's curious eyes and nodded. "Yes. But he wasn't pleased to see me. We knew each other under...difficult circumstances, a time neither of us wanted to remember. I hadn't seen him in eighteen years. He made it clear— I didn't want to mention in the article that we'd met before . . . so I didn't tell you."

Marjorie leaned back in her chair and tapped her teeth with her pencil. "I see."

Lynn was very much afraid that she did see. Too much. "Did they say— Is there any news on his condition?"

Marjorie shook her head. "I thought you might want to follow up on this, seeing as you did the first article. Of course, if you'd rather not—"

"No!" Seeing Marjorie's raised eyebrows, Lynn lowered her voice. "I'd like to take this. Have you got the name of the hospital?"

Marjorie pushed the news sheet across the desk. "It's all there. Take as long as you want on it."

"Thanks." Relieved that her legs appeared to be working again, Lynn pushed back her chair and stood. "Would it be all right with you if I went up there? I could probably find out more if I'm on the scene."

"Sure." Marjorie waved her hand in a gesture of dismissal. "If you leave now you can be there before dark."

Aware that her boss was being more than generous, Lynn managed a weak smile. "I really appreciate this, Marjorie."

Marjorie peered at her over the top of her glasses. "Just come back with a story, you hear?"

Lynn nodded, refusing to give in to the fear that threatened to destroy what little control she had left. "I'll do my best," she said and made for the door.

She had it open when Marjorie said softly, "Lynn? Try not to worry. These boys are tough. I'm sure you'll find your commander in good shape."

"I hope so," Lynn whispered, as she let the door close behind her. "Oh, God, I hope so."

He dreamed he was flying, high above a green-and-gold-checkered landscape—flying effortlessly, surrounded by a deathly silence. He knew it was a dream because he was out of the plane. He could see it far below him, spiraling down to earth, scarring the sky with a trail of dark smoke. It should have been screaming in its death throes, yet he could hear nothing.

But he could feel. The pain burst upon him without warning, vicious and inescapable. It tore at his head, behind his eyes. He groaned, but couldn't hear his own voice. Thick black clouds began to obscure the sun—smoky, evil-smelling clouds. They were choking him.

It wasn't a dream. It was real. He couldn't breathe. The thing he'd dreaded had finally caught up with him. He'd known it would happen one day. He was about to pay the price for what he'd done to Sarah. He was going to pay with his life.

He'd shut his eyes when the clouds enveloped him. Now he couldn't open them. His arms seemed to be trapped at his sides, too heavy to lift. His descent to the ground below accelerated. Faster and faster he plummeted, knowing that every second brought him closer to the unforgiving earth. At that speed his body would be crushed on impact...

Why couldn't he open his eyes? Forcing back the panic that erupted in his chest, he concentrated. His weighted lids flickered open and then closed. Again he struggled, and again, until at last his eyes were fully open. And still he couldn't see.

He was lying on something soft, in a darkened room. He knew he was awake now, and the dream, if it had been a dream, no longer clutched at him with grasping fingers. His head hurt like hell.

It must have been a dream. If it had been for real, he wouldn't be alive to remember it. But then, where was he? Not in his bed in his quarters, although he was in bed somewhere.

Someone had tucked the covers in tight at his sides, trapping his arms. Braced against the pain, he struggled for quite a while to release one of them. The other arm refused to budge, and he ran his hand over it. Apparently it was strapped to his chest.

He remembered now. He'd been approaching the final routine of the run. It had all gone smoothly up to then, like clockwork as usual. Then all hell had broken loose.

His body tensed at the memory, and he made himself relax. An explosion... aboard his plane. A moment of excruciating pain... then nothing... until his dream. He remembered reaching for the ejection handle. He must have pulled it... he couldn't remember.

He hadn't died. For a moment he regretted that. It wasn't over after all. He had to go on living with the guilt gnawing at his gut. He still had a life, but the knowledge that a beautiful young girl had taken hers because of him would not let him rest in peace. It might have been better had he died and paid his dues.

He heard a door opening and turned his head, expecting to see a shaft of light from the doorway. For a moment he thought he'd imagined the sound, then a voice spoke softly in the darkness.

"Commander Sullivan? I'm Dr. Alan Harper. How are you feeling?"

Ward frowned. The voice was close. Too close. He blinked, then jerked his head when he felt firm fingers on his face. "Turn the damn light on," he growled, annoyed that he could managed little more than a hoarse whisper.

He heard the sharp intake of breath, and the fingers stilled. His heart seemed to leap in his chest, then began pounding hard against his ribs. He blinked, several times, while his mind slowly absorbed the truth.

"Commander..." The doctor hesitated.

He heard his own voice. It sounded stronger and incredibly calm when he said quietly, "The light is on, isn't it?"

"Now I want you to relax—"

He shoved himself up on his elbow, oblivious of the excruciating agony bursting in his head and shoulder. "Tell me for God's sake! The light is on, damn it, isn't it?"

"Yes."

Fingers tightened on his arm as the doctor went on speaking. He couldn't hear the words. All he could hear was a dreadful roaring in his ears. So this was to be his punishment.

The cry of anguish that filled the room vibrated in his head, shuddering through his mind like the ungodly yell of some wild demented being. His body might have survived, but his soul had been destroyed. He might just as well be dead.

Lynn checked her tote bag to make sure she had everything she needed. She'd thrown in a change of clothes, expecting to stay at least one night. She couldn't seem to think beyond that.

Her mind kept painting pictures, terrifying visions of a shattered plane and a broken body. What would she find when she got to Seattle? she wondered, as she feverishly dialed her mother's number.

She had almost forgotten to call. Her mother would've thrown a fit if her daughter had left without saying where she was going. Never a day went by without one or the other of her parents checking on her to see that she was all right. They still didn't like the idea of their only child living alone.

Lynn grimaced at the memory of the fight she'd had to gain that little bit of independence. The constant phone calls

were a small price to pay for the privilege of having somewhere to relax without have to explain her every move. Not
that she could move far without checking in, Lynn thought
wryly.

Her father's voice spoke in her ear. "Is everything all
right?" he asked at the sound of her voice.

She curbed the spasm of impatience. "I'm fine. I just
wanted to let you know I'm leaving town. I've got a follow-
up on a story."

"Oh? Where are you going?"

"Seattle." Lynn waited while her father relayed everything back to her mother.

"Mother wants to know how long you'll be up there," her
father said.

"Overnight at least. I'll call you and let you know where
I'm staying."

"You don't have it booked? Wouldn't it be better to book
a room before you leave? Do you want me to book one for
you? I know a nice little—"

"Dad, I'll take care of it. Don't worry. And tell Mom not
to worry. I promise I'll call." She hung up before her father
could suggest she talk to her mother.

She begrudged the extra minutes it had taken to call them.
Yet, as always she reminded herself that they couldn't help
worrying about her. She was all they had left.

Once in Seattle, she pulled into a gas station and filled up.
She asked for directions, then drove immediately to the
hospital.

Her stomach churned as she lined up at the busy desk behind a buxom woman, whose strident voice grated on her
ears. How she hated hospitals, Lynn thought, as she heard
the intercom issue a sharp request for a Dr. Wilson. The
faint odor of disinfectant and new paint made her queasy.

In front of her the woman hefted an overflowing grocery
sack higher in one arm, while her other hand held on to a

squirming little boy. It seemed ages before the visibly harassed mother finally got the information she needed and
hauled the child, shrilly complaining, down the corridor.

Lynn stepped up to the desk and looked anxiously at the
tired-looking woman seated behind it. "I'd like to visit
Commander Edward Sullivan," she said. "Can you give me
his room number?"

The clerk tapped her computer keys with rapid fingers,
then shook her head. "I'm sorry." Her apologetic expression when she looked up filled Lynn with dismay. "Commander Sullivan isn't allowed visitors at present."

Disappointment robbed her of coherent thought for a
moment, then Lynn collected herself. "My name is Lynn
Barclay, and I'm Ward Sullivan's sister. I've driven up from
Oregon to see him. Can't you make an exception?"

The clerk shook her head again. "Sorry. You'll have to
talk to his doctor."

"And who's that?"

Again the quick fingers flew across the keys. "Dr. Alan
Harper. He's the surgeon."

Lynn curled her fingers into her palm. "Surgeon?"

The blond woman's expression softened. "The commander had surgery yesterday evening. He'd doing fine and
is as well as can be expected."

Somehow she'd managed to make the trite phrase sound
reassuring. Even so, Lynn's voice wavered when she asked,
"What kind of surgery?"

"Why don't you talk to the doctor about that?" The
other woman glanced at her watch. "He should be coming
off his evening rounds in about a half an hour. I'll tell him
you're waiting for him in the lounge."

Lynn nodded. "All right. Thanks. I'll go and get some
coffee."

The coffee, delivered by an impersonal vending machine, tasted bitter. Lynn sat on a black vinyl couch in the corner of the air-conditioned lounge. Opposite her, on an identical couch, a young man with a nervous twitch in his cheek tapped his fingers on the arm. A grim-looking elderly woman sat next to him, staring at a magazine without turning the pages.

Lynn sipped the coffee, grateful for its warmth, at least. Her entire body felt like an arctic wasteland. Outside, the dying summer still allowed enough sunshine to warm the evening. Yet it seemed like the heart of winter in that desolate room.

She realized she hadn't eaten since lunchtime. The thought of food sickened her, and she reached for a magazine on the table in front of her.

Surgery. For God's sake, what was the doctor going to tell her? She was still trying to make sense of the page she'd read three times when a pleasant, low voice spoke her name.

"Yes," Lynn answered, jumping to her feet. "I'm Lynn Barclay. Are you Dr. Harper?"

The man wore a white coat, and wariness hovered in his light brown eyes when he looked at her. "Yes. I'm your brother's surgeon."

For a moment she was confused, forgetting the lie she'd used in her desperation to see Ward. "Oh, yes...I'm sorry...I... Is he all right?" She swallowed hard. "What kind of surgery?"

The doctor glanced at the interested face of the young man on the couch, then took Lynn's arm. "Come with me, Mrs. Barclay. We can talk in my office."

She didn't correct him on the title. Since her name was different from Ward's, the doctor was bound to assume she was married. His quiet, calm voice spoke in generalities in the elevator. Lynn heard nothing he said.

She couldn't bear to think of Ward Sullivan's strong, healthy body crippled—or worse—paralyzed. By the time the doctor ushered her into a comfortable furnished office and closed the door, her lips felt too stiff to form the questions pounding in her brain.

"Make yourself comfortable," Dr. Harper began, motioning for her to take one of the deep leather armchairs facing a large, neat desk. Lynn perched on the edge of the seat and watched him walk around his desk and sit down. "I was under the impression that Commander Sullivan had no immediate family," the surgeon added. "At least, that's what Captain Phillips told me."

So he wasn't married, after all. Lynn shrugged, uncomfortably aware that it was too late to confess the truth now. "We haven't seen each other in a good many years," she said, hoping the doctor wouldn't pursue the subject. "I was horrified when I heard about the accident on the news."

"Well, I'm glad you came." Dr. Harper reached for a pile of folders and flipped through them. "Your brother was lucky," he went on, opening one of the folders. "Considering the circumstances—the speed of the plane and the height at which he bailed out—he got off remarkably lightly."

"You mean...he's not crippled or anything?" She hadn't realized she'd been holding her breath. It came out in a rush as the surgeon shook his head.

"No. Considering the explosion, his injuries were minor. Dislocated shoulder...some pretty extensive bruising caused by bailout at top speed...he managed to open his chute before blacking out but landed badly. He has a sprained ankle and severely torn ligaments in one arm. All of which will mend in time, though he'd going to be in pain for a while. The commander has recovered consciousness, and physically he's doing quite well."

Lynn tensed. "Do I hear a *but* in there?"

Dr. Harper laid down the folder. "There is one exception," he said carefully. "At the moment Commander Sullivan appears to have lost his sight. I'm afraid I can't say whether or not it will be permanent."

Lynn's shocked cry seemed to echo forever in the quiet room. "Blind? Ward is *blind*?"

The surgeon ran a tired hand over his thinning light brown hair. "Try not to upset yourself, Mrs. Barclay. Very often, when these problems are psychosomatic, they clear up in time. This could very likely be the case with Commander Sullivan, since there appears to be no physical reason for his condition."

Lynn shook her head, striving to understand. "You mean he imagines he's blind?"

"Oh, no. It's real enough." Dr. Harper leaned back in his chair and folded his hands across his chest. "But it could be caused by a psychological problem. Undue stress, some extreme trauma, such as the explosion aboard the commander's plane, are often the cause of psychosomatic illness. It's called posttraumatic stress disorder. The patient's mind creates the problem to avoid facing the reality of a certain situation, and the body believes it. We see it a lot in wartime. It's sometimes known as shell shock."

"I see." Lynn frowned. "How long does something like this usually last?"

The doctor shrugged his thin shoulders. "It's difficult to say. Sometimes a few days of rest and therapy work miracles. Sometimes it takes longer. In some severe cases, the patient never recovers."

Lynn leaned forward. "Are you telling me that Ward might never regain his sight?"

"Never is such a definite word, Mrs. Barclay. I'm simply trying to cover all the possibilities. One thing I will tell you, the majority of cases are resolved within a short time."

She nodded, only slightly reassured. "How is he taking it?"

The doctor shrugged. "Pretty much as I'd expect him to take it. He's angry, frustrated and scared, though he'd be the last one to admit it."

She drew a shaky breath. "I want to see him."

Dr. Harper looked at his watch. "I'm sorry, he's heavily sedated and won't wake up until the morning."

"I'd still like to see him."

"He won't know you're there."

Lynn stood and leaned her hands on the desk. "Please, Doctor. I've come a long way. I won't disturb him, I promise, but I won't sleep tonight if I can't see him and convince myself he's all right."

Dr. Harper climbed to his feet and gave her a weary nod. "All right. Five minutes, no more."

Following the doctor's directions, Lynn found the right floor and followed the signs to the desk. Dr. Harper must have cleared her with the nurse, as the petite dark-haired woman led her to the room and left her at the door, whispering, "You have five minutes, then I'll have to ask you to leave."

Lynn nodded, afraid to trust her voice. Her throat ached when she saw the still figure lying on the bed. A white bandage covered his forehead, another his shoulder and left arm. Bruises darkened his face, and one cheek looked puffy and swollen.

He lay so still that she watched his chest anxiously for a moment, before she saw the slight movement under the blankets that told her he was breathing.

She wanted to touch him, to let him know she was there. Mindful of her promise not to disturb him, she resisted the urge and contented herself with just looking at him.

The hard lines of his face had smoothed out under the influence of the medication. The years melted away as Lynn stared down at his firm jawline and his sensitive mouth, which used to break into a smile every time he saw her, lighting up her day.

It was Ward who had dried her tears and carried her into the house the day she'd fallen off her bike. She wasn't that hurt, but when he'd swept her up in his strong arms, she hadn't uttered a word of protest.

She'd been too young to understand the odd sensation his closeness had given her. He'd set her down on her feet and chucked her under her chin.

"One day, Charlie," he'd promised her, "you're gonna forget about keeping up with the boys. And they'd better watch out when you do."

She'd watched him turn to Sarah and draw her into the circle of his arm. It was the first time she remembered being jealous of her sister. And she wasn't sure why. She only knew that after that day she could never look at Ward without a quivery feeling in her stomach.

A dedicated, fearless leader she'd called him in her article. It was strange, Lynn thought, but even now, though he lay flat on his back and helpless, she could see the strength and pride still stamped on his features. And the bitterness, too.

Somehow, without the ability to disguise it, the ravages of a painful past seemed more evident in the hard contours of his face. If only he'd listened to her, Lynn thought, she could at least have set his mind to rest on that score.

She caught her breath. Maybe he would listen to her now. He needed someone now. She could be his eyes, his friend, anything he needed, until he was back on his feet. It would be her way of making up for all the pain her family had caused him so many years ago.

When he'd recovered his sight and had his strength back again, she'd show him the diary. Then she would apologize for all the dreadful things she'd said, all the misunderstandings, and ask for his forgiveness. Maybe after that they could both have peace of mind.

Feeling better by the minute, she pressed a kiss to her palm and gently blew it across the bed. "I'll see you in the morning," she promised in a soft whisper. Then she let herself quietly out of the room.

Pausing at the desk, she asked the nurse to let Ward know she'd been to see him and that she would return in the morning. Then she went to find somewhere to stay for the night.

She found she could eat after all. The family restaurant next to the motel where she'd booked a room served unpretentious but adequate meals, and she actually managed to enjoy the chicken she'd ordered.

She hadn't expected to sleep, but when she opened her eyes to see sunlight filtering through the flimsy drapes in her room, she realized she'd slept much longer than she'd intended. She reached for the phone and dialed the hospital's number, and her spirits lifted when she heard the polite voice on the other end assure her that Commander Sullivan was now allowed visitors.

After a quick shower she pulled on the white cotton pants and yellow shirt she'd brought with her. She didn't stop for breakfast, deciding to grab something at the hospital.

The sun sparkled on the leaves of a tall mountain ash still damp with morning dew as Lynn climbed out of the car. She paused for a moment, filling her lungs with soft summer air that carried just a hint of the sea.

He was going to get well, she told herself as she hurried across the parking lot and through the main doors of the hospital. It was impossible not to feel optimistic on such a gorgeous day. She couldn't wait to see him and tell him she'd stick around until he'd fully recovered.

She didn't bother to stop at the main desk. Instead she took the elevator and rode it to the third floor, oblivious of the silent people crowded in with her. Wishing she'd thought to bring something with her, though she had no idea what it would be, she hurried up to the nurses' station.

An older woman with a stiff back and thin eyebrows sat behind the desk, barely bothering to glance up as Lynn asked breathlessly, "I'm Lynn Barclay. Would it be all right if I went in to see Commander Sullivan now?"

"No. I'm sorry." The nurse kept her eyes on the report she was working on. "Commander Sullivan is no longer in this ward."

"Then where is he? I'd like to see him."

"Ms. Barclay." The nurse looked up at her with cool, blue eyes. "The commander left a message for you. He is not giving interviews to the press and has left specific instructions that you be barred from his room."

One look at the nurse told her she would get no help from that quarter. Shaken by the curt message, Lynn made her way to Dr. Harper's office. As she lifted her hand to tap on the door, the surgeon opened it and looked at her in surprise.

"They won't let me in Ward's room," she blurted out, too distracted to notice his frown of disapproval. "I'm sure he didn't mean to stop me from going in."

"I'm afraid he did. I can't say I blame him."

"But I don't understand."

"The commander is upset that you pretended to be his sister."

She couldn't ignore the reprimand in the surgeon's voice. Lifting her hands in a helpless gesture she protested. "I only wanted to help him."

"And you felt it necessary to lie in order to do that?"

Lynn flushed. "It was the only way I could find out how he was doing."

"Mrs. Barclay. Had I known you were a journalist—"

"That has nothing to do with it." In her anxiety to reassure him she grabbed hold of his sleeve. "Dr. Harper, I'm here as a friend. A very old friend. Ward and I have known each other for more than eighteen years. I was anxious about him, that's all. I had no intention of doing a story about him."

That bit, at least, was true, she realized. She couldn't possibly subject Ward to any kind of publicity—not now.

The doctor rubbed a hand over his jaw. "Well, I guess no real harm was done. But you can forget about helping him or even seeing him. He's flatly refused to have any contact with anyone outside of the hospital staff. He's adamant. Apart from his commanding officer, Captain Phillips, he won't talk to anyone. At this point, in view of his unstable condition, I have to respect his wishes."

"Then I'll have to wait until he will see me." Sick with disappointment, Lynn turned away. She hated to give up so easily, but what could she do? Ward apparently wanted nothing to do with her, and she couldn't risk upsetting him at this stage. She had to find some way of changing his mind.

Deciding she could use some coffee, Lynn trudged down to the lounge. A man in naval uniform stood outside in the corridor, talking into one of the public phones on the wall. Her pulse quickening, Lynn waited just inside the lounge for him to finish the call.

"Are you Captain Phillips?" she asked quickly as the officer moved away from the phone. He was a tall man, with a heavily lined face and a thick brown mustache that twitched when he looked at her in surprise.

"Yes," he admitted, giving her a curious stare. "And you are...?"

"A friend of Ward Sullivan's. A close friend." It wasn't exactly a lie, Lynn thought as she held out her hand. Though she seemed to be telling a couple of them lately. "My name is Lynn Barclay."

The officer took her hand with a small frown. "I'm afraid Ward hasn't mentioned you. I didn't think he had any civilian friends."

"We haven't seen each other in quite a while." Lynn managed an anxious smile. "I'm very disturbed by Ward's refusal to talk to anyone. I was wondering if he had a special friend who could persuade him to change his mind."

Captain Phillips gave her a rueful shake of his head. "As far as I know, Ward doesn't have any close friends. He's well liked by the men, especially his crew, who I know trust and admire him. But Ward is very definitely a loner. He simply prefers his own company. Some men are like that, especially in the military."

"That's very sad," Lynn said, half to herself.

"I agree." The captain pulled his cap from under his arm and tugged it onto his head. "Being grounded like this must be killing him. I've never seen a man more crazy about flying than Ward Sullivan. It seems to be all he lives for." He sent Lynn a brief smile. "I have to get back to the base, now. I hope you can change his mind—he's going to need a friend."

Lynn watched the captain's tall figure stride down the corridor, feeling more worried than ever. How could she possibly help Ward if he refused to talk to her? How could anyone help him?

She fed quarters into the machine and watched the steaming liquid rattle into the paper cup. The tangy flavor of strong coffee did little to revive her spirits as she sipped from the cup. There had to be something she could so, she thought, perching herself on the arm of the couch. She couldn't just give up and walk away from him now.

Over the rim of her cup she watched a young girl bustling down the corridor, dressed in a pink-and-white striped uniform. The girl carried a huge vase of flowers in her arms, and the bright yellow and white chrysanthemums almost hid her face.

Lynn watched her disappear around the corner, wondering what had prompted a young girl like that to be a volunteer. Had it been something in her personal life, some kind of tragedy that had prompted a need to respond, or did she just have a deep sympathy for people in need and felt compelled to help?

Lynn stood and tossed her cup into the waste bin. She could do nothing more here, she thought, her shoulders feeling weighted with depression. She might as well pack up and go home.

She had reached the main doors when the idea struck her. She stopped short and spun around, nearly colliding with the two young women behind her. She'd been thinking about the little volunteer in the pink and white uniform. A volunteer.

Dr. Harper had said that Ward wanted nothing to do with anyone outside of the hospital staff, Lynn remembered in mounting excitement as she hurried back up the corridor toward Dr. Harper's office.

So, that's what she would pretend to be—a volunteer visiting vets in the hospitals. Surely Ward couldn't object to that? As long as he remained blind, she could spend time with him and be there for him until he recovered.

And he would recover, she told herself fiercely. She would not let herself, or Ward, believe otherwise. Full of enthusiasm, she rapped on the doctor's door.

On the third floor, Ward lay listening to the surgeon's quiet voice, wishing he would go away and leave him alone. He didn't want to hear the careful sentences, the assurances that his body would heal, that no permanent damage had been done. What the hell did the fool know, anyway? It was all very well for him to stand there spouting platitudes; he wasn't lying helpless in a dark abyss of hell.

How could someone possibly know what it was like unless they'd had their sight snatched away overnight? How could this patronizing idiot possibly know what it was like to face a future full of uncertainties and unknown terror?

A malfunction in the fuel system, Phillips had said. A miracle he'd survived. But what good was survival without his eyes?

"There's a good chance you'll recover your sight in time," the doctor said from out of the black mist the world had become.

Ward tensed as he felt the surgeon's cool fingers probing at his eyelids. "Good chance? What does that mean? Fifty-fifty? Less?"

"Now, you know I can't be that specific. Psychology isn't my field. I wish you'd agree to talk to a psychologist—"

Ward brushed away the offending fingers with an irritable hand. "I told you, Doc, there's nothing wrong with my mind. It's my eyes that are screwed up, so if you can't fix that, maybe I need another surgeon."

"I've told you that I can find no physical damage to your eyes, other than some slight bruising." The mattress relaxed by Ward's side, and he knew the surgeon had stood. "Of course," the doctor added mildly, "if you want a second opinion, that can be easily arranged."

"I want a second opinion." He didn't want to sound ungrateful, Ward thought with a twinge of conscience, but hell, it was his sight and he wasn't going to take one man's word for it no matter how brilliant he was supposed to be.

"Very well. I'll send in Dr. Wilson, he's an excellent surgeon and you can trust his judgment. I'll be in to see you later."

Ward let out his breath in a hiss when he heard the door close. His head hurt again, but he knew he wouldn't get any more medication for at least an hour. He could put up with it, he thought, lifting his good arm in an attempt to massage his neck, if only he knew he wasn't going to be blind forever.

If only they'd stop skirting the subject, talking about chances and maybes, and give him something definite to hold on to.

He was afraid to hope. He couldn't live his life hoping for miracles that never happened. If he was permanently blind, he had to start learning to accept and deal with his disability, or he'd never be independent again.

And yet, without hope, how bleak his life promised to be. To accept his blindness as permanent meant accepting the fact he would never fly again. The thought terrified him.

He felt trapped. If he didn't recover his sight, he would never again escape the constant battle his life had become. There would be no respite, no freedom from the bonds that hampered his life on the ground.

He let out a small groan as he struggled to turn on his side. If that was to be his fate, he'd rather not know. They could forget about sending a psychologist. He wouldn't talk to anyone.

He knew the window was in front of him; a nurse had told him so. He stared into the blackness yawning before him and searched desperately for a tiny chink of light—a pinpoint— anything that could offer him a reason to hope.

After knocking on Dr. Harper's door and waiting several moments for a reply, Lynn realized he had left his office. Undaunted, she hurried back to the main desk and asked if she could speak to the surgeon.

"He's on his way to surgery," a pretty nurse told her. "He'll be tied up for the next three or four hours."

Frustrated, Lynn asked urgently, "Can you give me Commander Sullivan's room number? I have an important message to deliver." It was closer to the truth than the sister story, and it worked.

"Room two twelve," the nurse said, after consulting a sheet of paper. "But—"

"Thanks." Lynn dashed away from the desk before the nurse could finish, determined not to be prevented from carrying out her plan. She couldn't hang around for another four hours waiting for the doctor to give her permission. She had to take a chance and pray that it worked out.

She stabbed impatiently at the elevator button with a finger. She'd make it work out, she vowed silently. She would not let Ward Sullivan down again. He needed someone—anyone—who could help him through this disaster. He needed a friend, and she was determined to be one. Whether he wanted her or not.

She stepped out of the elevator into the quiet corridor. The nurses were talking quietly to each other just a few yards away. She could hear them, but couldn't see them. Nor could they see her.

Quietly she edged along the wall to Ward's room, holding her breath when the phone rang at the desk. As one of the nurses reached for it, Lynn slipped past the station.

Afraid to knock on the door in case one of the nurses heard her, she grasped the handle. She'd have to convince Ward she was a hospital volunteer and hope that he wouldn't throw her out.

There was always a chance he would recognize her voice. A little over a month had gone by since she'd last spoken to him. Not long, but a lot had happened to him since then. Hopefully it was long enough. Sending up a silent prayer, she twisted the handle and pushed open the door.

Chapter 3

Lynn decided not to disguise her voice. It would be too much of a strain trying to keep it consistent. She had to trust in the hope that Ward wasn't thinking too clearly and wouldn't remember.

Even so, she winced at the false brightness in her voice as she approached the quiet figure on the bed. "Commander Sullivan? My name is...Lee, and I'm with the Northwest Hospital Volunteers. I visit servicemen in the military hospitals, and I've been asked to add your name to my list."

She had no idea if such an organization existed, but it sounded good. She held her breath as Ward gave no indication that he'd heard her. He lay with his back to her, but she knew by the rigid set of his shoulders that he wasn't asleep.

Praying he hadn't recognized her voice and was simply ignoring her, Lynn repeated, "Commander Sullivan?" He wore no hospital gown, and the smooth tanned skin of his back looked dark against the stark white of the bandages.

Someone had removed the one on his head—a reassuring sign, Lynn thought as she moved closer.

"Who asked you?"

The muffled demand took her by surprise. "Er...Captain Phillips. I met him in the lounge downstairs." She'd told the truth in a roundabout way. That made her feel a little better. "He seemed very worried about you. He thought you might like someone to talk to."

"I don't feel like talking to anyone."

"That's fine. I understand. I'll talk and you can listen."

"Forget it, I'm not interested."

"It's not good for you to be alone. You'll get depressed."

"I prefer to be alone. Is that clear enough?"

Lynn tightened her mouth. She wasn't about to give up that easily. "Look, I want you to know that I don't discuss my patients with anyone, if that's what you're worried about. My lips are sealed, just like the doctor's. But you can't lie there in total silence all day, it's bad for your vocal chords. You need someone to talk to, and since you won't allow any of your friends in, you'll have to make do with me."

She waited several moments without getting a response. "I don't care if you swear and curse or hurl insults at me, just as long as you're making some kind of noise. Okay?"

He mumbled something she didn't catch. Deciding it might be better if she didn't ask him to repeat it, she reached for the glass on the table. With a clatter of ice cubes she poured water into it from a small jug. "Would you like a drink?"

"Gin."

This time she did identify the hoarse growl. With a small grin she said briskly, "Now you know that's not allowed. But it might help that throat of yours if you drink some ice water."

A long moment of silence followed. Shrugging, Lynn carefully put the glass back on the table. "All right, maybe later. Now, what shall we talk about? The weather? Would you like me to describe what I can see from your window?"

Without waiting for an answer, which she knew probably wouldn't be forthcoming, Lynn walked over to the window and drew back the drapes. The room overlooked the rear of the hospital, where gardens had been laid out like a small park.

Lynn uttered a small sound of pleasure. "It's beautiful out there. I can see wide paths winding between flower beds thick with chrysanthemums and dahlias, all different colors, and little white daisies. There are carpets of marigolds, rhododendron and camellia bushes, and people sitting on white benches beneath the trees. I'm not up on trees, but I think they're maples, I can see a willow and what I believe are several mountain ash."

She dropped the curtain and turned back to the bed. "As soon as you're well enough, I'll take you out there. You'll feel so much better with the sun on your face—"

"For God's sake, button it."

She broke off, her throat constricting. Again she wondered if he'd recognized her voice. She looked at him. His face still bore the cruel bruises. A wide strip of plaster covered one eyebrow. But above all, his eyes captured her attention. They were open, staring sightlessly in her direction. The intense light in them that she remembered was gone, and his face expressed the agony of his loss.

For the first time she began to understand a little of his suffering. She felt as if a fist closed around her heart, and she took a small step toward him before she caught herself. She couldn't touch him. She must remember she was a stranger—a hospital volunteer, nothing more.

"The next time I come, I'll bring a book so I can read to you. What kind of books do you enjoy?" Speaking carefully, she moved around the bed until she faced his back once more. Looking at his face had just about broken her heart.

He didn't answer, and she tried again. "Mystery? Western? Horror? How about Hemingway? I have a large collection of historical romance, how about one of those?"

If she'd hoped to get a reaction from him she was disappointed. His broad back remained impassive, his bandaged shoulder hiding his face.

Her fingers itched to plump up his pillow, or straighten his covers. Anything to let him know she cared about his comfort. She was terrified that if she touched him, he'd have her thrown out. It would be easy enough for him to do—the bell hung just above his head, within easy reach of his fingers. It would take him seconds to find it and bring the nurses running.

Desperate to find a subject he might be interested in, she blurted out, "What kind of sports do you like?" Good going, she thought with a grimace. What little she knew would fill a postcard, if that.

Still he didn't answer.

"Ah, well, I'm not really up on football or baseball," she amended. "Actually, I didn't know much about basketball until the Blazers started winning... Oh...that's right, you're from California, I don't even know what team—"

She broke off as Ward, with a grunt, turned on his back. "What's it going to take to shut you up?"

She flicked an uneasy glance at the bell. "Newspapers?" she asked hopefully. "I could bring in a newspaper and read it. Magazines? There must be at least one magazine you'd like me to read to you. How about letters? Is there anyone you'd like me to write—"

"No! No letters, no magazines, no books." His drawn features emphasized his hard mouth as he tilted his head toward her. "Look, I know you're only doing your job, but I'd really appreciate it if you'd do it somewhere else. Okay?"

It wasn't okay. But there didn't seem to be much she could do about it at the moment. "I'm sorry you won't let me help you," she said, wishing she could find some way to get through to him. "It isn't a crime to need someone, you know. But if you're determined to wallow all alone in your misery, that's your choice. After all, it takes a big man to admit he needs help."

She had reached the door when he spoke again. "What did you say your name was?"

Her pulse skipped. "Lee." She shouldn't have picked a name so close to her own, she realized as she waited for him to speak again. She should have given it more thought.

"I appreciate the offer."

She let out her breath slowly. "You're welcome, Commander Sullivan." His tone hadn't changed—he still sounded stiff and unfriendly—but the words helped a little. And apparently he hadn't recognized her voice.

For a long moment she thought he wasn't going to speak again, and her heart sank. Was he going to add her to his list of unwelcome visitors after all?

"I guess . . . if you're going to be by this way sometime . . . I could stand a little headline news."

It was a grudging consent at best, but the small victory had Lynn's heart soaring. "I'll be back," she promised softly, and slipped out of the room.

She had barely closed the door when she heard the doctor's voice behind her. "Just what do you think you're doing?"

With a start she turned and looked up with a frown of warning. "Shh!" she whispered, her finger on her lips.

"He's sleeping." The last thing she needed was for the surgeon to blurt out her name outside Ward's door.

Dr. Harper scowled at her. "I want to talk to you," he muttered and marched down the corridor to the elevator.

The nurses looked at Lynn in surprise as she followed the doctor past the station, and she sent them a shrug of apology. She hoped they wouldn't get into trouble for her unapproved visit.

Inside the surgeon's office, he waited until she'd sat down before asking curtly, "Now, maybe you'll explain what you were doing in Commander Sullivan's room, when he'd left express wishes that you not be allowed in there?"

"He didn't know it was me. He thought I was a volunteer."

"Oh? More lies?"

Lynn took a deep breath. "Dr. Harper, Ward needs a friend, whether he admits it or not. He won't see anyone who knows him. This is the only way I could see to help him."

"It wouldn't have helped him one bit if he'd realized who you were. In any case, the commander has made it very clear he doesn't want to talk to anyone. He won't even talk to a psychiatrist."

"Then he needs me even more." She leaned forward and stared earnestly into the doctor's wary eyes. "If his problem is in his mind, then he's going to need someone he can trust, someone he can talk to and confide in, or no one is going to be able to help him. I know Ward better than any stranger could know him. I know how his mind works and how to get through to him."

She crossed her fingers in her lap. "I know I can build up his trust, if he gives me half a chance. At least he didn't throw me out just now. And he even suggested I bring a newspaper with me the next time. That's more than anyone else has managed to do for him so far. I'm the only one he's talking to right now."

"Are you sure you're not just looking for a story?"

Lynn stifled her resentment. It was a logical question for someone as careful as the doctor to ask. "I swear to you, I just want to help Ward. And if the only way I can do it is by pretending to be someone else, then I'll do it. And I promise I'll be careful. He'll never know who I really am."

The surgeon sat stroking his jaw for so long that Lynn's neck ached with tension. "Well," he muttered at last, "I don't like it, but you're right. No one has been able to get through to him. Maybe you can. In any case, I can hardly stop you visiting him as long as he's agreeable."

He sat up in his chair and looked hard at her. "I have to warn you that if Ward Sullivan realizes who you are, things could get nasty in a hurry. He could take out all his frustration and bitterness on you—just because you're there. In his present frame of mind, there's no telling what might happen. Under these circumstances people don't always behave as they would normally."

With a leap of her pulse Lynn nodded. "I understand. I'll be careful. But I'm not going to walk away from him now, not while he needs me."

"Whatever his reason for not wanting anyone he knows, and particularly you, near him, it has to be a strong one. I hope, for both your sakes, that it's not because of some animosity between you. I don't want him upset."

"Neither do I," Lynn said fervently as she got to her feet. "Believe me, I'll do everything in my power not to upset him."

The doctor stood, doubt still visible on his face. "Mrs. Barclay, if you should upset him in any way, I will be forced to terminate your visits immediately. Do we have an understanding?"

Lynn held out her hand. "Please call me Lynn. And thank you, Dr. Harper."

"Don't thank me. I just hope I'm doing the right thing for my patient." He took her hand and squeezed it.

Elated, Lynn practically ran down to the lounge area. The phones were all occupied, and she fidgeted impatiently while she waited.

She called Marjorie first. The editor's voice quavered with curiosity. "Been waiting to hear from you. How's the commander?"

"Doing fine." How many more lies would she have to tell before this was all over? Lynn wondered helplessly. Marjorie was her friend, which made it twice as hard, but she was also an editor. And Ward's blindness would make a great follow-up story.

"He's recuperating nicely in the hospital," Lynn added. "He was lucky, he got away with minor injuries, so I guess there's no real story."

"That's too bad." Marjorie's disappointment sounded clearly over the phone. "Could have given you quite a boost to have had a follow-up on that piece you did on the Blue Angels."

"Tell me about it." Lynn closed her eyes briefly. If the news got out it wasn't going to be from her. She was passing up a great opportunity to capitalize on the story, but for once her career wasn't important. Preserving Ward's wishes and his dignity was what mattered now, and she would protect him at all costs.

Promising to be back in the office the next day, Lynn hung up, then dialed her parents' number. This time her mother answered and quickly accepted the collect call.

"Sorry about that," Lynn apologized, "but I'm on a public phone. I thought I'd call while I had the chance."

"Where are you?" her mother asked.

Without thinking, Lynn answered, "I'm at the hospital—" She silently cursed when a shocked gasp sounded in her ear.

"Hospital! Which hospital? What happened? Are you all right? Wait! I'll get your father—"

"Mom . . ." Lynn sighed when she realized she was talking to empty air. Her father's worried voice boomed on the line. "Lynn? For heaven's sake what—"

"Dad, it's not me. It's...a friend. I heard he was hurt and wanted to see him."

"A friend? Who is he? How come you've never mentioned him before?"

"I haven't seen him in years. I was up here doing the follow-up on the story and heard that he was here in the hospital." There she went again, Lynn thought miserably.

"What's wrong with him?"

Lynn chewed her lip. She didn't know if her parents were aware that Ward flew for the Angels, but if they did, and she mentioned the accident, it wouldn't be long before her father put two and two together.

"Nothing serious," she said casually. "He's going to be all right."

For years she'd put up with her parents' constant probing into her private life, always making allowances for them, always conscious of the fact that she was all they had. Although Sarah's name had never been mentioned since the day her father had handed over the chest, Lynn knew that neither of her parents had truly recovered from the tragedy. They were terrified of losing touch with their one remaining child.

As she fended off her father's insistent questions, Lynn had one thought in mind. For the first time, she really had something to hide. If they knew that she intended to be by Ward Sullivan's side until he recovered, it would destroy them.

All the painful memories would be dragged out in the open again, and Lynn wasn't sure that her father could handle that now. She knew her mother wouldn't be able to endure the trauma. She was a frail woman; the distress could make her ill.

Finally Lynn was able to reassure her father that she would be back in Portland that night. She had something to do before she drove back home, and no one was going to stop her. Least of all Commander Ward Sullivan.

Lynn spent the long afternoon wandering among Seattle's downtown stores, and then had an early dinner. The official visiting hours at the hospital were from seven till nine, and she wanted the entire two hours to spend with Ward.

The evenings were probably the toughest on him, she thought as she dabbed a light touch of lipstick on her mouth. He couldn't read or watch television, and although he had a private room, he had to hear the visitors arriving at other rooms on his floor.

It would be a couple of days before she could come back again. She wanted to spend this one evening with him, and hopefully, give him something to look forward to.

She was uncomfortably conscious of the fact that Ward neither expected her, nor particularly wanted her there. The knowledge gave her cause to be a little apprehensive as she approached his room, but it certainly wasn't enough to stop her. A herd of wild elephants wouldn't be enough to stop her, she thought wryly as she tapped on the door.

His muffled answer could have been anything, but she took it as an invitation and pushed open the door. Shock snatched her breath away when she caught sight of him.

He sat propped up against the raised head of his bed. His hair tumbled over his forehead in an unruly tangle of black curls, and dark stubble covered his jaw. His chest was bared above the covers, except for the white sling that supported his arm. And he looked straight at her as she walked in.

"If you're a doctor," he said hoarsely, "I need my medication. If you're a nurse, get the doctor and bring me a razor. If you're anyone else, get the hell out of here."

Lynn recovered her poise. He'd only appeared to be able to see her. Now that she was closer, she could see his eyes were unfocused. "And good evening to you, too, Commander Sullivan," she said brightly.

Ward groaned. "Oh, God, not you again. Where the hell is that doctor?"

Lynn peered at him anxiously. "Are you in pain?"

"Of course I'm in pain. My head feels like a walnut in a nutcracker." His voice had risen to a roar, and Lynn spun around. "I'll go get a nurse," she said quickly, and rushed out the door.

A friendly faced nurse with silvery hair smiled at her when she reached the station. "It's Commander Sullivan," Lynn sputtered in her haste to get the words out. "His head is hurting and he's yelling for the doctor."

The nurse pulled a face. "I know. He's been ringing the bell every half hour. He's not due for medication until 10:00 p.m. He knows that. I think he's just testing us."

Lynn frowned. "Testing you?"

The nurse nodded. "Patients do that sometimes. It's a form of paranoia. They want to be sure that someone knows they're there and they're not being abandoned or ignored. It's worse in the commander's case because he can't see. He just needs the reassurance that we're out here."

"But he said his head is hurting him," Lynn insisted, still not convinced.

"Anxiety, that's all." The nurse leaned over and patted her hand. "Don't worry, he'll be fine. You're his friend, Mrs. Barclay, aren't you? I recognize Dr. Harper's description of you."

Lynn nodded. "Yes, but Ward doesn't know that. He thinks I'm a volunteer."

"So the doctor told me." The nurse gave her a look of sympathy. "I hope you know what you're doing. You've got a tough one on your hands there. I wish you luck."

"Thanks," Lynn said soberly. "I've got a feeling I'm going to need it."

Tucking the newspapers she carried more securely under her arm, she marched back to Ward's room. He hadn't moved, and sat glaring in her direction when she closed the door.

"Doctor?" he asked sharply, as she laid the papers down on the table next to his bed.

"Nope. You'll have to make do with me until he gets here."

His head swung in her direction. "I thought you were going to get me a nurse."

"I talked to her. She said she'll bring your medication when it's due. In the meantime, I brought you some newspapers. I thought you might like me to read to you."

"What I would like," Ward said, his voice harsh with bitterness, "is to be able to read them myself. Failing that, I would really like a razor. This beard is driving me nuts."

"And how do you propose to shave without cutting off your nose?"

She'd offered the lighthearted remark without thinking, and was devastated when Ward said nastily, "I don't need you to remind me of my limitations, thank you. Believe me, I'm fully aware of them."

"I only meant..." She pulled in a short breath. She was going about this all wrong. If she was going to help him, she would have to be as tough as he was.

She pulled a chair up to the bed and settled herself on it. "All right, so why don't you ask one of the nurses to shave you?"

"I did. She said they only shaved patients in the mornings."

"Then I guess you'll have to put up with it until then." She unfolded the first newspaper to the front page and began to scan the headlines. She was startled when Ward said abruptly, "Why don't you do it?"

"Pardon?"

"Shave me. Or isn't that in your job description as a volunteer?"

The newspaper rattled in her hands. Of course. As a volunteer she should expect requests like that. Excitement nudged her when she realized that Ward was actually asking her for help. The sensation flared into something else when she thought about performing such an intimate task for him.

She swallowed. Hard. "Ahh...I haven't had too much experience—"

"You shave your legs, don't you?"

Embarrassed, she muttered, "Yes."

"Well, it's the same thing, isn't it?"

She stared at him, at a loss for words.

"Look," Ward said irritably, "I'll probably hate it a lot more than you will, take my word for it. But I'll hate it even more if I have to go all night with this itchy jaw. So what do you say we give it our best shot?"

Lynn folded up the newspaper and laid it back on the table. "Electric or blade?" she asked, not quite steadily.

"Electric. It'll be a hell of a lot safer."

Amen to that, Lynn thought as she rose to her feet.

It took her several anxious minutes to locate a razor. The nurses could offer her only disposable razors, and short of buying an electric one, Lynn was faced with the possibility of having to use one of those.

To her immense relief, a passing male intern heard the conversation and handed over his razor, which apparently he carried everywhere he went.

"I'm on duty for thirty-six hours at a time," he explained. "I have to shave whenever I can get the chance."

Promising to leave the razor at the nurses' station when she was finished with it, Lynn thanked the intern and hurried back to Ward's room.

"I don't suppose you're the doctor," Ward muttered, when she closed the door behind her.

"I'm the next best thing," Lynn answered cheerfully as she approached the bed. "I have in my hot little hand one electric razor."

"Well, well, things are looking up."

She ignored his sarcasm and examined the razor. She'd never used an electric one before. Maybe she should have stuck with the disposable ones after all, she thought, examining the lethal looking weapon in her hand.

"So, what are you waiting for? It'll be down to my chest if you don't get on with it."

Her glance strayed to his chest. His lean build was deceptive. The sling almost hid a sprinkling of dark chest hair, but she couldn't help noticing his muscles were well developed, like the biceps in his good arm. A ripple of awareness disturbed her, and she turned away.

"Wait, let me get a towel." She started toward the tiny bathroom when his growl stopped her.

"I don't need a damn towel. Just get on with it."

She knew how much he was hating the situation. She could hear it in his voice. She looked from the razor in her hand to his tense jaw and said faintly, "Maybe you could manage it yourself if I guided you."

"I'm left-handed, for God's sake—a fact I have to keep explaining to the fool therapist, who's trying to teach me how to take care of myself."

"Oh." She eyed his left arm in the sling and sighed. "All right, but I can't promise to do a professional job."

"Lady, I'm not going to be lining up for inspection. I just want to get rid of the itch."

Taking a deep breath, Lynn plugged the cord into the outlet above Ward's head. She flicked the tiny lever on the razor with her thumb and was rewarded with a faint buzz. "Okay, Commander, brace yourself," she murmured, and reached for his jaw.

Ward forced himself not to jerk away when he felt the soft, cool fingers on his face. He tried to relax his facial muscles, knowing it would make things easier for this determined little volunteer who wouldn't leave him alone.

The humility of having to depend on someone like her for something as mundane as shaving infuriated him, and he was trying very hard not to take out his frustration on her.

He knew that most of the volunteer staff were teenagers, experimenting with the nursing profession before making up their minds whether or not they wanted to make it a career. He didn't want to send an overemotional young girl from his room in tears, and incur the wrath of the head nurse, who was a formidable dragon.

Yet he wasn't sure that this volunteer was a teenager. Her voice sounded more mature, and the sophisticated fragrance that drifted by his nose reminded him less of a sweet young thing and more of a seductive, earthy woman.

Whatever made him think such a thing? he thought irritably. He hadn't had those kinds of thoughts for some time. It had to be the long hours he'd spent flat on his back with nothing to think about but the stark blackness surrounding him.

Or maybe, he thought uncomfortably, it was the velvet grip of cool fingers holding his chin while the razor slid slowly down his throat. Up until now he'd never imagined that shaving could be an erotic experience.

Furious with his treacherous mind and too-responsive body, he put it down to his weakness. Once he got out of this damn hospital—

Reality punched his stomach like a cold fist. What if he never saw again? What then? What was he going to do when he left the hospital? How was he going to survive?

He could feel beads of ice cold sweat breaking out on his brow. He wasn't sure he wanted to survive without flying. That's what scared the hell out of him—that he'd be tempted to end it all. He jerked his head away from the gentle, yet firm fingers. "Okay, that'll do."

"But I'm not finished," the pleasant, mellow voice protested.

"Oh yes, you are. I've taken about as much as I can stand."

"Well, you're entirely welcome, Commander Sullivan."

He heard the faint resentment in her voice and was immediately angry with himself. He wanted to yell at her to get out of his room and leave him alone to suffer in peace.

He wanted to tell her not to waste her precious time with someone who neither appreciated nor cared what she did for him. He wanted to order her not to come back, to tell her that it drove him crazy to hear a voice and not be able to see a face behind it.

He did none of those things. Instead he tried to make up for hurting her feelings by saying, "Didn't you bring a newspaper with you?"

Lynn stared at him in surprise. His sudden outburst had unnerved her. She'd been shaky enough holding his chin in her nervous fingers, terrified she was going to hurt him. When he'd jerked away from her, she'd fully expected him to tell her to get out.

"Yes, I did. Would you like me to read it?"

He gave a curt nod. "Out loud."

She felt a smile tug at her mouth. "I wasn't intending to read it to myself." She reached for the paper and settled herself once more on the chair. "All right, let's see." She unfolded the front page and studied it.

The news headlines looked so depressing. The latest problems with unemployment, drug busts in California and Florida—surely there had to be more cheerful news than that. She turned to the local pages and began scanning the stories in there.

"How old are you?"

His abrupt question shocked her. "I beg your pardon?"

"What are you doing here, anyway? Haven't you got anything better to do than hang around hospitals at night? Don't you have any boyfriends?"

He sounded angry, as if she'd offended him in some way. He'd turned his head in her direction, his gaze aimed several inches above her head. Her heart turned over with sympathy for him.

How awful it must be, she thought, not to be able to see the person he was talking to. It must be like living in a void with no beginning and no end. Just vast, black empty space.

And how much worse to have his sight taken from him so suddenly, without warning. Bad enough when a person is born without sight, but to know what he's missing, to be afraid he might never see the world again, must be terrifying. And the thought that he might never fly again had to be destroying him.

The revelation dissolved any resentment she might have felt at his direct questions. "I'm thirty," she said quietly. "How old are you?"

She knew perfectly well how old he was, but she wanted to see how he'd react to her throwing the ball back in his court.

His mouth tightened to a thin line. "Okay, rude question. I'm sorry."

Elated that he'd actually apologized, she said firmly, "You didn't answer my question."

"Thirty-six."

"Isn't that a little old to be throwing tantrums?" She held her breath as a flush of temper swept across his face.

"Excuse me for blowing off a little steam. You know what they say—if you can't stand the heat, get out of the kitchen."

Lynn smiled. "Commander, I can take all the heat you're willing to dish out. You know why? Because I truly believe that under that gruff, grizzly bear attitude of yours beats a warm, caring heart, and that as soon as you're feeling better, you're going to be smiling at me. And I'm going to hang around to see that day."

"Why?"

That was a good question. She sought for the right answer. "Because that's my job. That's why I'm here. And once I start something, I'm the type of person who has to see it through to the bitter end."

"What if I don't want you around until the bitter end?"

Her heart seemed to stop beating. "Just say the word, Commander, and I'll take you off my list."

The seconds ticked by in the silent room. Outside the door a burst of feminine laughter seemed incongruous as Lynn waited for his answer.

"Well, I guess I can put up with you—on one condition."

Her pulse quickened. "What's that?"

"That you stop calling me Commander. It reminds me too much of where I should be, instead of lying in this damn hospital. My name's Ward, okay?"

She grinned with relief and sheer delight. "You got a deal, Ward."

"You never mentioned your last name."

Taken off guard, she hesitated a fraction too long. "I guess we won't need it if we're on a first-name basis. I hope you'll call me Lee?"

He frowned but didn't pursue the subject and she relaxed. "By the way," she said, "in answer to your question, I do not have a boyfriend so my time is my own."

"Married?"

He'd thrown in the question casually, but she sensed a certain alertness in the way he tilted his head, waiting for her answer.

"Once. Not anymore. How about you?"

It was natural that she ask, she told herself. He would have wondered why she hadn't. Even so, she found herself tensing as he pinched his lips together.

"No. I never got around to it. The navy put too many restrictions on my life..."

His voice trailed off, and Lynn decided that was enough questions for one day. It was more than he'd told her at the interview. She wasn't sure she was comfortable with that fact.

How would he feel, she thought nervously, if he found out he'd been talking about his personal life to not only a journalist, but to someone he regarded as an enemy?

He mustn't find out, she warned herself, as she searched through the paper for something to read. Whatever happened, he must never know that his helpful, willing volunteer named Lee was in reality a woman he once knew as a gangly child called Charlie. At least not until he was able to cope on his own.

She finally decided on a heartwarming story about a dog who saved the lives of three children when their house caught fire. She finished reading and glanced up. "Now that's the kind of—"

She broke off. Ward's chin rested on his chest, and he'd closed his eyes. He was breathing deeply, his face relaxed in sleep.

Unexpected tears sprang in Lynn's eyes, and she dashed them away with the back of her hand. Tears weren't the way to help him. He wouldn't thank her for being weak. He was a powerful man, and in spite of everything he'd been through, in spite of his occasional lapse into a frustrated outburst, that power still emanated strongly.

It was that strength, that gritty courage, that was going to see him through this nightmare. And it was the formidable force that burned inside him that would help him survive if, God forbid, he should lose his sight forever.

Whichever way it went, Lynn thought as she folded the paper and rose quietly to her feet, she was going to be there for him. She'd hold his hand, bear his moments of temper, listen to his complaints and try to be strong for him. Until she knew he could manage without her.

She crept silently across the room, then turned to look at him. He hadn't moved, and in sleep he seemed incredibly defenseless.

Please, she prayed silently. *Please, give him back his sight.* He didn't deserve this, she thought, carefully closing the door. He'd been through so much already.

As soon as he was well enough, she promised herself, she would tell him all of it. About the diary and about how her parents were so wrong to blame him. And how sorry she was for not trying to contact him all those years ago. As soon as he was well enough.

As she hurried across the parking lot to her car, she was already wishing the hours away until she could see him again. She was lucky, she reminded herself, that she worked part-time at the office.

It scared her to know how intensely she needed to help Ward. She was getting in deep. Somewhere along the line the schoolgirl crush had begun to mature into something much stronger. That bothered her.

But as she climbed into her car and started the engine, she was sure of one thing. She was committed now, and no one, not even Ward himself, could turn her away. Not until she knew without a shadow of a doubt that Ward no longer needed her. Nosing the car out into the street, she turned south and headed for home.

Inside the hospital Ward grunted and rubbed the end of his nose with his good hand. His eyes flickered open and, as always, the jolt of his blindness caught him unaware. How long would it be, he wondered, before his system got used to the shock of opening his eyes and seeing nothing but a black wall?

Remembering the little volunteer, he tensed. Tilting his head to one side to listen, he asked quietly, "Are you there?" Silence greeted him, and he was disturbed to feel a twinge of disappointment. She'd gone. After the way he'd treated her he'd be surprised if she ever came back.

He settled himself more comfortably on the bed and stared up at where the ceiling would be. He'd miss her cheerful voice, he admitted, a little shaken by the knowledge. He didn't want to miss anyone. He didn't want to be that dependent.

He had to learn independence all over again, a very different kind of independence, and he didn't need to start leaning on other people. Somehow he would have to learn to manage for himself, or he would never be in control of his life again.

He would tell her, he promised himself as he drifted back toward the blessed relief of sleep. If she came in to visit him again, he'd tell her he didn't want her coming back. The decision gave him no pleasure as his body succumbed to the exhaustion creeping over him. No pleasure at all.

Chapter 4

The hours seemed to drag on interminably, and Lynn found it hard to concentrate on her work. She fought the temptation to call the hospital, knowing that she would get nothing more than a stock answer. She would have to wait until she visited Ward again to know how he was progressing.

Getting ready to leave for Seattle again, she dreaded calling her mother. She wasn't used to being elusive with her parents, and it worried her. She managed to escape from the barrage of questions by more or less hanging up on her mother, something she would never have done under normal circumstances.

But these weren't normal circumstances, Lynn reminded herself as she drove into the hospital parking lot. In fact, she doubted if anything would be the same again, now that she had reencountered Commander Ward Sullivan.

She went straight to his room, afraid that she might be

stopped if she made inquiries at the desk. Heart thumping, she tapped on the door and slowly eased it open.

Her spirits soared when she saw him sitting upright on a chair by the bed. He wore headphones, which were hooked up to a small tape recorder, and he sat with his eyes closed. A look of intense concentration tightened his features, and the fingers of his right hand moved restlessly over the arm of the chair.

He had more color, she decided, and the dark shadows under his eyes had faded. He wore a maroon-colored robe buttoned over the sling, and blue pajama bottoms covered his long legs. Leather slippers protected his feet, while a heavy bandage encased one of his ankles.

His face, though still marred with purple bruises, had lost the puffiness of two days ago, and he sat with his back stiff and straight. Smiling, Lynn advanced toward him and lightly touched his arm.

His expression changed immediately, becoming alert and wary as he lifted his hand to remove the headphones. "Who is it?" he demanded, obviously annoyed at being interrupted.

"It's Lee, your friendly barber, though it looks as if someone is doing a better job than I could." She touched his jaw with light fingers and was dismayed when he jerked his head back.

"Then I guess you're released from duty." He scowled in her direction. "Thanks for dropping by, but as you can see I'm managing quite well now. So you're free to go and find someone more deserving of your time."

Lynn tried not to let her voice reveal her anxiety. "Now, is that the way you talk to someone who's come all this way to brighten your day?"

"All what way?"

Angry with herself for the slip, she said casually, "Clear across town. I made a special trip to see you. I've brought today's paper to read to you and Robert Parker's latest novel. You're not going to tell me you don't like Robert Parker. Everyone loves Spencer.''

"I don't need you to read to me." He held up the headphones still clutched in his hand. "Ever heard of books on tape? They're narrated by experts.''

She winced at his put-down. A faint stirring of temper warmed her cheeks, but she held it down. She wasn't going to let his bluntness get in the way of her purpose. She was going to see him through this thing whether he liked it or not.

Though she had to be careful, she warned herself. One wrong word from him and Dr. Harper would be breathing down her neck. "Well," she said brightly, "that's nice. But can your experts read the stories in the newspaper? Aren't you just a little bit curious to know what's going on behind the headlines?''

"Not in the least. Now if you wouldn't mind leaving me alone..."

She didn't know what she would have answered if the door hadn't opened at that moment and a dark-haired nurse with oversized spectacles breezed into the room.

"Now, Commander Sullivan," the nurse said cheerfully, "it's time for your spin around the gardens.''

"I'm not going anywhere," Ward said. "I'm quite happy to stay here and listen to the rest of this novel, if everyone would just leave me alone.''

The nurse clucked her tongue. "That's not the attitude I want to hear. It's a beautiful day outside, just what the doctor ordered. Plenty of sunshine and fresh air. It will give you an appetite. Then maybe you'll eat your food instead of sending it back to be thrown out.''

"If you had to eat the garbage they serve in here you'd send it back, too.''

The nurse glanced at Lynn and pulled a face. "Well, I'm sorry, Commander, but I have to take you outside again. I have my orders, and you of all people should know that orders have to be obeyed. You can listen to your novel out there."

"Do you leave him alone outside?" Lynn asked, guessing that without walls surrounding him, Ward must lose his sense of security.

The nurse nodded. "He's fine. We have wardens walking about to keep an eye on him."

"Yeah, they're making sure I don't do wheelies across the lawn."

The dry comment earned a sympathetic smile from the nurse. "Believe me, Commander, if you cooperate like a good boy, you'll be doing those wheelies in no time. Now I'll go and get the wheelchair." She turned her back on him, which was just as well, thought Lynn, as Ward sent a murderous look in her direction.

She could hardly blame him. How he must hate being patronized. "Excuse me," she said abruptly as the nurse reached the door. "Could I take him outside? I have time to stay and talk to him, maybe that will help?"

She glanced at Ward, holding her breath. His face looked like a thundercloud, but to her relief, he didn't say a word.

The nurse glanced at her watch. "Well, I am short of time. You sure you can manage?"

"She's a hospital volunteer," Ward said, surprising Lynn. "She should be able to handle a wheelchair."

"Oh, in that case, I'll get the chair," the nurse said, obviously relieved.

She left, and Lynn sent a guilty glance at Ward. He had unknowingly lied on her behalf. Again she wondered how he would react if he knew the truth. Pushing the thought away, she asked, "Does this mean you're willing to put up with my company for a while?"

"It means," Ward said, "that I'm settling for the lesser of the evils. At least you don't talk to me as though I'm in kindergarten." He rubbed his jaw with his good hand. "Besides, I hate bossy women. Especially ones with authority."

The door opened, and the nurse surged through, propelling a wheelchair in front of her. "Okay, Commander, upsy-daisy."

Lynn hid a grin at the disgusted look on Ward's face as the nurse grabbed his arm and tugged. The grin faded as the nurse hauled him into the chair with seemingly little concern for his discomfort. Apart from a small grunt as his feet were tucked into the footrests, he made no sound of protest, though the hollows in his cheeks had deepened with pain.

Lynn could feel knots in the back of her neck by the time the nurse stepped back and said brightly, "He's all yours. Turn right in the hallway and take the elevator at the end. It will lead to the garden doors. If you have any problems, just signal to one of the wardens. They're wearing white coats and blue arm bands."

"And packing 45s, no doubt," Ward muttered.

The nurse punched him lightly on the arm. "Cheer up, Commander, this isn't the State Pen, you know."

"You could have fooled me." He straightened his shoulders and turned his head in Lynn's direction. "I'm ready if you are."

Lynn stepped around the back of the chair and hooked her purse higher up her arm before grasping the handles. "Do you want to take the recorder?"

"No. I can't concentrate out there." He flapped his right hand at her. "All right, let's go."

It was easier than she'd feared. The elevator was roomy and the chair surprisingly easy to maneuver, considering the weight of the man seated in it. In no time, it seemed, she had him through the doors and out into the balmy summer afternoon.

"Do you want to sit in one place, or shall we go for a walk?" she asked him as she wheeled the chair down a wide pathway between heavily scented flower beds.

"It really doesn't make any difference to me," Ward said, lifting his shoulders in a shrug of indifference.

"Of course it does. You don't have to see to appreciate the change of scenery." She pulled the chair to a stop. "Listen. Tell me what you hear."

He was silent so long she thought he wasn't going to answer her. Then, in a low, husky voice that just about broke her heart, he said slowly, "Birds. I can hear the birds. I wish I could be up there with them."

"Can you hear the leaves rustling in the wind? They're maple leaves," Lynn said unsteadily. "Big fat green leaves that look like they're dancing." She moved the chair forward, concentrating on finding the words that would make him see what she could see.

"The sun is changing their pattern. Their shadows are spread out over the grass, like huge green umbrellas."

Ahead of her she saw a small gathering of people seated on benches beneath the trees. She pushed the chair closer, talking all the time. "There's a group of women under the trees, all talking at once. One of them talks with her hands, she must be excited about something, her cheeks are flushed and she looks as if she's conducting an orchestra."

Lynn kept quiet as she passed the group, so that Ward could hear the voices. She wished she could see his face. Though with his stoic expression it would be hard to tell if he was enjoying the trip.

"I think this would be a good place to rest," she said, pulling the chair to a halt beneath the sweeping arms of a willow. "It's in the shade. It'll be nice and cool."

She put the brake on the chair, then sat on the bench next to it. "You can see the hospital from here. It looks lovely with the sun gleaming on the white walls."

She glanced at Ward's face and wished, with all her heart, that she could wipe away his look of despair. "The sky," she went on, struggling to keep her voice steady, "is a brilliant blue today, with those big white fluffy clouds that look like swans floating across a lake."

His face creased in pain, and she caught her breath. "Are you all right?" she asked anxiously.

"Fine. Your descriptions are vivid. You should be a writer."

Caught off guard, her face froze. She'd been speaking like a writer. Had she given herself away?

She was still trying to compose an answer when he added bitterly, "I'd prefer not to be reminded of how the sky looks. I'm more used to seeing it from a different angle, anyway."

She drew a shaky breath. "So why don't you tell me what it looks like from up there?"

"I don't think I can describe it with justice. All I can tell you is that it's like nothing on earth. It's more than just a view, it's a feeling, a sensation of being free—like breaking away from the ordinary boundaries and entering a whole new dimension where all the rules are changed and you're the one setting new ones..."

His voice trailed off, and Lynn swallowed past the lump in her throat. "I think you describe it very well."

He gave a short derisive laugh. "It's all I've got left now—the memories."

She couldn't bear to see that lost expression on his face. What if he never regained his sight? How could he live a full life without the one thing in the world he loved—his job? But no matter how bad she felt for him, she couldn't let him dwell on it.

"Until you go back, you mean."

"There's a good possibility I might never go back."

"There's every possibility that you will." She leaned forward in her urge to reassure him and laid her hand on his restless fingers. "Ward, you must believe that. Set your mind and soul on that one thought and never let it go."

He let her hand rest for a moment or two on his, then pulled his fingers away from her touch. "So tell me," he said in an obvious attempt to change the subject, "what made you want to spend your spare time hanging around hospitals?"

Once more at a loss for words, Lynn dug in her purse for her sunglasses. Putting them on, she said lightly, "I'd rather you told me why you chose to fly for a living. That sounds a lot more interesting."

"Speed," Ward said, after a moment. "It's always fascinated me. I wanted a motorbike when I was younger. I used to watch the riders flying along the highway and imagine how it would feel to be going that fast with the wind in my face."

And the bike would have been an impossible dream. She knew that he'd grown up more or less in the streets. Sarah had told her how Ward's father had died when Ward was small. His mother had been too busy working to make ends meet to supervise a lonely, restless boy.

But she could imagine him on a bike. She could see him sitting astride a gleaming machine, head thrown back in laughter, white teeth flashing in the sun. He had such a wonderful laugh, Lynn thought with a pang of nostalgia. How she'd love to hear it again now.

"When I joined the navy," Ward was saying, "all I wanted was to get as far away from home as possible. I wanted to see what the rest of the world was like. Then one morning I saw a blue and gold Navy jet streaking straight up to the sun. I watched its trail until it stretched clear across the sky, and it just about blew my mind.

"I knew then I'd never be satisfied until I knew what it was like to fly one of those machines and paint a trail across the sky. And then when I did, nothing meant more to me ever again than being up there—" His voice halted abruptly, and he tilted his head to the heavens, his useless eyes closed in despair.

Impulsively she reached for his hand and held it. "You'll fly again, Ward. You will. You just have to want to bad enough."

"Oh yeah?" He lowered his chin, tilting his face toward her. "I wish I could share your optimism. But I tell you, lady, you can't change things just by wishing. I found that out a long time ago, and no one wished harder than I did back then."

Lynn's pulse fluttered as she looked at his set face. He had to be talking about Sarah. If only she could tell him. The urge to confess who she was, to tell him the whole story, to let him know that Sarah hadn't meant to kill herself was so compelling, the words actually hovered on her lips.

She was still holding his hand. She looked down at the strong fingers, tense against her palm, and knew she couldn't say anything. Not yet. She couldn't take the risk of losing the fragile ground she'd gained.

As if she'd communicated her thoughts, Ward turned his hand in hers, giving her fingers a light squeeze before letting them go. The contact brought a warm flush to her cheeks.

Then, as if regretting his impulsiveness, he said sharply, "Don't let me keep you. I'll be fine here on my own. They'll come and get me when it's time to go in."

"I don't have anywhere else to go," Lynn assured him. "Besides, I'm enjoying talking to you."

He looked as if he was about to say something, but a sudden shout of laughter from the group of women turned his head. "They seem to be having a good time," he said, leaving Lynn to wonder what it was he'd been going to say.

She couldn't go on for long like this, she realized. Sooner or later she would have to tell him. Maybe now that he'd had time to think about it, he might be more receptive to talking to the woman whose sister he'd loved.

Deciding that it would do no harm to test the waters, Lynn said tentatively, "I understand that someone has been asking about you. A young woman who says she's an old friend of yours. I guess she's been asking to see you."

His face swung in her direction. "If you're talking about Carolyn West, I'm not interested. She's a reporter for some local town newspaper, and I refuse to have my personal problems splashed all over some cheap rag for the sake of sensationalism."

Waves of resentment surged through Lynn as she struggled for control. Surely he couldn't believe that all she'd wanted was a story? Had his bitterness affected him so much, he couldn't accept the hand of friendship she'd been willing to extend to him?

Even as the questions raged hot and angry in her mind, her heart was already making excuses for him. He was ill. He was blind for pity's sake. She had to make allowances.

Even so, she had a hard time hiding the resentment in her voice as she wheeled him back to his room.

He refused her offer of help in getting out of the wheelchair. "I can manage," he told her, weariness making his voice gruff. "I need the practice."

Lynn accepted his refusal without comment. She needed to get away, to have time to think about what she was doing and the risks she was taking.

"I'll be back tomorrow," she told him.

He nodded, apparently without enthusiasm.

At least he hadn't given her an argument about coming back, she reminded herself as she walked slowly across the parking lot to her car. Now all she had to do was decide if she was doing the right thing after all. His bitterness went a good deal deeper than she'd realized.

She wondered how much of that was due to his affliction, and how much of it was so deeply embedded from the past that she might never reach him. Her depression lasted for the entire drive back to Portland.

She spent the evening with her parents, having agreed to go for dinner. She regretted the promise long before the meal was over. She wrestled with her problem until Ward's agonized face filled her mind and she could no longer concentrate on her mother's chatter.

"You're awfully quiet," Ellen Barclay said, as Lynn struggled with the large helping of cherry pie on her plate.

"I'm enjoying this delicious dessert." Lynn lifted another spoonful to her mouth.

"I don't know." Her mother shook her head, rustling the faded blond curls that fell across her forehead. "I was saying to Daddy, I don't think you've been the same since you started chasing after this story in Seattle, didn't I, Daddy?"

Lynn's father peered at her over the top of his glasses. "You all right, kitten? Not overdoing it, are you?"

"I'm fine." Lynn reached for her napkin and dabbed at her mouth. "I'm also full. I can't eat another bite."

The older woman sighed. "You see what I mean? You always used to eat like a horse."

"That's when I was seventeen," Lynn said mildly. "I was still skinny then."

"So what's this story about?" her father asked for the umpteenth time.

"I'm sorry," Lynn said, trying to hide her exasperation, "I can't say anything about it until it's finished."

"Why not?"

"That's investigative reporting, Mother. It's one of the rules." She hoped fervently that her parents would accept the weak excuse. "Now, if you don't mind, I'm tired. I'll help with the dishes, then I think I'll go home and have an early night."

"You're not going back to Seattle tomorrow, are you?"

Lynn managed to smile at her mother's concerned face. "Yes, I am. I'm planning on staying there a day or two. I'm getting tired of the drive."

"I don't know why you can't find things to write about in Portland," George Barclay muttered, his fingers absently tracing what was left of his hairline. "All this running around."

Lynn breathed a long sigh of relief when she finally escaped to the solitude of her own apartment and could think about Ward without being afraid she'd speak his name.

The drive back to Seattle seemed endless the next morning. Lynn kept hearing Ward's harsh voice condemning her without a chance to defend herself.

How long could she keep up the pretence without letting something slip? How long could she swallow her pride, knowing that the frail relationship she had with Ward had been built on lies and deception and that the person he was beginning to respond to didn't exist? And how long could she live with the guilt of knowing that it was only because of his condition that she was with him now?

She was tense with anxiety as she tapped on Ward's door later that day, wondering in what kind of mood she'd find him.

Again he sat by the window in a chair, headphones securely covering his ears. He'd discarded the sling, though his arm was still heavily bandaged. She watched him for a moment, trying to gauge his disposition from his expression.

As always his features told her nothing. His hard mouth was set in a firm line, and his closed eyes could give her no clues. He'd tilted his head slightly to one side, as if he was concentrating, and Lynn wondered what he was listening to as she approached him. Very gently she touched his arm.

He reacted immediately, swinging his hand up to the headphones as he twisted his face toward her. "Yes?"

She wondered if she imagined the fleeting look of expectancy that crossed his face. "Hi," she said softly, "it's Lee. How're you doing today?"

His expression didn't change, but his voice sounded almost mellow when he answered. "Not bad. They had me walking around this morning."

"Well, that's great." If only she knew that he was pleased to see her, she thought. Just once she'd give anything to hear him say he'd missed her, or that he'd looked forward to seeing her again.

"Yeah, though I'm not ready to drive my car or buy groceries."

He'd said the words simply, making a statement of fact without any trace of self-pity. Yet the very simplicity of the things he could no longer do made it seem all the more heartbreaking.

He hadn't mentioned what was really important to him—his career and his love affair with flying. How it must hurt him to face the possibility that he might never again do the things he loved most.

Lynn made up her mind to speak to the doctor and find out exactly what could be done to help him. And if it meant that Ward should talk to a psychiatrist, then somehow she'd persuade him to do it.

"It's a beautiful day outside," she said, forcing a cheerful note in her voice. "How would you like to go out for a breath of fresh air?"

His chin lifted, and tiny lines creased his forehead as he turned his face in her direction. He seemed to be concentrating, and she felt a touch of fear. Had she unknowingly said something to give herself away? She was retracing her words when, to her relief, Ward said quietly, "I'd like that."

Her pulse leapt as she studied his face. It was the first time he'd indicated that he enjoyed her presence. Feeling buoyed up beyond description, Lynn patted his arm. "Just hold on, there, while I get a chair. I'll be back in a minute."

Ward heard the door close and relaxed his shoulders. She'd come back. For a while he'd been afraid she wouldn't. He didn't know why he hadn't stuck with his decision to dismiss her.

Maybe it was the thought of being abandoned all by himself. He imagined nothing but open sky and space around him and the thought gave him the willies. It was ironic that the one place where he'd always felt safe had now become an alien environment.

He'd reminded himself over and over how crazy he was to look forward to her visits. He couldn't afford even that small luxury if he was going to learn to take care of himself.

He was on his own now, and he refused to be dependent on anyone. Certainly not a cheerful little volunteer who didn't know how to take no for an answer and who would disappear from his life just as soon as he was on his feet.

So why was he sitting here feeling less miserable by the minute, just because some well-meaning good Samaritan was doing her job? Because he was stupid, he answered himself as he heard the door of his room open again.

The squeak of rubber wheels on the vinyl floor told him she'd come back. Just for a little while, he promised himself. It couldn't hurt to feel the sun on his face once more and the warm wind ruffling his hair, while he listened to the calm, steady chatter of the woman who had become his only link with the outside world.

Lynn winced as she bumped the wheel against the foot of the bed. Just as well he wasn't in the chair, she thought wryly. He'd probably lash her with one of his caustic comments.

"I saw the nurse down at the end of the hall," she said as she maneuvered the wheelchair around to the window. "I told her I was taking you out. I didn't want them sending out a search party for a runaway wheelchair with a determined Navy pilot at the helm."

"Fat chance of that."

His tone had been dry, but Lynn could have sworn she saw a slight tilt of his mouth. Delighted at this chink in his formidable defenses, she angled the wheelchair next to his chair and put on the brake.

"Okay, Commander. Your carriage awaits." She put her hand under his arm and prepared to brace herself for his weight.

He pulled away from her grasp and raised his hand in the air. "I can manage," he said with a faint note of impatience.

She stood back, prepared to help if he had any problem.

Using his good arm, he shoved himself upright and stood for a moment, apparently finding his balance. Lynn chewed her lip as he patted the empty air next to him until he found the back of the wheelchair. Carefully he traced his fingers down the arm and across the seat, then began to edge sideways into position.

Lynn's face creased in sympathy as she watched him. He looked remarkably unscathed after his ordeal. The bruises on his face had almost disappeared, and his body looked so strong and healthy it was hard to comprehend how helpless he was without his sight. Looking at him stand straight and tall, it was easy to imagine him striding confidently out of that room and back into his life as if nothing had happened.

Even as she thought it, his bandaged ankle struck the footrest protruding from the chair. With a muttered curse Ward reached out, searching for something to hold on to while he regained his balance.

She moved without thinking, throwing both arms around his upper body to steady him. She felt the weight of his arm clamp around her shoulders as his chest collided with hers.

His face was inches away, so close she could feel his breath on her cheek. His skin smelled of soap, a subtle, musky fragrance that seemed to enclose her in its intimacy.

His chest pressed warm and hard against her breasts, and she heard his sharp intake of breath as she shifted her weight against him to steady him. For a moment or two his fingers dug into her shoulder, and heat flooded her body as time seemed to pause, holding them captive together. Her own breath stilled as he raised his hand until his fingers rested on her cheek. For a wild moment she thought he was going to kiss her. Then he pushed himself away, and she dropped her arms.

"You okay?" she asked, cursing herself for the tremor in her voice.

"I will be, as soon as I get into that damn chair."

She was almost glad of his irritation. It helped to clear her blur of confusion. With a steady hand she guided him into the chair and watched him settle himself.

"There's a breeze today," she said, her voice a shade too high in her attempt to break the tension that seemed to crackle in the small room. "I'll get you a blanket."

He didn't answer, and she wished desperately she knew what he was thinking. Judging by his expression, she told herself as she tucked the blanket around his knees, he was most likely angry and frustrated by his clumsiness. Obviously the close contact hadn't affected him. She was the one overreacting to the incident; her pulse still rocketed like a warning flare.

She would have to be very careful, she reminded herself. She couldn't afford to give him any hint that he meant anything more to her than a name on her list of patients.

With that in mind she managed to keep up a determined stream of chatter as she pushed the wheelchair down the pathway with its bright borders of flowers. Ward sat silently with only the back of his head visible to her.

They reached the shade of the willow, and she pulled the chair to a stop, placing it alongside the bench so that she could sit next to him.

"Do you spend as much time with all your patients?" Ward asked suddenly. "Or am I enjoying special privileges?"

Lynn clung to that word *enjoying* with more pleasure than was prudent. Not knowing quite how to answer his question, she said lightly, "The privilege is mine, Commander. You're quite a celebrity around the hospital. Everyone asks me how you're doing." That much was true, she thought wryly. It seemed that every nurse on his floor took a keen interest in his welfare.

"And what do you tell them?"

She glanced at him, but could tell nothing from his expression. "Just that it's a pleasure to talk to you and that you're handling everything remarkably well, under the circumstances."

"Am I?" He sounded cynical as he turned his face in her direction and asked, "Aren't you giving me a little more credit than is due?"

"I don't think so. I can only imagine what you must be going through. I don't know if I could deal with it as well as you're doing."

His face twisted in a grim smile. "I don't really have much choice, do I?"

"But it might not be permanent. Dr. Harper said—"

"Doctors tell you what you want to hear." Lynn was about to protest, but his next words were uttered as an obvious attempt to change the subject. "So what does a hospital volunteer do in her spare time?"

Wishing she could find the words to give him some hope, she leaned back on the bench. Across the lawn the usual group of women chattered incessantly, while a young man in a white coat, wearing the arm band of a warden, strolled down the path.

A nurse appeared, leading an elderly gentleman by the arm. The old man shuffled along, looking neither right nor left as the nurse led him to a vacant bench and sat him down. Bending over him, the nurse spoke, then patted the frail shoulder before leaving him and striding purposefully back to the buildings.

Lynn watched the old man for a moment, her heart aching at the wistful expression on his face as he watched the group of women laughing together.

That's how Ward must feel, she thought, with a sudden stab of pain. Shut out, isolated, alone in his own little world of misery and fear. Yet to look at him now, except for the tense line of his jaw and the unfocused stare, he appeared normal in every way and utterly controlled.

He must have an iron will, she thought, looking at his tightly composed features. And yet he had to be living on hope, even if it was unconsciously. How would he cope if he knew he would never fly again?

Her pulse quickened when Ward tilted his head on one side. "You still there?"

For once she'd heard a note of uncertainty in his voice, and she hurried to reassure him. "Yes, I'm sorry. I was just enjoying the peace and quiet."

Again that wry smile flickered across his face. "Sometimes you can have too much peace and quiet."

Dismayed by her thoughtlessness, Lynn said again, "I'm sorry. What was it you asked me?"

"I was curious about what you do when you're not visiting patients. Do you work? Or do you have an understanding husband who doesn't mind sharing you with undeserving people like me?"

He was bound to ask questions sooner or later. He'd apparently forgotten she'd already told him she was divorced. She should have been more prepared. She wondered what he'd say if he knew she was giving up a long-planned trip to California to pay for her motel bills, just to be near him. He'd probably be scathingly blunt about her sanity.

Stumbling over her words as she groped for inspiration, she said, "No husband. And I have an office in my apartment where I free-lance, so that gives me plenty of spare time."

Hurrying on before he had time to ask what she free-lanced in, Lynn added, "I like to go to the movies, and I read. Mostly historical novels and biographies. I like listening to music—what I call mood music. I guess they call it easy-listening. I'm not much of a rock fan. What about you?"

She held her breath, then let it go when he shook his head and answered, "I'm more into country and blues."

Thankful to be on safe ground again Lynn said, "Really? I wouldn't have imagined you a country fan."

"No?" He shrugged his wide shoulders. "There was a time when I even used to play a little guitar."

The memory was sweet and infinitely painful. She'd forgotten how he'd sit on the back steps and play her sister's guitar. She remembered warm summer nights, a soft-scented breeze drifting over her bedroom windowsill, carrying the insistent croaking of bullfrogs blended with soft twanging chords of a country song.

She heard again Sarah's soft voice singing the simple tune, and the strange, warm sense of longing Lynn had felt spread through her body in a familiar ache of remembered torment. Her words were husky in her tight throat when she whispered, "My Summer Love."

"What?" He turned his head sharply, and she could see the tension in his braced shoulders.

How could she have been so stupid? she thought, searching in silent desperation for the right words to say. She hadn't even realized she was speaking aloud. "It used to be a favorite of mine," she said finally, throwing caution to the winds. "Do you know it?"

She waited in an agony of suspense, watching the emotion ripple across his face. Pain—so deep she could feel it. She had to tell him, she thought, twisting her hands together in unconscious indecision. She had to do something to wipe that awful look off his face.

She was still trying to form the words when Ward said abruptly, "I'm very tired. I'd like to go back to my room."

Pushing the chair back toward the building, Lynn wasn't sure if she was relieved or sorry that he'd forestalled her confession. The more time she spent around him, the more difficult it became not to let him know who she was.

She had so much she wanted to say to him, so much to share. She'd never been able to talk about Sarah with anyone, certainly not her parents. Now, for some reason, she felt a deep and compelling need to talk about what happened, to bring it all out in the open and examine her feelings.

She was tired of avoiding the subject, of trying to pretend that it never happened. It was like denying Sarah's existence, as if she'd never been born. But Sarah had lived seventeen beautiful years, and Lynn had shared twelve of them. She couldn't go on denying the memory of those years.

Only by reliving them, bringing them back into the light and examining them, could she ever hope to bury the ghost of her sister. And if Ward, too, was haunted by that ghost, he needed to share those years with the only person capable of doing so.

Soon, Lynn promised herself. Soon she'd be able to tell him. She'd work out the best way to break it to him and then pray that he would understand why she'd had to deceive him.

Feeling a little better, she navigated the door to his room and wheeled him to the bed. "Can I help you?" she asked, as he levered himself out of the wheelchair.

"I can manage."

She pulled the chair away from him and turned it toward the door. "Then I'll let you get some rest." As he straightened in front of her, another memory returned to torment her. The disturbing pressure of his hard chest against her breasts, his breath warm on her cheek, his mouth just inches from hers.

A deep, intense longing to know the touch of his mouth robbed her of breath. She pushed the wheelchair toward the door, struggling for composure. She couldn't afford such fantasies, she warned herself as she angled the chair through the doorway.

Turning, she glanced back at the bed. Ward sat on the edge of it, the thin fabric of his robe stretched across his broad back. He stared sightlessly into the space in front of him, his face pensive, his mouth pulled down at the corners.

It took all her willpower to stay where she was. She wanted so badly to go to him, put her arms around him and cradle his dark head on her breast. Unsteadily she said, "I'll see you tomorrow."

He nodded. "Thanks for the ride."

"You're welcome." She slipped through the door before her emotions got the better of her and she gave in to the unbearable need to comfort him.

She carried the memory of his touch, his hand on her shoulder, his body resting against hers, long after she'd left him. But in the endless hours of that restless night in her lonely motel room, she couldn't shake the conviction that she was heading for inescapable and devastating heartbreak. Yet she couldn't turn away now. She was in much too deep already. The discovery only deepened her depression.

Chapter 5

He awoke as he always did these days, lying with his eyes closed, afraid to open them. He had begun to dread the ugly disappointment that drained his energy every time he lifted his eyelids and found the black, empty space still imprisoning him. He let his mind wander, delaying the moment he would have to face the reality of his plight once more.

Almost at once the memory of a compassionate, mellow voice invaded his thoughts. That was something else that had become a habit. Even more so since those few seconds when he'd felt the soft contours of a warm female body pressed so enticingly against him.

He'd noticed that since the accident his other senses seemed to have intensified, as if making up for the loss of his sight. He'd never noticed it more than when he'd held Lee for a too-brief moment, his whole body reacting to the whisper of her breath, the subtle fragrance that reminded him of warm summer fields and the exquisite sensation of her rounded breasts against his chest.

He'd thought at that moment that he would suffocate. He'd tried to tell himself, over and over again, that his reaction was natural. How long had it been since he'd held a woman that close? Obviously too long.

But it was more than that. Lying here, bound by the dark void around him, he silently admitted that he'd begun to look forward to her visits with an intensity that was not only stupid, but downright dangerous.

He'd been intrigued to discover that she was taller than he'd imagined. Taller and softer. Oh, how he longed to know what she looked like. The longing deepened to torment when he acknowledged that the chances were he'd never know.

Bracing himself, he forced his eyes to open. The frustration was like a physical pain building in his chest, consuming his body until he wanted to scream. Pulling in a long breath, he fought to control the despair that engulfed him.

Damn them all. Damn the doctors who kept telling him his sight could return. Didn't they know that he could see through the tangle of lies? That he was fully aware the false words of hope were merely a prop until he was strong enough to accept the truth?

Why the hell hadn't he died in the crash, instead of dragging on like this, no good to anyone, least of all himself? All he knew was flying. All he'd ever cared about was flying. And no one ever flew a plane blind. He would have been better off dead.

"You fool," he whispered aloud to the spiritual force beyond the blackness surrounding him. "You took the wrong one."

Lynn hurried up the hospital steps, her hair lifting in the cool September wind that brought a promise of rain. She hoped it would hold off long enough for her to walk with Ward that afternoon. He had come a long way in the past few days. In fact, Lynn thought, with a quickening of her pulse, he was almost back to normal, except for his blindness.

Going up in the elevator, Lynn wished he would talk to a psychiatrist. He still flatly refused, saying he didn't believe in all that mumbo jumbo. Lynn sighed. Even Dr. Harper had given up trying to persuade him.

The doors slid open and Lynn stepped out into the corridor. When she'd talked to the doctor, he'd as good as told her that there was nothing more he could do. Now it was up to Ward himself. Yet it seemed as if Ward had accepted his condition and had given up all hope of recovering his sight. And no matter what she said or did, she couldn't change his attitude.

He seemed determined to make it on his own, in spite of his handicap. And watching his steady progress, she had come to believe that if he never regained his sight, he would at least achieve the independence he so badly craved.

Sooner or later he would no longer need her. And she wanted to enjoy what little time she might have left with him. She had already let the deception go on way too long. Once he realized who she was, the easy companionship she enjoyed and treasured would be instantly erased. She wasn't ready to face that moment yet.

Right now he still needed her. She was his only visitor from the outside, and she knew, although he'd never said as much, that he looked forward to her visits. She hated to give that up a moment sooner than she had to.

Her cold sense of shock when she opened the door to his room and found it empty unnerved her. Surely he hadn't been released already? She spun around, intending to ask at the nurses' station, and saw him limping slowly down the corridor, tapping his cane in front of him. A young nurse walked beside him, encouraging him with a quiet word.

Lynn curled her fingers when Ward turned his head and smiled in the nurse's direction. The glimpse of the dimple in his cheek stung her with bittersweet memories. For a moment she thoroughly disliked the pretty nurse.

Although angry with herself, she greeted the nurse with a smile as the petite woman guided Ward through the door.

"I guess I can leave him in your capable hands," the nurse said, then patted Ward's arm. "You're doing fine, Commander. You'll be getting your walking papers any day now."

Lynn's throat seemed suddenly dry when she said, "So they're going to spring you at last, huh? You finally got rid of the wheelchair."

He turned his head at her greeting, and once more she saw the dimple flash in his cheek. "I thought you weren't coming until tomorrow."

Lynn watched him tap his way to the edge of the bed and sit down. "I managed to get away a day early. Though it appears that you're doing just fine without me." She held her breath, willing him to contradict her.

"They still don't trust me to go outside on my own."

"By the looks of you it won't be long." He would never know how much it hurt to say those words. Once he could manage without her, she would have to leave. Remembering her reaction when she'd seen his empty room, she had a sudden vision of the long empty weeks yawning ahead with nothing to look forward to, and her throat ached with misery.

"Maybe. But until then, I still need your steady arm and cheerful voice to guide me."

He was looking her way with an air of expectancy. She thought back to the first time she'd come to his room. He'd done his best to get rid of her then. Now he seemed, if not eager, at least pleased to be with her. It made it all the harder to realize that her time with him would soon be over.

"Can you make it outside on foot?"

"Sure. As long as you don't mind walking at a snail's pace?"

"Of course I don't mind." She waited for him to stand, then reached for his arm to guide him out of the door. "It looks like rain, so we'd better make the most of it while we can," she said, trying her best to sound bright.

"I don't mind the rain," Ward assured her. He took a step forward before she was ready for him. His cane banged her ankle, then clattered to the floor, and her swift gasp of pain escaped before she could stop it.

"Sorry," Ward muttered, "that was clumsy of me."

Dismayed to see the sudden frustration on his face, Lynn laid her palms on his chest. "It was my fault," she said quietly, "I got in your way."

It had been an unconscious gesture to reassure him, but she felt his body tense under her hands. Before she could pull away, he reached up and covered her fingers with his warm palm.

"I'm glad you came today," he murmured and lifted her fingers to lay them against his cheek.

Warmth rushed through her body. Like most dark-haired men, his beard grew fast, and she could feel the slight prickle of his jaw against the sensitive pads of her fingers. She wondered if he could possibly hear the thunder of her heartbeat as those few precious moments held her breathless.

She could feel a pulse beating in his jaw, as wild and erratic as her own, and the urge to reach up and touch his lips with hers became unbearable. His clean musky smell swamped her senses, and she felt herself lean toward him. His initial start of surprise when her lips met his unnerved her. Before she could withdraw, he returned the pressure, sending a shaft of warmth throughout her body. It lasted but a second or two before he lifted his mouth from hers. Then he stood waiting, as if unsure what to say next.

Embarrassed, Lynn said quickly, "Those clouds are coming in pretty fast. We'd better make a move."

He was silent on the way down in the elevator, and she wondered what he was thinking. She wondered if he knew that her heart still raced with the memory of his touch, his kiss, and that his words kept repeating over and over in her mind. *I'm glad you came today.*

She'd recovered her composure by the time they stepped outside into a cool, damp breeze. "Summer's almost over," she remarked, as they began to stroll slowly down the pathway. "The maple leaves are beginning to turn. They'll be a riot of color in a couple of weeks, if this cool weather keeps up."

She felt a shiver chase down his arm, and glanced at him. His face was set in the grim lines she'd come to dread, and she searched in her mind for something to say to soften that expression.

"I like the winters," she went on, forcing a positive note into her voice. "There's something so cozy about sitting in front of a crackling fire with the wind blowing outside and snow blowing against the windows."

"Have you always lived in Seattle?"

He'd said it with the air of someone determined to make light conversation. Normally she avoided his personal questions, but his wistful expression touched her heart, and she found herself answering. "No. I grew up in Oregon."

"Really? So did I. What part?"

"Klamath Falls." The necessary lie slid smoothly from her lips. She was getting entirely too practiced at it, she thought miserably.

"I've only been through there on the freeway. Tell me what it was like growing up in Klamath Falls."

"Pretty much like anywhere else in Oregon, I guess." She hesitated. Then, as he waited expectantly, she added, "It was fun, actually. I had a great childhood. Though I think my parents despaired of me ever growing up to be a lady. I was a little too wild, and hopelessly independent."

"In what way?"

"Well, I once packed up a lunch and left home to hitchhike to California."

"What happened?"

"The police picked me up. I was causing a lot of attention walking down the freeway."

"How come?"

"I was only four at the time."

His soft chuckle delighted her. Encouraged by the success of her story, she dug into her memories to find more. As long as she kept to her childhood years, before Ward had met Sarah, she would be safe, she told herself. There would be nothing to connect her with the kid he'd once called Charlie.

Steering him across the grass toward the small lake, she told him about the Halloween night she'd dressed up in an old sheet and had climbed an elderly neighbor's tree to frighten the rest of the kids.

"The old lady had been getting ready for bed," Lynn explained, "and happened to look out of her upper-story window. She came close to having heart failure when she saw a ghost floating in midair."

Ward's laugh rang out as she finished the story, and Lynn's pulse leapt at the sound. The dimple deepened in his cheek as he turned his face toward her. "And you must have given your parents heart failure," he said, still smiling. "Were you an only child, or were there more at home like you?"

"Oh, that wasn't the worst of it," Lynn said, deliberately ignoring the question. Gently, she turned him back toward the building. "There was the time I experimented with a cigarette in the bathroom. I dropped the match and set the toilet roll on fire. I tried to smother it with a towel, and that caught fire and I shoved it into the toilet—are you all right?"

She clutched Ward's arm as he stumbled, concern tightening her muscles when she saw his strained expression.

"I'm all right." His voice sounded strangled, but he managed a smile as he twisted his face toward her. "It's the ankle, it still does that at times. I guess it's not completely healed..."

His voice trailed off, and Lynn's heart skipped a beat when she saw his white face. His tense jaw convinced her he was in pain, and she said quickly, "I'd better get you back. It's starting to rain, anyway. Can you manage?"

He limped heavily, but nodded at her question. "I'll be fine."

She would have liked to stay and read to him, but his face looked drawn and tired, and his listless voice confirmed his weariness when she got him back to his room.

She left him, worried by the fast deterioration of his stamina. Obviously he wasn't as strong as he wanted everyone to think. She cursed the fact she had to be back in the office the next day. Her time was so precious now, she hated to waste one minute of it away from him.

The moment was fast approaching when she would have to tell him the truth. She couldn't leave him now without telling him everything, whether he wanted to hear it or not. She owed him that much at least. The prospect of how he would react when she did tell him kept her nerves jumping long after she arrived in Portland.

He lay tense and unyielding in his bed as the doctor prodded and probed his eyelids. The questions, repeated so often he despised the sound of them, pierced his mind like red-hot needles.

"No," he muttered through gritted teeth, when the specialist asked if he could see anything. For God's sake, didn't the idiot know that if he could see anything at all other than the dense black curtain smothering him he'd be screaming for joy at the top of his lungs?

At last the ordeal was over, and they left him alone. He'd asked for Dr. Harper, but the gruff voice that had answered him had told him the surgeon was at a conference and wouldn't be back until the end of the week.

When he'd told them why he wanted to speak to Harper, they had murmured those idiotic phrases that he knew were meant to be reassuring but only increased his frustration.

He wanted out. Out of the hospital, out of Seattle, as far away as he could get. And he wanted it now. Not at the end of the week.

The gruff voice had been apologetic but adamant. He was Dr. Harper's patient, and only that surgeon could release him. They would be sure to convey the commander's wishes to the doctor as soon as he returned.

Damn her. He didn't want to be here when she came back. Damn the deceitful, devious, lying witch. She was up to her old game again, hiding behind a false identity just to get near him.

If Sarah hadn't told him the story about the fire in the bathroom, he'd never have guessed that his loyal companion of the past few days was in fact Sarah's sister, the dedicated journalist.

All the time she'd led him on with her sweet voice and her soft touch, pretending to be his friend, pretending to care, when all the time she'd been prying, probing, wheedling words out of him he never would have uttered to another living soul.

How he'd managed to hide his shattering shock had been nothing short of a miracle. He'd been stunned, too confused to think it all through properly.

Hell, he'd told her things he'd never admitted to himself before now. He'd even been tempted to tell her about Sarah. Wouldn't she have loved that—hearing him confess how her sister's death had haunted him, and how he'd never been able to forget the injustice of her family.

How he'd spent years of his life wondering how he could prove to them that Sarah had never told him about the baby. God, he would have begged Sarah to marry him if he'd known. How could they believe that he'd walked out on her? He'd loved her so much, so damn much....

He squeezed his eyelids together. Sarah... Why had she done such a crazy thing? Why hadn't she trusted him enough to know that he would have taken care of her? He should have known, when she started finding reasons to avoid him, that something was wrong. He'd gone over that day to find out why she'd been acting so strange. He'd found out all right. One day too late. What had he done to make her so afraid to tell him?

He swung his legs over the side of the bed and sat up. If only he could see something, faint shadows that could guide him through the mine field of obstacles that lay in his path, he'd damn well walk out of there tonight.

Only he knew that would be suicide. And he'd come too far and suffered too much, to surrender this hellish life that had stubbornly refused to let him go. If this was his punishment for his past sins, he would make it work for him somehow. There had to be a reason he'd lived, though it was beyond him at the moment. But he was damned if he was going to give up on it till he knew what it was.

He stretched out his hand and groped for his cane. His fingers found it and he gripped it hard. This slender piece of wood was going to be his lifeline, and he might as well get used to relying on it.

He still had something to prove, and by God he was going to finish it. And the sooner he started working on his new life, the better.

He stood, pausing until the disorientation he always felt at first faded. Once his head was clear he swung the cane from side to side in front of him. Meeting no resistance, he stepped forward and repeated the process.

He had taken four steps when his cane tangled in something and tripped him. Thrown off balance, he felt himself falling, and he knew a moment of panic before crashing into the wall.

His injured shoulder took the full force of his weight, and the white-hot pain spiraling down the length of his back made his senses swim. He fought the nausea as he awkwardly righted himself.

Dazed with pain, he found he'd lost his sense of direction. Cursing, he dropped to his knees and began to crawl, one hand testing the floor in front of him. His fingers closed around his cane, and he lifted it, swinging it in a wild arc around him until it hit something. Raw, powerful anger erupted in his chest when he pictured himself huddled like an animal on the floor.

A low growl rumbled from his throat as he hauled himself to his feet. With the cane held in front of him, he moved toward the object he'd struck. It proved to be a chair, and he grasped it to steady himself. Taking a shuddering breath, he made an effort to control the waves of fury consuming him.

She had reduced him to this. Was this what she'd wanted all along—revenge? Was that why she'd played this cat-and-mouse game, pretending to be his friend, waiting all the time for the opportunity to smash what little self-respect he had left into a million pieces?

Was she even now writing every word down, dragging his past, and God help him, his miserable future into the lime-light for everyone to enjoy?

She'd chosen the ultimate retaliation. Once more he'd be examined and judged without a chance to defend himself. History repeating itself, only far more cruelly.

Well, two could play at that game. Now it was his turn. He wouldn't let her know he'd discovered her charade. He'd lead her on, pulling her deeper into her nest of deceit, until he knew for sure why she had gone to all this trouble. And then he was going to cause her more grief than she'd ever imagined.

Even as the ugly thoughts seized his mind, he recognized the real source of his anger. It wasn't the cruel deception so much as the discovery that the woman he'd begun to care for, in a way he hadn't felt since Sarah, didn't exist. And it hurt. It hurt more than he would have thought possible.

With an inhuman howl of rage, heedless of the agony in his shoulder, he grabbed the chair and flung it as hard as he could. He heard a splintering crash and knew he'd hit the window. In the next second the door opened behind him. He recognized the nurse's voice, high-pitched with concern, and he cut her off with a thunderous roar.

"Get out! Get the hell out and leave me alone."

Lynn couldn't shake the odd sense of foreboding that had tormented her ever since she'd left Seattle. She knew that Marjorie was worried about her, though the laconic editor would never put it into words. Lynn however, was fully aware of Marjorie's furtive gaze following her every move when she was in Lynn's office.

Lynn couldn't bring herself to tell Marjorie about Ward. Much as she wanted to share her problem with her friend, she knew that the editor was bound to pressure her for a story.

And what a story it would make, Lynn thought, as she skimmed through her account of the fund-raising party given at the governor's home. It could make her career. Who wouldn't be moved by the courage of an undaunted Navy pilot, who'd had more than his fair share of tragedy?

She could never write it of course. Apart from the obvious immorality of making Ward's misfortune public news, the story was far too personal, and she was far too close to the subject.

She laid down her pencil with a sigh. Far too close was right. And the problem had begun to make itself felt in more ways than one.

Her parents were not blind or stupid. Their questions about her frequent trips had become more insistent, until at last Lynn had confessed that she had met a man and was dating him. Her mother had immediately suggested she invite him down to Portland, as they were anxious to meet him.

It had taken Lynn several minutes to convince her parents that the friendship was a casual one and would never amount to anything more. It was strange how she'd never realized, until lately, how protective her parents were. It had never bothered her before, but now she felt smothered by the constant questions and concern, even though she knew the reasons behind it.

She hated being forced to resort to lies. But how could she expect them to accept the fact that the man she was falling in love with was the same man they blamed for their daughter's death?

Besides, she told herself wearily as she gathered up the sheets of paper on her desk, there was no point in dredging up all that pain and agony again. In a very short time now, Ward would be leaving the hospital. And once she told him the truth, her relationship with him would almost certainly be over.

She assumed he would be sent to a rehabilitation center somewhere. Probably in California. And knowing Ward as well as she did, she had no doubt that it would be no time at all before he was fending very well for himself on whatever path he chose.

She wondered what his options were at this point and if he'd settled on anything. She would ask him, she decided, the next time she saw him.

The foreboding still clung to her, slowing her steps as she entered the hospital foyer. The sensation deepened when she knocked on Ward's door and, receiving no answer, pushed it open to find the room empty.

Only this time, Lynn realized, aware of her skin prickling with apprehension, the room was really empty. It looked unlived in. The bed had been stripped of its covers, and everything had been cleared off the top of the small chest.

Lynn gasped as she realized the reason Ward had vacated the room. Someone had taped a thick sheet of clear plastic over the window, covering the missing lower pane. Whatever had caused that much damage must have had considerable force behind it.

She slid her tongue over lips that had gone dry. Clamping down on the wild visions running rampant through her mind, she made for the door. Someone would be able to tell her what had happened. Someone would tell her where he'd gone.

Dr. Harper. She'd have to talk to him—if she could find him. Damn, it didn't matter, she'd find him if she had to search the entire hospital.

The nurse sitting at the station shook her head when Lynn blurted out the doctor's name. "Sorry," she said, her smile fading to a look of concern. "Dr. Harper won't be back until Friday. Is there something I can help you with?"

Lynn drew in a slow breath. "Commander Ward Sullivan," she said more calmly. "He isn't in his room. Can you tell me where he is?"

"Oh, yes," the nurse answered, nodding. "He's been moved to the ground floor. You'll find him in the psychiatric wing. They'll tell you which room."

Stunned, Lynn could only stare at the round face in front of her. He would never have gone there voluntarily. He would have fought it all the way. He was probably tearing the place apart right now. Muttering her thanks, Lynn backed away from the desk.

She quickly found the psychiatric wing and hurried down the corridor. A nurse stopped her at the main doors.

"I have permission from Dr. Harper to visit Commander Sullivan on a regular basis," Lynn explained, praying that the privilege still held.

The nurse frowned. "Well, the doctor's not in the hospital, and I'm not sure the patient wants to talk to anyone. He—"

"He'll want to see me," Lynn urged, hoping desperately that was true. "Just tell him it's Lee. Please?"

After a moment's hesitation the nurse disappeared behind the doors. After what seemed like hours, but in fact could only have been minutes, she returned.

"You can go in, but don't stay too long. Commander Sullivan needs plenty of rest right now."

Her heart thumping with anxiety, Lynn followed the stiff back along the narrow corridor. Pausing at the door, the nurse turned the handle. "No more than a few minutes," she warned in a whisper, then pushed open the door.

He sat in a padded swivel armchair, his back toward her. Lynn saw the slump of his shoulders in the maroon robe, and her heart ached for him. She wanted to put her arms around him and tell him that whatever it was that troubled him, she was there to help. Instead she stood looking at his dark head for a moment, wondering exactly what to say to him.

"Hi," she said softly, in the end. "I guess you've got a new room."

He lifted his head sharply at her voice, and she saw him square his shoulders. "I had a little...accident with the other one."

"So I saw." She walked toward him, worried by his bleak tone. "What happened?" she said quietly.

"I needed some fresh air and I was too lazy to go outside."

If he hadn't sounded so bitter she could have smiled at that. She sat down on the bed beside his chair. "What really happened?"

He turned his face toward her, and she saw his grim expression. "*I* say it was a little healthy display of frustration. *They* say it was an indication that I'm cracking up."

Lynn felt a cold finger of fear. "I'm sure they didn't tell you that. Have you talked to Dr. Harper?"

Ward shook his head. "He won't be back until Friday. When he gets here, I intend to release myself."

She frowned. "To where?"

"Back to the base. Home. To my apartment."

"Are you ready for that?"

"You bet I'm ready for it." He jerked his left hand viciously in the air and winced. "They keep sending some half-baked shrink in here. Hell, I'm more sane than she is. All those asinine questions she keeps asking..." He shook his head in disgust.

Lynn felt sorry for the psychiatrist. "Can you tell me exactly what happened?"

He sat for a long time, his fingers playing restlessly along the arm of the chair. "I got mad," he said finally. "I happened to be holding on to a chair at the time."

"You threw a chair at the window?" Her incredulous voice sounded loud in the quiet room.

His shoulders rose and fell. "I didn't know the window was there."

Something in his attitude unnerved her. There seemed to be something he wasn't telling her. "Did you explain that to the psychiatrist?" she asked, barely holding on to her resolve not to touch him.

"I'm not explaining anything to a shrink." His voice was gruff with suppressed anger. "Before you know it, she'd have everything I say turned around, and they'd be dumping me in some institution. I'd die before I let them do that."

"So would I," Lynn said grimly.

An odd expression crossed his face. "You sound as if you mean that."

"I do." Unable to hold back any longer, she leaned forward and patted him on the arm. "Don't worry, they can't do anything until Dr. Harper gets back. And he's not going to let them put you away in any institution. Besides, I won't let them."

"And you think they'll listen to a hospital volunteer?"

Lynn stared at him. Again something in his voice made her uneasy, but she couldn't put a finger on it. "I'll make them listen," she said, putting conviction in her voice. "I'll call Captain Phillips and have him do something. I'll call the president of the United States if it comes to it, but I promise you, they are not going to dump you in any institution."

For a moment she had the uncanny feeling he could actually see her. He sat very still in his chair, his eyes narrowed, as if he was doing his best to see her face.

"Why?" he asked, in a low voice.

Her heart skipped a beat. "Why what?"

"Why are you doing all this?"

She swallowed. "Because it's my job."

Again he seemed to be focused on her face. "Aren't you going a little above and beyond the call of duty?"

"I don't think so. The welfare of all my patients is important to me—"

She'd suddenly had enough of the lies. No more. She couldn't go on lying to him anymore. She had to tell him who she was and exactly why she was there. Bracing herself, she look a long breath. "Ward, I—"

The door opened and the nurse stuck her head inside. "I'm afraid you have to leave now," she said, glancing at her watch. "Commander Sullivan is due to take his medication."

"Just a moment longer?" Lynn pleaded.

The nurse shook her head. "Sorry."

"They have to put me out," Ward said nastily, "in case I get violent on them again."

"Now, now, Commander, it's just a mild sedative, to help you sleep."

"It's the middle of the afternoon, for God's sake," Ward muttered.

"You need lots of sleep, if you're going to get well." The nurse advanced into the room, giving Lynn a meaningful look.

Reluctantly Lynn rose. "Maybe they're right," she said, laying a hand on Ward's shoulder. She gave him a gentle squeeze. "Don't worry, I'll be back this evening. You'll let me in for a little while, won't you?" She looked pointedly at the nurse.

"I'll see what I can do." The plump woman took a small container from her pocket. "As long as the commander behaves himself . . ."

Lynn escaped from the room before she vented her anger on the unsuspecting nurse. They were treating him like a child, for heaven's sake. How he must hate that. She had to talk to Dr. Harper just as soon as he got back. They were going about this all wrong. . . .

She pushed her way through the swinging doors, taking great gulps of cool, fresh air. Something had to be bothering Ward a lot to have set him off.

Maybe it was just as well she hadn't had the chance to tell him the truth, Lynn thought as she drove back to the motel. If his emotions were as unstable as his treatment suggested, the last thing he needed was another shock.

Wondering when this whole charade was going to end, she parked the car outside a fast-food restaurant. She'd get some food inside her, she decided, then maybe she would take a nap as well. Something told her she was going to need all her wits about her to deal with this latest development.

A few blocks away in the hospital, Ward lay in the fuzzy world somewhere between consciousness and the deep sleep the medication induced. Released from his control, his mind wandered back and forth, replaying Lee's fervent assurance that she would fight to save him from an institution.

Lynn, he reminded himself. Her name was Lynn. She was Sarah's sister. A journalist. On one level he was well aware of all that. On another his mind was utterly confused.

In the hours he drifted through a half sleep, the person he'd known as Lee somehow kept getting mixed up with the tall, elegant woman a kid called Charlie had become. It wasn't a faceless volunteer's voice he heard, soothing, encouraging, understanding—it was Charlie's. How could someone with that much patience, that much compassion, be the vicious, self-serving fiend he'd portrayed her to be?

She couldn't, his rational mind insisted. Underneath the anger, the self-righteousness, he'd somehow known that. That's why he hadn't told her he'd discovered her deception. He first had to find out why she was doing this. Why she had spent so much time in Seattle, helping him fight every step of the way. If it wasn't his story she wanted, what did she want from him?

A thought pierced through the fog, rousing him from his artificial sleep. Was it pity that kept her coming back? He groaned out loud. No. He didn't want her pity. He didn't want anything to do with her.

She was part of his nightmares that kept returning again and again to torment him. Her family had blamed him for Sarah's death, and in doing so had laid a guilt on him too heavy to ever escape.

He might not have deserted Sarah, as they had so wrongly accused him of doing, but he had failed her just the same. He couldn't forgive them for what they had done to him, and he could not forgive himself. That was the legacy Charlie and her family had left him.

He would tell her, he promised himself, the second she stepped through his door again. He would tell her he knew who she was, and then he would tell her to get out of his life and leave him alone to rot in his own guilt.

He didn't need her pity, and he was damned if he was going to let her use his story. Sleep, at last, claimed him, soothing his troubled mind, and when he awoke again his thoughts were crystal clear.

He didn't have to wait long. Shortly after they'd cleared away the barely touched food from his room, the light tap he'd come to recognize so well alerted him. He kept his back to the door when he heard it open. His fingers gripped the arms of his chair as her low, pleasant voice greeted him.

"Hi," she said, her shoes whispering across the floor as she approached. "Did you have a good sleep?"

His mouth twisted in a wry smile. Forcing his voice to remain calm, he said clearly, "Hello, Charlie."

Chapter 6

She'd known. Somehow, deep down, she'd been expecting it. But that didn't make it any easier. The tiny flicker of fear she'd refused to acknowledge erupted in a flood of emotions—guilt, apprehension, desperation that he wouldn't give her a chance to explain and, most of all, the devastating fact that it was all over. Her time had finally run out.

"Ward, I . . ." She took a step forward, then stopped, reaching for words that weren't there. He swiveled the chair around to face her, and her heart faltered at the animosity stamped on his harsh features.

"How long did you intend to go on with this ridiculous pretense?" Though his eyes focused past her left shoulder, the burning contempt in them seemed to sear her skin.

"Until you were well enough to tell you the truth."

His derisive laugh grated on her quivering nerves. "And tell me, Miss West, just what do you call the truth? If you even know the meaning of the word, that is."

She wished her knees would stop trembling. Slowly she edged over to the bed and sat down, her fingers gripping the covers with the need to hang on to something. "I wanted to help you, that's all. I knew you wouldn't let me if you knew who I was—"

"Damn right I wouldn't. I'd have had you thrown out before you got one foot inside the door."

She felt so cold. Yet deep inside her a tiny ember of resentment began to burn. Everything she had done she had done for him. He had no right to treat her as if she were a criminal. She pushed herself off the bed and made herself walk toward him, until she was standing only inches away from his knees.

"You needed help," she said, her voice low and clear. "You needed someone to talk to, someone who'd listen and understand. I understand you like no one else, because I know who you are. How many people know you, Ward? How many people have you turned away because you're too stubborn, too angry at the world, to give anyone a chance to get close to you?"

The muscles in his jaw tensed. "I've had my reasons, and you know why."

"No, I don't know why. I don't understand how you can let a tragedy rule your entire life. You have to let go sometime. We've all had to let go. And our loss was every bit as painful as yours. If not more so."

"Did that give all of you the right to condemn me? To judge and convict without giving me a chance to defend myself? Even a murderer has his rights, you know."

Her throat hurt so badly she couldn't speak. Is that the way he saw himself, as a murderer? What in God's name had her family done to him?

"Ward, I'm sorry." She sat on the edge of the bed again, knowing that she could put it off no longer. It was time he knew the truth.

"I don't know if this is going to help," she said quietly, "but there's something you should know. Sarah never meant to kill herself. She was afraid to tell my parents about the baby because she knew how they felt about you. She was afraid they'd do something to drive you away. She took the pills and the alcohol because a friend had told her it was the way to get rid of the baby. That's all she meant to do."

The silence in the small room seemed to spread beyond the bare white walls. Outside, the world went on. People talked and laughed and cried. Birds sang, cars sped by on the street, and somewhere high above the clouds, jets droned on their way across the sky. But all Lynn could hear was the echo of her heartbeat thudding in her ears and the painful whisper of her breath.

Ward sat motionless, his face carved in stone. She couldn't even tell if he was breathing, he sat so still. Finally, in a voice brittle with pain, he muttered, "How do you know all this?"

"She left a diary." Lynn swallowed, wishing desperately she had the right to go to him, hold him, anything to disturb that awful stillness in him. "She was hoping to get rid of the baby, then she wouldn't have to tell you. She just didn't want to worry you, Ward. She wanted you both to be happy. She loved you so much.... Her last words were 'I love you, Ward.'"

When had she started crying? Lynn wondered, as the sobs tore at her throat. Her face felt wet with tears, and she pulled her purse toward her, intent on finding a tissue.

"Then you knew." He swung in her direction, his face a mask of pain. "Damn it, you all knew she hadn't told me."

"No, not then." Lynn blew her nose, still talking, in her anxiety to tell him all of it. "My parents didn't want to read the diary, so they gave it to me. I didn't read it until five years later."

Ward swore, making her flinch. "Eighteen years," he muttered. "For eighteen long, miserable years I thought Sarah had deliberately taken her life, rather than trust me to take care of her and the baby. For eighteen years I blamed myself for her death, for failing her in some way I didn't understand."

His head swung in her direction, and his eyes were the color of an Arctic sea. "And you knew. You could have saved me thirteen years of hell, dammit!"

His voice had risen on the last word, and Lynn's nervous fingers tore the tissue to shreds. "I had no idea where to find you, I—"

"I wasn't on another planet. You could have found me if you'd wanted to. What about your father? He's an enterprising businessman, he could have tracked me down. Or did he get some kind of perverse pleasure out of letting me suffer?"

Ward's fingers closed in a fist. "They wouldn't believe I didn't know about the baby. Did they forget they'd blamed me for Sarah's death? Didn't it occur to any of you how I'd feel?"

"No, wait!" Lynn jumped to her feet. "They don't know. I never told them."

His stunned expression made her feel sick. "Why not?"

"I couldn't bring all that pain back again." Forgetting he couldn't see, she held out her hands, willing him to understand. "It had been five years. They hadn't mentioned Sarah's name in all that time. If you had seen my mother after—"

Lynn gulped, fighting to control the tremors in her voice. "I couldn't put her through all that again. It would have destroyed her."

His expression frightened her. "So, just when do you plan to tell them?"

She shook her head. "I...I can't Ward. You don't understand..."

"You've got that right. Is that the version you're going to use when your big story hits the stands? Are you going to forget to mention that I knew nothing about the baby? You must let me know so I can get someone to read it to me. I'm sure everyone will get the utmost pleasure in learning all about my lurid past."

Shock held her rigid for several seconds before she found her voice. "Damn you." Her voice broke, and she gulped back the sob that threatened to destroy her hard-held composure. "How could you even think that I would have so little respect for people's feelings? Do you really believe I would degrade my sister's memory and hurt everyone for the sake of a story?"

Anger did what all her resolve had failed to do. The tears dried on her face. "I guess you're in the right place after all, Commander Sullivan. You're irrational and overwrought, and you need help. Certainly more than I could give you."

His face was a white blur in front of her eyes, his voice a tight growl. "No one asked for your help, lady. And if you're not doing all this for a story, then why the hell have you been hanging around here? Tell me that."

She fought for control. She would die before she told him how she felt about him. Even now, after all the cruel words he'd flung at her, her heart was breaking at the thought of never seeing him again. She could understand his torment, and she was powerless to help him.

She blinked the last of the tears from her eyes. "For Sarah," she said brokenly. "I wanted to help you through all of this to make up for everything my family had done to you. Because I knew that's what Sarah would have wanted."

Her vision cleared, and she saw him turn away. But not before she saw the sparkle of tears clinging to his dark eyelashes. The sight nearly destroyed her.

That this man, so formidable, so unrelenting, could resort to tears was unmistakable evidence of how much he'd loved her sister. Unable to bear any more, she spun away from him and stumbled to the door.

She thought she heard him mutter something as the door closed behind her, but she was too shattered to even care. Half-blinded by tears once more, she fled down the corridor, past the surprised nurse at the doors and out into the cool September night.

She walked for hours, unaware of the dark, empty streets, or of the shadowy dangers that might be lurking there. Lights from the street lamps swelled and faded, and tinkling music spilled from the restaurants and coffee shops as she passed, all of it part of another world.

She let the night breeze cool her burning cheeks and the dark sky soothe her raging thoughts. And when she finally made it back to her car she was exhausted, but resolved. She had one more thing she could do for him, then she would walk out of his life without looking back. She just hoped she could go through with it.

She drove back to Portland that night, forcing herself to stay alert. Dawn had painted broad bands of peach and dusty rose across the sky by the time she pulled up in front of her apartment block.

She hardly remembered dragging off her clothes. She crawled into a cold bed and pulled the covers over her chilled shoulders. Her pillow was wet with tears long before she slipped into a fitful sleep.

She awoke around midday and put in a call to the office. Marjorie answered, her voice sharpening with concern when Lynn wearily told her she wouldn't be in for the next couple of days.

"You sick? Man trouble?" the editor asked. "Can I help?"

"Thanks, but I'll handle it." Lynn wondered briefly just how much Marjorie had guessed. It didn't really matter. After tomorrow it would be all over, anyway.

She spent the rest of the day taking care of household chores, and that evening she went to visit her parents. They were both surprised to see her.

"What is it?" her father asked the moment he answered the door and saw her standing there. "Is something wrong?"

Everything, Lynn wanted to say. Instead she smiled and tucked her hand in her father's arm. "Can't a daughter visit her parents without something being wrong?"

"Of course you can." He patted her hand and led her into the living room.

Her mother's face reflected her surprise as she got up from her armchair to turn off the television. "Are you all right?" she asked anxiously as Lynn sat down on the couch.

"I'm fine." How was she going to begin? she wondered. How did she tell these two unsuspecting people that their daughter had died, not because her boyfriend had walked out on her, but because she'd been too afraid and too ashamed to confide in her own parents?

How did she tell them that they had been wrong to accuse the young man who had loved their daughter so much, and that because of what happened his entire life had been shattered?

"Something *is* wrong," Ellen Barclay said, peering at Lynn's face. "You look awful."

"What is it, kitten?" Lynn's father dropped a hand on her shoulder. "We can't help you unless you tell us."

She struggled with the words. They had a right to know, she told herself. Ward had a right that they should know. An injustice had been done, and it was up to her to right it.

She stared at her mother's face, noticing for the first time the deeply etched lines and sagging skin. Pale blue eyes stared in growing anxiety from a fragile face.

She loved these people, Lynn thought. They had been hurt so much already. How could she sit and watch those eyes fill with pain and see that gentle face crumble with the agony of those terrible memories? Her parents meant well. They had loved both their daughters, and when Sarah had died, their love had been poured into the one who was left.

"I'm just tired," Lynn said softly. "You'll be happy to know that after tomorrow, my Seattle story will be finished. I won't have to go again."

Her mother looked even more dismayed. "What about your friend? Is that why you're so upset? You've had a fight about something?"

Lynn shook her head. "Nothing like that. As I told you before, I never expected that relationship to come to anything. We were just casual friends, that's all."

"Oh, I'm so glad." Ellen Barclay's anxious face cleared. "I've been so worried about you driving all that way back and forth. Can you tell us what the story's about now?"

Lynn shook her head. "Not yet. But as soon as I can, I'll tell you." She changed the subject then, directing the conversation to safer topics.

Her father went with her to the door after she'd wished her mother good-night. "You know, you can tell us anything," he said, dropping a kiss on her forehead. "We might be getting on in years, but we'll do our best to understand."

"I know." Her throat tight, she patted his arm. "Don't worry, I'll be fine."

He nodded, but as she drove away, Lynn was uncomfortably aware that her father, at least, could see through her facade. Wishing she could be sure she was doing the right thing, she headed for home.

Just before she went to bed, she drew Sarah's diary from its place in her desk drawer. There was one thing she could give Ward, she thought, her thumb caressing the smooth cover. Something that had meant a great deal to Sarah.

He might not be able to read it yet, but God willing, he would someday. And Sarah would have wanted him to have it. It belonged to him. Neither she nor her parents had any use for it now. Blinking back the tears, she packed it into her overnight bag and went to bed.

Overcast skies followed her all the way to Seattle the next morning. Turning up the collar of her camel coat against the cool wind, she trudged up the steps of the hospital. Dr. Harper would be back today she'd been told when she'd called to find out if Ward was still at the hospital. She wondered if Ward had told him what had happened and hoped they would still let her in to see him.

She was halfway down the corridor when she heard the voices. She recognized the bland tones of Dr. Harper, almost drowned out by Ward's strident voice. Reaching the door, she heard the angry words.

"It's my life, dammit, and I'm the one who's going to say how I live it."

"No one's telling you how to live your life, Ward. All I'm saying is that I'm responsible for your health. I simply can't release you under the present circumstances. Surely you must understand that?"

"I understand nothing." Something fell with a splintering crash to the floor. "All I know is that I want out of this place, now."

Hearing the anguish in the harsh voice, Lynn did something she would normally never have done. She didn't stop to think that Ward might not thank her for interfering. Whatever battle he was fighting, he was losing. She could hear it in his voice. And all her natural instincts urged her to jump to his defense.

Pushing open the door, she said brightly, "I hope I'm not interrupting?"

Two heads swung in her direction. Ward sat on his swivel chair, his hands gripping the arms. A broken tumbler lay in pieces at his feet. Doctor Harper stood nearby, his expression impassive.

"Good morning, Lee," the doctor said politely, while Ward muttered something unintelligible.

Lynn nodded briefly at the doctor, her gaze riveted on Ward's grim face. "It's all right, Doctor," she said evenly, "Ward knows who I am."

There was a short silence. Ward's expression had turned glacial, and Lynn glanced at the surgeon. He was watching her with narrowed eyes.

"I see," he said. "That explains a lot."

"That has nothing to do with it." Ward shot an angry glare in Lynn's direction.

"To do with what?" Lynn asked, looking directly at Dr. Harper.

The tall man sighed and tucked a pen into the top pocket of his white coat. Glancing down at the clipboard he carried, he said, "Commander Sullivan is insisting on being released. I have explained to him that I cannot release him until he has undergone extensive therapy. I am responsible for his condition and in my opinion he is not ready to function on a day-to-day basis on his own."

"The hell I'm not. I can fix myself a sandwich and I can get myself to the bathroom. What else do I need to do?"

"You are going to need a lot more than basic functions, Ward." Dr. Harper's normally calm voice showed signs of wearing thin. "You have to learn how to keep yourself and your surroundings clean. You have to be able to shop for your needs, and you must have the necessary skills to take care of emergencies."

He moved closer to the chair, as if to impress his words on Ward's stubborn mind. "You also have to train for some kind of vocation. Unless you recover your sight, you will no longer be eligible for the United States Navy. I'm sure that someone with your exceptional intelligence can see the logic in that."

Lynn bit back a protest at the surgeon's apparent cruelty. Her glance flew to Ward's face. Two red spots burned high in his cheeks, and his eyes were slits of chipped ice.

"Why does everyone think that because I've lost my sight I have also lost my mind?" He lifted a hand to rub furiously at his jaw. "I know what kind of therapy you're suggesting, Doc, and I'm not about to submit to your subtle tactics. Just because I had a little accident with a chair doesn't mean I'm a psycho. I am not going to talk to any shrink."

"And I'm not going to release you from this hospital until I know you are capable of taking care of yourself."

"Then I'll damn well release myself."

"Can I say something?" Lynn moved forward, compelled to try anything to settle the argument.

The doctor shrugged. "Go ahead."

Ward simply looked belligerent.

"Would it be possible to have someone look in on Ward?" Lynn asked tentatively. "A nurse or someone who could make sure he's doing all right? Maybe they can arrange something at the base for him?"

"I'm not going back to the base," Ward said sharply. "It's the last place I want to go."

"But you said—"

He cut her off with a curt "So I changed my mind."

"I couldn't allow it, anyway," Dr. Harper said. "Even if I agreed to release him on an out-patient status, someone would have to live with him full-time until he could manage on his own. And it would have to be in this district, where we could keep a strict eye on him. Plus he would still have to have vocational training eventually."

"I don't need—" Ward began.

"Yes, you most certainly do need," the doctor interrupted vehemently. "I pay a very large portion of my salary out for malpractice insurance, and I do not intend to have the military breathing down my neck because I didn't do my job. You might as well accept it, Commander, you are going to a rehab center whether you like it or not."

He glanced at his watch, and his voice was calmer when he added, "Now, if you'll excuse me, I have other patients to attend to."

He had reached the door when Ward's angry growl stopped him. "Wait a minute. What if I can find a volunteer to stay with me until I can find my own way around?"

The doctor turned, his expression skeptical. "Where do you propose to look for one?"

"I don't have to look," Ward said deliberately. "I've got one right here in this room."

Lynn's gasp was audible in the silence that followed. Surely he couldn't mean her?

As if reading her mind, Dr. Harper glanced at her, then back at Ward. "Are you talking about Lee?"

"No," Ward said, his voice heavy with sarcasm. "I'm talking about Miss West. Or her real name, Lynn Barclay. She has so many I forget which is which."

"That's not fair, Ward," Lynn said, exchanging another incredulous glance with the doctor.

"Since when have any of you played fair?" Ward's embittered look was aimed at her alone. "You said you wanted to make up for everything. Well, now's the time."

The doctor cleared his throat. "Maybe we should all discuss this another time—"

"No. We discuss it now. What do you say, Doc? Will you agree to let me out if Lynn stays with me?"

Doctor Harper shook his head at Lynn as he answered, "I don't think that's a good idea. Miss Barclay isn't qualified for the job."

"She has two perfectly good eyes and a strong arm. Besides, she's been a . . . constant companion ever since I got here. We know each other well. If anyone understands my limitations and abilities, she does. She's the perfect choice."

The doctor's eyes telegraphed a warning as he said, "Perhaps we should ask Miss Barclay how she feels about it?"

Lynn stared back helplessly. How could she possibly do such a thing? Ward had made no effort to hide his hostility toward her. How could he expect her to agree to live with him and take care of him, knowing how he felt about her?

"Dammit, Charlie," Ward muttered, "you owe me. Here's your chance to pay up."

Maybe if he hadn't called her Charlie. Maybe if she hadn't heard the tiny break in his voice that told her he wasn't nearly as confident as he sounded. Whatever it was, she heard herself say slowly, "All right. If that's what Ward wants, I'll be happy to take care of him until he can fend for himself."

"I'll want to talk to you in my office," Dr. Harper said. "Around four?"

"I'll be there," Lynn promised. She was preoccupied with watching Ward's face. He showed no sign of being pleased with the arrangement. She had a moment of uneasiness when she wondered if he was planning some kind of revenge, then dismissed it. Ward Sullivan would never be that devious.

She was a means to an end, that was all. A desperate means, but there was no doubt in her mind that Ward was a desperate man. The thought gave her no comfort at all.

Wondering what had possessed her to agree to such a crazy idea, she waited until the door had closed behind the doctor. "Are you sure this is what you want?" she asked quietly.

"No, I'm not. But if it's the only way I can get out of this…prison, then I'll take it. I just hope we don't kill each other in the process."

"That will be entirely up to you, Commander." She pursed her lips and looked down at him. "I should warn you, I don't intend to be intimidated by you. If you don't behave, I'll bring you right back here."

"Then you'll be bringing back a dead body, because that's the only way I'm coming back."

"That," Lynn said carefully, "is something I'll be sure to consider."

She felt a small stab of satisfaction when she saw his start of surprise. If the way to deal with him was to attack, then attack she would. She had no illusions about the situation. But one thing was clear—he'd been right when he said she owed him.

She'd made him a promise the first time she'd seen him lying in that hospital bed. And he still needed her. Whatever it took, she'd be there for him. And she could only hope they would both survive the experience.

"Do you have any idea where we'll be staying?" she asked, aware of an acute flicker of apprehension. The enormity of what she was contemplating had begun to hit her. The very idea of sharing living accommodations with him, no matter in what respect, was enough to raise the hairs on the back of her neck.

Had he considered the full ramifications, the lack of privacy—the intimacy—of such an arrangement? She wondered what he was thinking as he sat silent, a small frown creasing his forehead.

"I guess I'll have to leave all that up to you," he said finally. "I'll pay for all the expenses, of course. I'm sure my insurance will cover most of it."

She sat down on the edge of the bed. "What do you have in mind?" she asked, her heart sinking when she realized this was only the start of her problems. "Something temporary? Do you plan on going back to California once you're well enough?"

"I don't know. I guess, since I have to stay here for the time being, I might as well settle for something more stable than a motel room."

Thank goodness for that, Lynn thought, wondering how she would have survived in such a cramped environment. "An apartment, then?" she suggested.

"Yeah, I guess so. Something close to shops, since I'll have to find my way there and back."

Her throat closed at the thought of him feeling his way along a busy street. Surely, *surely*, she thought, this blindness couldn't be permanent? Yet everyone seemed to have given up on his sight returning. Including Ward himself.

She pushed herself off the bed. "Well, I'd better get on it. It would be nice if I could find something before I talk to the doctor, but don't bet on it."

"Okay." He seemed almost subdued as he turned his head in her direction. "And thanks."

Not sure exactly what he was thanking her for, she twisted her mouth in a wry smile. "Don't be premature, Commander Sullivan. You may well regret this before it's over."

"Don't worry," he murmured, dropping his chin, "I fully expect we both will."

Not too auspicious a beginning, Lynn thought ruefully, as she let herself out of the room. But her apprehension over Ward was only a part of her problems. She now had to deal with Marjorie, and then her parents. How on earth was she going to explain this? she wondered as she made her way to the public phones.

You owe me, he'd said. Did he have any idea what he was asking from her? Probably not, but in any case she had made her own decision. Whether it was the right one or not would remain to be seen.

Marjorie picked up on the first ring, and concern laced her words.

"I want to take a month's leave of absence," Lynn told Marjorie, hoping that was all the time she would need.

"Do you want to tell me why?"

Lynn hesitated, wishing she could confide in her friend. In anyone, for that matter. "Would you be upset if I told you it's extremely personal, and that I'm really sorry I can't talk about it right now?"

"Are you in some kind of trouble?" Marjorie sounded genuinely concerned. "Maybe I can help—"

"No trouble," Lynn said quickly. "Really. I hope that by the time I come back, I'll be able to tell you everything."

"You're not in Portland, then?"

"I'm in Seattle," Lynn answered, knowing that Marjorie would gather a lot from that.

"I see." There was a slight pause. "I'll see you in a month, then."

Lynn let out her breath. "Thanks, Marjorie."

"Sure. Oh, and Lynn? Give my regards to your Navy pilot."

Lynn's smile was rueful as she hung up.

She waited a long time for her mother to answer. Her father, she knew, wouldn't yet be home from the office.

As she expected, Ellen Barclay was dismayed and suspicious when Lynn explained that she was staying in Seattle for a while. "I thought the story was finished," she protested, before Lynn had finished speaking.

"It is." Lynn drew a long breath. "I've been invited to spend some time with a friend up here, so I thought I'd use my vacation time. I never know what to do with it, anyway."

"A friend? Is it that man you told us about? I thought you were going to California on your vacation."

"Yes, well, California can be a lonely place when you're on your own."

"Your father and I would have gone with you."

"I know, Mother," Lynn said, wincing at the plaintive tone, "but you shouldn't have to worry about holding my hand. I'm a big girl now."

"You're still our little girl."

Lynn sighed. "Look, I promise I'll call at least twice a week, okay?"

"Why, how long do you expect to be up there?" her mother demanded in obvious alarm.

"About a month. Look, I have to go now, but I'll call later, all right?" Lynn hung up, feeling terrible. Sooner or later she would have to give her parents some kind of a story, but right now she had more important things on her mind.

She glanced at her watch. It was a little more than two hours before her appointment with Dr. Harper. She could at least get started on her search. Wondering where she was going to start, she headed for the door.

On the other side of the building, Ward sat drumming his fingers on the arm of his chair. What had he done? He must have been out of his mind.

He had deliberately set himself up for all kinds of trouble. How could he stand to be around her twenty-four hours a day? Hell, he had enough trouble being around her for twenty-four minutes. Not only was she a constant reminder of everything that had tormented him for the past eighteen years, she was partly the cause of it. She and her sanctimonious parents. She had even refused to clear his name with them.

Not that he cared. They could go to hell. They could all go to hell. It would serve her bloody well right to have to play nursemaid to him for the next week or two.

Ward groaned aloud and buried his face in his hands. He was the one being punished. It went against everything he'd ever believed in to be forced into asking for help. Especially from her. But he'd had no choice. He wanted out of there. He wanted to start living his own life again, under his own steam. And he wanted that more than he wanted to be rid of her.

Dropping his hands, he lifted his sightless gaze to the ceiling above him. That wasn't all of it. He might as well admit it—he still couldn't let go of the feelings she'd stirred in him whenever she'd come close enough to touch. The feelings had remained even after he'd known who she was. And that was the cruellest joke of all.

His body reacted in direct confrontation with his mind when she was there. How was he going to be around her twenty-four hours a day, without wanting, in the worst way, to take her in his arms and crush that soft, warm body against his?

How was he going to stop the blood rushing to his head every time he heard her voice or smelled the familiar fragrance that always made him think of dew-covered grass drying under a warm summer sky?

And how was he going to sleep at night, knowing she was in the next room, so close and yet so totally out of reach?

Willpower, he told himself. He'd always prided himself on his control. He would concentrate on learning everything he had to know to survive on his own as quickly as possible. And the minute, the very second, he could convince Harper he was ready, he'd ship her back home. Maybe then he could get on with his life.

Maybe. His snort of self-contempt echoed like a sardonic taunt in the quiet room.

* * *

Two hours later Lynn tapped on Dr. Harper's door. She answered his brief summons and stepped inside the room, feeling apprehensive. Well aware of the surgeon's reservations about the arrangement, she wondered what he planned to say to her.

He didn't keep her guessing. Waving her into a chair, he said without preamble, "I hope you realize what you're getting into."

Lynn shrugged. "I'm not expecting it to be easy."

"Easy?" The doctor shoved his chair back. "My dear, you haven't the faintest notion of what you will be up against."

"So why don't you tell me?" She met his gaze with more composure than she felt. The last thing she wanted him to know was how jumpy her nerves were and how much she wished she didn't have to go through with her hasty decision.

"Ward will be like a baby. He will have to learn to use all of his senses in a way he never has before. He will have to learn to wash, dress and feed himself and, if he doesn't want to grow a beard, how to shave.

"He will have to learn new skills and forget old ones, and you will have to help him. He will resent that, in more ways than you can imagine. It will take the patience of a saint, the strength of an Amazon and a will of iron to stand up to him and give him the encouragement he will so badly need."

"I understand."

"Do you?" Dr. Harper narrowed his eyes. "I'm asking you, Miss Barclay, not if you want to do this, but if, deep down in your heart, you truly believe you *can* do this."

"Yes," Lynn said evenly, "I can." She didn't know where the resolve had come from, but it was there, strong and sure. She had made a promise, and she would see it through.

"In that case," the doctor said, "we have a lot of work to do." He stood and held out his hand. "I admire your courage, Lynn. I wish you luck, and we'll be here to help in any way we can."

Lynn grasped the strong fingers. "I'll remember that. Thanks."

"Now," the doctor asked briskly, "I'd better take you down to Dr. Williams's office. She's Ward's psychiatrist and will tell you what to expect emotionally from him. After she's talked to you she'll take you to Beryl Adams, who's a physical therapist. She'll be the one explaining everything you'll need to know in that aspect. In the meantime, have you found somewhere to stay?"

"Not yet." Lynn followed the tall figure out of the office. "I did wonder if a mobile home would work better than an apartment? I saw a park not far from here, with a small general store on the grounds. I thought it might be better for Ward than trying to navigate a busy street. I think he could manage the pathways in the park more easily."

Dr. Harper nodded. "Sounds good. Just make sure the manager is aware of the problem and is willing to accept a blind person as a tenant. We don't want to get tangled up with insurance policies and have to uproot Ward again."

"I'll do that." How much more, Lynn wondered, would she discover out there to trip her up and make things difficult? And she had barely started yet.

She didn't see Ward in the two days it took to learn everything necessary to take over his rehabilitation. Both Dr. Williams and Beryl Adams pointed out the possible pitfalls and impressed upon her to call for help anytime she needed it, night or day.

The manager of the mobile home park turned out to be sympathetic and helpful. The rental he showed to Lynn was a little farther from the store than she would have liked. But it stood apart from the main bulk of homes and proved to be roomy, with two bedrooms and a compact kitchen that would be easy for Ward to manage. The manager promised to have the phone hooked up by the end of the week.

Finally, everything was ready. She'd arranged to have Ward's clothes, and anything else he might need, flown up from California. She'd made a quick trip back to Portland and packed what she needed into her car, leaving again without contacting her parents. There would be time enough for that later, she decided.

All she had to do now was pick up Ward and the few belongings that he'd had with him when he'd arrived in Seattle from his base two weeks earlier.

Her foot tapped against the newly mopped floor as she waited in the lobby. Now that the moment was here, the doubts had begun crowding in.

What if he hurt himself while she was supposed to be looking after him? What if he couldn't control his hostility and refused to do the things she would have to ask him to do? How was she going to be with him all the time and not let him know how she felt about him?

The doors to the psychiatric wing swung open, and a nurse walked through, one hand under the arm of the tall, dark-haired man beside her. He wore jeans and a light-colored jacket over a blue shirt. He looked different somehow. Stronger. More formidable in his street clothes.

Lynn took one look at his face and one last question tugged at her heart. How in the world was she going to have the strength to walk away when all this was over? Slowly she moved toward him, knowing she didn't have the answers. All she knew was that she was going to help him stand on his own two feet again. And for now that was all that mattered.

She reached him, smiled at the nurse and took hold of his arm. "All right, Ward," she said quietly. "Let's go home."

Chapter 7

He wasn't sure how he felt. The sensation of movement seemed strange to him as he sat next to Lynn in the car. He knew they were traveling along busy streets; he could hear the muffled roar and squeals of traffic all around him.

He knew by the steady thwack of the windshield wipers and the swish of the tires outside that it was raining. He wondered if that was why he felt so depressed. Or maybe it was the realization that his body was a lot weaker than he'd expected it to be. It had to be due to all the inactivity of the past weeks.

He would have to get on some kind of exercise program, he told himself, his depression settling even deeper when he realized how limited his choices were.

He shifted his weight in the seat, tensing when Lynn's concerned voice next to him said, "Are you all right? Are you warm enough?"

"I'm fine." He knew he sounded abrupt. He hadn't meant to. It was just the indignity of the situation. He would have to rely on her quite a bit at first, until he could find his way around. Dr. Williams, as well as Harper, had impressed upon him how important it was to control his frustration.

"You need to work together," Dr. Harper had warned, "if you expect any real progress. You must remember that this is as new to Lynn as it is to you. She is determined to help you as much as she can, but you'll have to work at it just as hard, if not more so."

He knew that, Ward thought, trying to control his rising irritation. Didn't they all know how desperately he wanted his freedom, his independence? Did they really think that he would do anything to slow that process down? He couldn't wait until he could tell Lynn Barclay that he no longer needed her.

Beside him Lynn said quietly, "We're almost there. I expect you're anxious to s—get settled—in your new home."

"Just because I can't see doesn't mean you can't ever use the word. If you're going to stumble over every other word you're going to make yourself miserable."

"I'm sorry."

"And don't apologize for everything. I'm not brittle. I won't break."

He heard her sharply indrawn breath and silently cursed. He was angry with himself, so why was he taking it out on her? And why was he angry with himself?

He knew why.

It was her perfume, filling the car with sunshine and breezes across a summer meadow. It was her voice, vibrating along his highly attuned senses. It was the brush of her arm against him, acutely reminding him of the few brief moments he'd held her soft yielding body.

Against his will a picture began to form in his mind—her upturned face, tears clinging to feathery lashes that framed eyes the color of a morning sky, a gentle mouth that was made for smiling, quivering with grief instead.

He could see again that empty parking lot, hear the echo of her poignant voice as she spoke his name. And once more he felt that same fierce stab of regret when he'd watched her drive away.

Stop it, he urged himself. *Stop it.* The words kept repeating over and over in his mind, becoming part of the insistent drumming of his heartbeat, until they no longer had any meaning. He was weak with relief when he felt the car slow to turn a sharp corner, then roll to a stop.

"We're here," Lynn announced, and he winced at the tension in her voice.

He was beginning to feel sorry for her. He couldn't afford that. Once he started worrying about her feelings, he would soft-pedal his own. He needed the anger, the frustration. He needed that kind of desperation to drive him, so that he could get this over with as soon as possible.

Once he was on his own, he could let up. But until then he was going to drive them both as hard and as fast as he was capable of going. And when it was over, he'd be as good as new. Almost. As good as he could possibly be without his sight. And never again would he have to be dependent on another living soul. Never again.

This wasn't going well, Lynn thought as she led him up the small path to the mobile home. She could feel the taut muscles in his arm. In an effort to relax him, she described the red bricks lining the path and the weeds that would have to be dealt with. "I'll have a go at them when it stops raining," she told him.

He didn't bother to answer her, but nodded his head instead.

Reaching the door, she fitted the key into the lock. "You have two steps up," she told him, watching as he explored the territory in front of him with his cane.

He managed the steps more easily than she'd expected, then took a careful step inside the doorway.

Joining him, she felt a sudden quiver of apprehension as she closed the door behind her. He seemed taller, bigger, more imposing in the small area of the living room.

She started to edge around him, just as he swung to face her, and his hip collided with hers. "I'm sorry," she said quickly. "There isn't much room here. It's a mobile home—I thought it would be easier for you to manage. I rented it furnished, so you have everything you need for the moment. Perhaps you should sit down while I describe the room to you."

"No. Walk me around it and tell me where everything is."

Of course. She should have thought of that. She had to stop thinking of him as an invalid. Once more she slipped her hand under his arm. "All right, take a step to your right. There's an armchair there just in front of you and a small table next to it."

"Okay. Is there a television?"

"Yes, I brought a small portable from home. I thought we . . . you . . . might enjoy listening to the news."

Again he gave her a brief nod. She went on describing the contents of the room, then led him through the kitchen, the bathroom and finally, his bedroom. She felt awkward, watching him sit on the side of his bed, his hand patting over the quilt.

"Where did the bed covers come from?" he asked, punching lightly at the pillows.

"I had everything you need sent up from the base."

"What about your bed?"

"I brought my own stuff up from Portland."

The look of relief on his face suggested he'd worried there might be only one bed. Lynn's face burned at the thought. "Captain Phillips wants to talk to you about your future arrangements," she said hurriedly. "I told him you'd call him as soon as you were settled."

Ward gave a snort of derision. "I don't have any future arrangements. I'm hardly going to be flying an F-18 anymore."

"You don't know that," Lynn protested sharply. "You can't just give up hope."

"And I can't go on basing my life on pipe dreams. If I don't convince myself that this is the way it's going to be, I won't be putting everything I've got into learning how to manage."

He had something there, Lynn had to admit. Even so, it upset her to think he'd given up. Somehow she had the conviction that if he wanted his sight back—really, desperately wanted it—he could make it happen. He was that kind of man.

"We have all kinds of problems to work out," she said, getting back to the practicalities, "so we'd better get started."

"Right." He pushed himself to his feet, and she noticed that he no longer had to find his balance before moving forward. "Door right ahead of me, right?"

"You're doing well, Commander," Lynn said lightly. She followed him down the narrow hallway, murmuring a word here and there as he made his way back to the living room.

That afternoon she shopped in the general store, armed with a list a mile long. Ward had wanted to go with her, but she'd been adamant. He still needed his rest, she told him, and this first time in the store, she needed to be on her own to study the layout.

Relieved that the second part of her excuse had convinced him, she hurried up and down the aisles, throwing things in her basket in her hurry to get back to him.

Turning a corner, she almost ran over the pink toenails of a plump woman with long, straggly blond hair.

"Hi, honey, aren't you the new tenants in number thirty-four?" the woman asked in the dry, raspy voice of a chronic smoker.

The odor of stale nicotine caused Lynn to wrinkle her nose. "Yes," she admitted cautiously, "we just moved in today."

The woman nodded, and light glinted off the dangling silver hoops in her ears. Her dingy white T-shirt stretched a message in huge red letters across her full, drooping bosom. *If you've got it, flaunt it.* Lynn read silently, her lip twitching in wry amusement.

"Well, I couldn't help noticing your hubby is blind," the woman said, her eyes glistening with curiosity. "My name's Jamie Morris, and I live in number forty-seven. Let me know if I can be of any help, okay, honey? We all take care of each other in this here park."

"That's nice," Lynn said, watching the woman's dark brown eyes fasten on her left hand, which lay in full view on the handle of the basket. "I'm Lynn Barclay."

"Oh, I thought your name was Sullivan. That's what Bill, the manager, told me."

Lynn eyed the woman's smirk with distaste. "Thanks for your offer," she said politely. "I'll keep it in mind."

"Sure, honey," Jamie Morris drawled. "Anytime."

Something about the way she said it made Lynn's flesh crawl. She couldn't wait to get out of the store, and even cut her list short in her haste to escape into the damp afternoon air.

Fitting the key into the lock of the front door, she was startled when it swung open under her hand. Ward stood in the doorway, his silver gaze uncannily accurate on her face.

"Want some help with the groceries?"

He held out his hands, and Lynn said sharply, "How did you know it was me?"

"I heard the wheels of the cart. Anyway, who else is going to come visiting? The only people I know up here besides you are hospital staff, and they don't make house calls."

Lynn thought of the woman at the store and shivered. "Well, in future, ask who it is before you open the door. You don't know who could be on the other side."

"Well, that's a chance I'll have to take." He stepped back, a scowl darkening his face. "You're not going to be hanging over my shoulder forever, you know."

He'd made it sound like an insult, and she flushed. "This was your idea, remember?" She reached for a loaded sack of groceries and pushed past him, forgetting for a moment he couldn't see her. He stumbled back, bumping into the door, and she felt a stab of dismay.

Shoving the heavy sack onto one hip, she grasped his arm to steady him. He shook her off with a low curse. "Forget it," he muttered. "I'm all right."

She felt sick as she carried the groceries into the kitchen. How long could she put up with his attitude without striking back? she wondered. How much should she let him get away with, before she decided he was overstepping the boundaries?

Taking a deep breath, she said carefully, "The store owner seems to be a nice man. I'm sure if you take a list over to him he'll be glad to pick out the things you need. He has just about everything there as far as food goes."

"Fine. How do I know what I've got when I get it back here?"

"We'll work out a system. But first you have to memorize what will be in each cupboard." She packed the groceries away, then began the task of teaching Ward where she'd placed everything.

Long after she was ready to quit, Ward insisted on going over and over it again. He took things out and put things back. He opened packages and smelled the contents, he traced shapes with his fingers and drove Lynn crazy with constant questions and demands.

"You don't have to learn it all in one afternoon," she told him, after he'd correctly identified a package of cereal for the third time. "You have to be more easy on yourself."

"The faster I learn it all," Ward said, taking an egg out of the tray and fitting it back in again, "the faster you can get back to your own life and I can get on with mine." He took the egg out again. "I bet if I practiced I could make a darn good omelette."

She didn't want to admit his remarks hurt. She should be happy he was so determined to gain his independence. "We'll give it a shot tomorrow," she said, plucking the egg from his fingers. "But tonight we have stew."

"Home cooked?"

"I made it last night."

He tilted his head on one side. "You a good cook?"

"I guess you'll find out soon." She made him go into the living room where she switched on the television. "Sit there and listen to the news," she told him, "while I get the dinner."

At least he seemed to be making more of an effort to be pleasant, she thought as she placed the stew in the microwave oven and tapped out the code on the panel. He was obviously determined to make the best of a bad situation.

She wasn't sure how that made her feel. He could be devastating when he was being pleasant; it was easier to deal with her reactions to his irritation.

She did her best to relax during the meal. It wasn't easy. All things considered, Ward managed the task of transferring food to his mouth with surprising ease. He seemed to be enjoying his stew and even launched into a discussion about the land-use controversy he'd heard about on the news.

Lynn answered his comments with only half of her mind on the subject. She found herself watching his every movement, tensing when he spread out his long fingers to feel for his water glass or took a little too much time to chase a piece of meat around his plate.

Her fingers itched to do it for him, and she practically had to sit on her hands. By the time he'd finished eating, she'd barely touched hers. Her neck ached from hunching her shoulders.

"That was very good," Ward remarked, swiping at his mouth with his napkin. "And a big improvement over the mess they call food at the hospital."

The praise warmed her as nothing else could. "I'm glad you enjoyed it." She whisked the plates away and headed for the kitchen. "Coffee?"

"Yeah, but I want to make it." He pushed back his chair and reached for his cane.

Lynn set the plates on the counter. "No, let me. You must be tired—"

"I want to."

"Maybe tomorrow."

"I want to make the coffee. I want to do something useful besides memorize the contents of my cupboards."

Hearing the edge to his voice, she hurried over to him. "All right, if you insist." She tucked her hand under his arm, but he pulled away from her.

"I can manage. I have to learn to move around this place on my own. I'm not going to do it if you insist on leading me everywhere."

"I'm sorry," she said, more sharply than she intended. "I'm just trying to help."

"I know. And your help is killing me." He backed away from her, catching the leg of his chair with his foot. It tipped back, and she lunged at it, grabbing it before it fell.

"Well, I'm doing my best," she muttered, righting the chair. "I'm just trying to save you from wrecking the place."

"If you gave me more room I wouldn't keep bumping into things."

She glared at his mutinous face. "Fine. If you're not happy with this arrangement, I'll be happy to drive you back to the hospital. I'm sure that Dr. Harper will be pleased to transfer you to a rehab center, where you'll have nurses hovering over you twenty-four hours a day."

Seconds ticked by, with only the sound of his harsh breathing in the room. Outside, the roar of a motorbike engine shattered the silence.

"All right," Ward said heavily. "I apologize. But you have to understand that I must do these things for myself. It's the only way I'm going to learn."

She met his apology with one of her own. "I'm sorry, too. I just don't want you to hurt yourself."

"Sometimes we have to get hurt to learn our hardest lessons."

She stared at his back as he moved slowly away from her, wondering exactly what he'd meant by that remark. One thing was clear, she thought as she suffered through the agony of watching him wrestle with the coffeepot—he was bent on doing everything himself. And she had to let him try.

She kept reminding herself of that during the long evening, as Ward prowled endlessly around the rooms, going in and out of doors and up and down the hallway, until she thought the tap of his cane would drive her out of her mind.

She was thankful when finally he announced he was tired and was going to bed. She heard him bumping around in the bathroom, but wisely decided not to interfere. There were some places, she warned herself, where he would have to learn to fend for himself.

Alone in his room, Ward lay on the bed, feeling as if he were buried beneath a ton of rocks. It wasn't going to work. It simply wasn't going to work. Every step she took, every word she spoke had his nerves jumping all over the place.

It was no wonder he bumped into things and couldn't seem to get his hands to work in unison. He couldn't seem to concentrate on anything knowing she was just a few feet away—so provocatively close, yet so far out of his reach.

No matter how hard he tried to control his thoughts, his body ached to hold her. Every time her fingers touched him he had to fight the urge to grab her and haul her into his arms. This was only the first day, for God's sake. How long could he expect to hold things under control if he couldn't be in the same room with her without wanting her in the worst way?

With a quiet groan he turned his face into the pillow. He *had* to control himself. He had to survive this somehow. Anything was better than being stuck in a rehab center. That was something he couldn't deal with.

He would just have to live with it somehow and hope it wouldn't be too long before he could manage on his own. Praying that he hadn't made the biggest mistake of his life, he forced his mind off Lynn and did his best to fall asleep.

The next morning Lynn awoke with a start, her ears already attuned to the sound of movement before she was fully awake. She heard the light buzz of an electric razor and smiled. So he'd found it. She'd bought it for him after discovering only a safety razor in his travel bag.

She came fully awake, pushing herself up on an elbow when she heard the muttered curse clearly through the thin walls. She was still wondering what to do about it when she heard the bathroom door open and the tap of Ward's cane along the hallway.

Reaching for her turquoise terry robe at the foot of the bed, Lynn slipped it on over her short cotton nightie and opened her bedroom door.

She couldn't see him, but she could hear him moving around in the kitchen. The distinct sound of water rushing into the coffeepot brought another smile to her face. Just as she reached the doorway, she heard another sharp curse, followed by a loud, shattering crash.

Looking in, she saw him standing by the sink, dressed in jeans and a gray shirt. His dark eyebrows almost met above his stormy eyes; his mouth was set in a grim line. At his feet the coffeepot lay scattered in jagged pieces.

"Don't move," she said sharply. "I'll get some shoes on and clear it up."

"I'll do it."

She stood her ground. "No, Ward, you won't. You'll cut yourself. Be sensible. This is one of the times you'll have to let me do it."

His look of agonized frustration brought tears to her eyes, and she fled back to her room for her slippers. She shoved them on her feet, then raced back to the kitchen, terrified he'd ignore her warning and try to pick up the pieces.

To her relief he stood where she'd left him, a look of grim resignation on his face. She swept up the shattered glass into the dustpan and emptied it all into the garbage can under the sink. "Now you can move," she said, stepping back out of his way.

"I was looking forward to that cup of coffee."

Her heart ached at the despondent note in his voice. "I have some instant, and we'll buy another coffeepot today." She took her first good look at him. "You missed a spot on your chin when you shaved," she said unsteadily. "And your shirt is buttoned wrong."

Without thinking, she moved closer to him and began to undo the buttons. "You need to start from the bottom and work..." her voice trailed off.

He stood as stiff as a fence post as her fingers bared his chest. For a long moment she stared in fascination at smooth skin and the light fuzz of dark hair that covered it. He'd used an after-shave lotion, and his clean, masculine fragrance seemed to seep into her pores. She could hear his uneven breathing and fought to control her own.

Unnerved, her hand jerked, brushing his bare flesh. His chin lifted sharply, and his breath hissed through gritted teeth.

"I can manage," he said, pulling away from her. He ran his hand along the counter until his fingers collided with his cane. It slipped from his grasp and crashed to the floor.

Lynn reached to pick it up, and his ears must have detected the movement. "Leave it," he muttered. "I don't need it."

She watched him blunder through the hallway and wanted to cry. He couldn't bear her to be near him. He was so anxious to get away from her, he was collecting bruises.

All right, she told herself. If that was the way he wanted it, so be it. From now on she would try to keep her distance, unless he did something desperate. The best she could do was try to stay out of his way, yet be close enough to step in if he needed her.

He'd found the rough spot on his chin, she noticed, as she later served him pancakes and bacon. She felt somewhat appeased by his obvious enjoyment of her offering, and although his conversation was more stilted than the previous evening, he seemed content enough to let her read the headlines of the newspaper she'd ordered delivered to the door.

"I'd like to go to the store this morning," Ward said, as she was clearing away the breakfast dishes. "I have to buy a new coffeepot anyway."

"All right." She knew there was no point in arguing, and in any case, he had to venture out sooner or later. She showered, pulled on jeans and a pale blue sweater and took her jacket from the closet.

Ward was sitting on a chair by the window when she walked into the living room, his fingers impatiently tapping on the arm. He'd zipped his light jacket over his shirt, and his shoulders spanned the width of the chair. Once again she felt the disturbing aura of a powerful man straining at the invisible bonds that held him so securely.

"Ready?" she asked lightly, and made herself stay where she was as he got to his feet, his fingers grasping his cane.

"Let's go," he said, turning away from her. She held her breath as he made his way to the door, reached for the handle and found it with ease. Turning it, he pulled open the door and stepped back to let her go through.

His actions were so fluid, so sure, she could almost believe he could see. It brought home to her how quickly he was learning and just how determined he was to reach that point when he no longer needed her. Her throat ached as she walked past him and out into the misty morning air.

Jamie Morris met them when they had gone no more than a few yards. It was almost as if she'd been waiting for them, Lynn thought, eyeing the heavily made-up face of the blonde with suspicion.

"Oh, is this your hubby?" Jamie gushed, as she halted directly in front of them.

Ward stopped dead at the sound of the voice. Standing close by his side, Lynn could feel the tension vibrating from him. Instinctively she slipped her hand under his arm. He'd been guiding himself with his cane tapping along the edge

of the pathway, and she'd been fighting the urge to touch
him until now.

"Ward," Lynn said evenly, "this is a neighbor, Jamie
Morris. She's kindly offered her help if we need it."

Jamie reached for Ward's free hand and pumped it. Lynn
saw the slight grimace of pain at the jolt of his newly healed
shoulder and gritted her teeth.

"So nice to meet you," Jamie purred huskily. "I was
saying to your wife, I couldn't help noticing your problem
and—"

"She's not my wife."

The sharp words bit into the cool mist, and Jamie feigned
innocence. "Oh? I'm sorry, I thought—"

"Well, you were mistaken." Ward sent a lethal glare in
Lynn's direction. "I appreciate your concern, Mrs. Morris,
but I assure you I do not need your help. Now if you'll excuse us?"

"It's Miss . . ."

Jamie's voice trailed off as Ward rapped his cane sharply
on the edge of the pathway, dragged his arm from Lynn's
grasp and took a decisive step forward. He narrowly missed
the bulky frame of the blond woman in front of him.

Lynn shrugged an apology she didn't feel and hurried to
catch up with him. "Slow down," she admonished him,
grabbing his elbow. "Do you want to fall off the path in
front of her?"

"You didn't waste any time," Ward snapped, striking the
path with unnecessary force. "Still playing your double-
identity games, I see. What're you doing, lining up potential candidates to interview?"

It took her a moment for his meaning to sink in. Letting
him go, she whirled on him and muttered in a low, furious
voice, "You still won't believe me, will you? You still think
I'm planning to write a story about you. Well, let me tell
you, Commander Sullivan, I wouldn't waste my precious

time or insult the intelligence of my readers by writing about an egocentric bore, who is bound and determined to step on anyone who dares to offer a helping hand.''

"Pity, you mean." His face was white with temper as he stared blindly in her direction. "I don't want your pity, dammit. I don't want anyone's blasted pity." He turned on his heel, misjudged the edge of the pathway, and his injured ankle turned over.

Lynn saw the flash of pain that transformed his face for a second before he controlled it. Ignoring all her good intentions, she grasped his arm again. "Now look what you've done," she said crossly. "You'll be limping again for a week."

"The hell I will." He pulled himself up straight, shook her off and grasped his cane. "I'm going to the store. So you'd better tell me how to get there."

Aware of Jamie Morris a few yards behind them, avidly watching the scene, Lynn said quietly, "I'll show you."

Her fingers had barely touched his arm before he backed away. "I'll get there by myself, without your help."

Gritting her teeth, she muttered. "You're facing the right direction. Straight for about a hundred yards, then left. If you keep the cane on the left side of the path, you'll know when you reach the turn. The store is a few yards farther, on the right. Your cane will hit the step when you reach it."

A flicker of triumph crossed his face. "Fine. Thank you."

"You're welcome. And I'll be right behind you, just in case you fall flat on your face. After all, that is my job."

She knew by the set of his rigid shoulders that she'd hit where it hurt. She was past caring. For the moment at least, she was mad enough not to care what he was thinking or feeling.

Even so, part of her mind registered the fact that whatever it was costing him, his limp was barely noticeable. Stubborn, she thought, with a flash of resentment. Stubborn, irritating, awkward and intolerable. So why, she asked herself, as she followed him down the pathway, did she love him so much?

She almost stumbled as the full impact of the realization hit her. How long had she been in love with him? And why on earth did she have to discover that fact now, after he'd made it so clear that he couldn't wait to get rid of her?

The visit to the store was not a great success. Lynn guided Ward up and down the shelves, explaining each section they were in and how to identify the various departments. Even though Ward wrinkled his brow with intense concentration, she knew that he absorbed only half of it.

After buying the coffeepot and a few other items they needed, she suggested they return to the mobile home. The relief on Ward's face confirmed her suspicions. Something was bothering him, and she had no doubt she'd find out what it was before too long.

She was right. He barely waited for the door to close behind them before demanding, "Why did you tell that woman we were married?"

For a moment she was speechless. She'd been so angry at his crack about her story, she'd forgotten the remark about the double identity until now. "I didn't," she said, indignation tightening her voice. "She simply assumed we were married, I guess, since we are living together."

She refrained from voicing her suspicions about the woman's deliberate misunderstanding. But then she wished she could take back the words when she saw his startled expression.

"Good grief," he muttered, "I hadn't thought about that."

"If you're worried about my reputation," Lynn said dryly, "forget it. There's no one here I'm trying to impress."

He didn't answer, but she couldn't help noticing that he renewed his efforts to take care of himself with even greater impatience than before. The knowledge depressed her no end.

By the end of the week, she was ready to throw in the towel. Nothing she did seemed to please him. In an effort to keep the peace, she crept around him on tiptoe, half-afraid to let him know she was there.

She'd driven him to the hospital one morning, for his check-up. Afterward, he'd refused to answer her questions, but she knew by his set face that the news hadn't been encouraging.

Things deteriorated rapidly, finally coming to a head one evening when she served the steak dinner she'd prepared for them. His exasperation materialized when he had trouble cutting up his meat.

"Let me do that for you," Lynn said, reaching for his plate.

"Thanks, but I can manage."

He sounded like a broken record, Lynn thought. Every time she offered to help he gave the same response. She watched him struggle without success for several minutes, while irritation simmered to a slow boil. Finally she could take it no longer. Reaching for his plate, she muttered, "For God's sake, it'll be cold by the time you get it in your mouth."

She cut it up for him, but noticed he left more than half of it on his plate when he pushed it away a few minutes later.

Biting back her resentment, Lynn picked up the plates and headed for the kitchen.

"I'll do the dishes tonight," Ward said behind her.

She hesitated. She didn't want to start another war by refusing to let him do what he wanted. He invariably ended up doing it, anyway. But this would be his first time handling the dishes, and she wasn't sure he was in the right frame of mind to tackle it.

She turned back to look at him and knew by his fierce expression that he wasn't about to take any argument from her. "All right," she said mildly. "Do you want me to run the water?"

"No, I'll manage."

Then go ahead and manage, she thought, with a rush of rebellion. Let him make a mess, and she'd make damn sure he cleaned up.

Ward pushed back his chair from the table and stood. He no longer used his cane to move around the home. He'd learned where every stick of furniture, every potential obstacle lay, and he'd become expert at moving through the rooms.

He wore a black sweater with his jeans, and somehow it gave him a rugged, wholly masculine image as he moved toward her with a confidence she wouldn't have believed possible three days ago.

Unnerved by the thought, she moved out of his way. Even so, his arm brushed hers as he passed, sending the usual quiver up her arm and down her spine. The heat of her reaction took her by surprise. She must be especially vulnerable to his male charisma tonight, she thought, wishing she could cure herself of the hopeless feelings she couldn't seem to control.

Ward reached the counter and ran his long fingers over the faucet. With his left hand he felt for the handle of the dishwasher and released it. Fascinated, Lynn watched him reach unerringly for a plate and rinse it under the running water.

Deftly he transferred the plate from one hand to the other, then bending from the waist, felt for the slots in the dishwasher and slipped in the plate.

Lynn slid her gaze over the denim fabric straining across his buttocks and swallowed. For some reason everything about him seemed to be tormenting her tonight. In an effort to cool her racing pulse, she turned her back on him and reached for the kitchen towel. She still had her back to him when she heard the sound of glass smashing into splinters, followed by a sharp curse.

Spinning around, she saw Ward shake his hand, then bring a finger to his mouth. With a cry of dismay she leapt across the floor and snatched his hand away to look at it. "Oh, Ward, I knew something like this would happen. Look at that, you've cut your finger now. I shouldn't have—"

"Is the finger still attached?"

She lifted her head, warned by his tone. "Yes, of course. But it's bleeding—"

"Then I'll live?"

Conscious now of his sarcasm, she dropped his hand. "There's no need for that tone of voice. I was concerned, that's all. You're going to need a dressing on that—"

"Fine. I'll get it. Bathroom cabinet, right?" Sucking at his finger again, he turned his back on her and walked steadily out of the kitchen.

Burning with resentment, she cleared up the pieces of glass in the sink. Intent on her task, she didn't hear him come back until she heard his voice behind her.

"Leave that," he said quietly. "I'll do it."

"I've got it. Go and sit down."

Shock rippled through her as she heard him take three swift strides across the floor. His hand skipped across her shoulders, then slid down to grasp her arm. "I said leave it."

She turned to face him, her heart beginning to pound. "For pity's sake, Ward, what is the matter with you? I'm only trying to help you."

"I don't need this much help." He waved his free hand in the air, narrowly missing her head. "You're suffocating me with your help. Everywhere I turn, every step I take, you're there in front of me, behind me, at my side, waiting for me to make a mistake, waiting to leap in and help me like some ridiculous guardian angel."

She tried to pull her arm free, but his fingers tightened their grip. "That's why I'm here," she protested. "This was your idea. You practically begged me to come and take care of you—"

His voice rose to a roar. "I never beg!" He must have felt her start of apprehension and added more calmly, "The only reason I asked you to stay was because I didn't want to be imprisoned in some rehab center for the next six months. I didn't figure on being smothered by your paranoid fears for my safety."

"Paranoid?" She gave her arm another vicious tug, without result. "You ungrateful, ill-tempered baboon—"

"I'm not ungrateful, dammit, I just can't deal with your constant babying, that's all."

Incensed beyond belief, Lynn shoved at his chest with her free hand. "Can't you see—" She shut her mouth with a snap, horrified at the forbidden word she'd uttered. "Oh, I'm sorry, Ward, I didn't mean—"

His furious growl stopped her. "You see what I mean? Listen to you. You watch every word you say, you walk around me like I'm made of fine china, liable to break into little pieces if you so much as touch me."

He grabbed her fingers still pressed against him and pounded her hand against the hard wall of his chest. "Look, Lynn, I'm not going to break. I'm tough, I can take it."

"Stop it," Lynn demanded, trying in vain to drag her hand from his grip. "You're just being childish."

His entire body seemed to go rigid. Still holding her in his firm grasp, he said with deadly calm, "Is that right?" Taking her by surprise, he shifted his grip, finding the back of her neck with disturbing ease. Before she could move, he pulled her against the length of his body, and with a quick side step, trapped her against the counter.

"Well, lady, it's about time you faced a few facts. Just because I can't see, doesn't mean I'm helpless. I'm an adult, able-bodied man, and capable of doing just about anything any other man can do. And in case you have any doubt of that—" He ran his other hand sensually up her arm to grasp her chin.

She realized, a second before he lowered his head, what he intended to do. She was powerless to stop him. In a kind of helpless fascination, she waited for his mouth to claim hers, her body quivering in anticipation of his touch.

Chapter 8

He bent her backward with the force of his kiss, his mouth hard on hers, his hips slamming her against the counter. His body potently demonstrated his urgent need, and she lost all desire to resist him. Drowning in the fierce pleasure of his touch, she gave herself up to the sheer enjoyment of it.

His mouth forced her lips apart with a kind of ruthless purpose that took the strength from her limbs and reason from her mind. Helpless against his determined onslaught, she returned the insistent demands of his tongue, excitement forging a stream of fire throughout her body. She felt shock and intense disappointment when he let her go and stepped back.

For a moment he stood white-faced and silent, except for the rasping sound of his harsh breathing. Then, with a muttered curse, he twisted away from her. He bumped an elbow against the stove and swore again, then headed into the living room.

Lynn pressed a hand to her mouth when she heard him crash into a table, sending everything on it flying. He was cursing in earnest now, and suddenly she'd had enough. With a strangled cry, she fled across the room to the door, dragged it open and slammed it behind her.

Shutting everything from her mind, she took off at a fast jog. She kept to the pathway, wary of the night closing in on her, and didn't stop until her breath sobbed in her throat and her lungs felt ready to burst.

Inside the mobile home Ward lay on his bed, doing his best to relax his tense muscles. Furious with himself, he tried to analyze what had goaded him into doing something so stupid. If he were really honest with himself, he thought, he'd admit that his frustration had nothing to do with being blind. Or maybe it did. Maybe it had everything to do with it.

The last visit to the hospital had upset him. Dr. Harper had tried to soften his words, but the verdict had been all too clear. His condition showed no signs of improving. And the longer it continued, the less chance he had of ever regaining his sight.

Ward turned on his side in an effort to dispel the knot of despair in his chest. He'd thought he was resigned to his handicap, but he must have been nurturing a thread of hope. The news had hit him like a physical blow. And he knew why.

He lifted himself up on an elbow and punched the pillow. He should never have suggested this insane arrangement. If he'd given himself time to think about it, he would have avoided it at all costs. Even if it meant putting up with the surgeon's lousy rehab center.

He'd acted on impulse, out of desperation, and look where it had landed him. Right in the middle of a situation he didn't know how to handle.

Smothering a groan, he turned onto his back. He couldn't
stop thinking about her. Every step he took, every move he
made, strung his nerves tight as he wondered if he was going to bump into her. And wondered how he was going to
keep his hands off her if he did.

Every tiny sound she made drove him crazy. Every time
she came close enough for him to smell that wildflower fragrance, he wanted to reach out and grab her. And the worst
of it was he knew she felt it too. He'd known it long before
he'd finally given in to his urge to kiss her. He could sense
it in her voice and in the subtle way her body tensed whenever he brushed too close.

She'd demonstrated it beyond all doubt when he'd kissed
her. He didn't need eyes to know when a woman was re-
sponding to him. He could have taken it all the way, and she
wouldn't have stopped him.

As he struggled to dispel that particular fantasy, he heard
her key in the lock. Holding his breath, he lay still, half of
him hoping she'd go straight to bed, the other half hoping
she'd want to talk.

No light showed from the windows as Lynn returned to
the mobile home. Half-afraid of what she would find, she
opened the door carefully and switched on the lights.

Ward had righted the table, she saw at once, and replaced the magazines on it. He wasn't in the living room, the
kitchen or the bathroom. Standing in front of his bedroom
door, Lynn gave it a light tap.

"Come in."

The muffled response unnerved her and she froze, her
knuckles still on the door. "I just wanted to make sure you
were all right."

"You can come in—I'm not going to attack you again."

His irritation gave her the courage to open the door. "I'm
quite sure of that, I just didn't want to disturb you." Aware

that her own turmoil had sharpened her voice, she added more calmly, "Can I get you anything?"

In the pause that followed, her eyes became accustomed to the darkness. The security light outside threw a faint glow across the bed, illuminating his bare chest as he turned toward her.

"Nothing, thanks."

She started to close the door, then stopped as he said urgently, "Lynn?"

She waited, heart pounding, for him to speak again. Her fingers curled on the door handle as the seconds ticked by, then he said quietly, "Good night."

The anticlimax almost suffocated her. She muttered an answering "Good night" and closed the door. What had she expected, she asked herself, a declaration of love? Angry with her adolescent emotions, she marched into her bedroom and closed the door—hard.

With a quiet groan Ward threw off the covers and sat up. God, how he wanted her. He'd almost told her that. He didn't know when he'd forgiven her for all the secrecy and the pretenses. He'd thought a lot about it, in the long, lonely hours of the night. About the woman he'd thought she was, before he knew the truth. The woman who'd sat by his side, ignored his bad moods and made him laugh when he had never felt less like laughing.

In spite of the things she'd done, or hadn't done, it didn't make any difference to the kind of woman she was. Gradually the things he liked most about her had outweighed all his suspicions and doubts.

In a way he could understand why she hadn't told her parents. It wouldn't change much, anyway. It wouldn't change the fact that Sarah had died, trying to get rid of his baby. Even though it was an accident, he was still responsible for her death.

Lifting his face to an invisible ceiling, he ran both his hands through his hair. Lynn's reaction to his presence still mystified him. Hers was a chemical response, perhaps, to the close intimacy of sharing such small living quarters. Or maybe her feelings were tied up in guilt, and she was subconsciously trying to make amends. Maybe, God forbid, she felt pity for him.

With a muffled groan, Ward swung his legs over the edge of the bed. That was the one answer he feared—the one answer he couldn't take. *For Sarah,* she'd said, when he'd asked her why she'd stuck with him. But why? Because she felt sorry for him? Because he was no longer the man her sister had loved?

He'd actually felt tears when she'd said that, but he wasn't sure why. Maybe he, too, felt he was no longer a whole man. That's why he'd tried so hard to prove his independence, to prove that the loss of his sight didn't make him less of a man. It was the reason he'd resented all her efforts to help him; he couldn't rid himself of the fear that she was doing it all out of pity.

Yet he owed her so much. He would never have survived these last weeks without her patience and that special brand of gentle humor. Her warm, infectious laugh had lifted his spirits, and her strength and compassion had become his lifeline. What on earth was he going to do without her?

Shoving himself upright, he patted the bed to find his robe. He would have to learn to do without her. What did he have to offer a beautiful, young, vibrant woman with her whole life ahead of her? How could he tie her down to the kind of life he faced if his sight never returned?

He couldn't do that to her. He sought the door handle. He couldn't do that to himself. He would end up destroying them both. Finding the knob, he turned it.

His hostility toward her had become an ironic farce. He found it almost impossible to stay angry with her anymore, no matter how much he reminded himself of his doubts.

Somehow, he had to keep up the pretense. Soon he would be able to satisfy Harper that he could take care of himself. And until that day, he would have to find the willpower to stay away from her. He just prayed he was strong enough to do it.

Lynn heard the door of Ward's room open and lay still, scarcely breathing as she listened to him walk quietly down the hallway to the living room. She had never felt so helpless in her life.

Everything had backfired on her, and Ward's meaningless display earlier had only proved that his emotional problems had not improved. If anything he was becoming even more frustrated and irritable.

And it was probably all her fault, Lynn thought miserably. She must remind him all the time of a part of his life he'd rather forget. No wonder he was so anxious to get rid of her.

Yet she couldn't leave, knowing nothing had been resolved. He seemed to have lost all hope of getting better. At the moment the sheer necessity of learning to fend for himself kept him going. But once he'd conquered that, he would need hope if he was going to survive. Otherwise he'd have nothing left to fight for. Somehow she had to give him the will to go on fighting, something to hang on to, something to reach for.

She stared at the shadowed ceiling. Maybe she could plan a surprise for him; it was worth the try.

It took only a couple of calls the next morning to find what she wanted, and she sent up a silent prayer as she put down the phone. It had to work.

She could smell the biting fragrance of coffee as she walked toward the kitchen. It seemed to emphasize the familiarity of their situation. Now that the moment was at hand, she felt nervous about seeing him again. After last night, their relationship was more strained.

"Good morning," she said lightly as she paused in the doorway. "It looks as if the rain has stopped again."

He reached in the cupboard for the mugs and took them out, setting them on the counter in front of him. He'd tucked his black shirt inside his jeans, and her gaze skimmed over the firm flesh above his waist. Somehow he'd managed to keep in shape, in spite of the long hours of inactivity.

Her skin tingled as she remembered those narrow hips pressed intimately against hers, the searing pleasure of his hot, eager mouth... She jerked up her gaze as he turned to face her.

"Look..."

"Ward, I..."

They'd both spoken at once, and Ward lifted his shoulders. "Go ahead."

"No, you first." All at once it seemed important to know what he'd intended to say.

"I just wanted to say that if you want to go home, don't let me stop you."

She stared at him, not sure how to take his offer. If it was his way of apologizing, she thought with resentment, it was a pretty lousy way of going about it. "We made an agreement," she said stiffly, "and I'll keep my side of it. Until Dr. Harper releases you, I'll stay."

He nodded, and she couldn't tell if he was relieved or disappointed. "Well, I want you to know that I'm sorry, and it won't happen again. Last night I mean."

"I know what you mean." She had no trouble analyzing her own feelings. Much to her dismay, she actually felt disappointed. She had to be crazy.

He'd kissed her in anger, in a display of rebellion against what he perceived to be his limitations. She'd realized that at the time, but it hadn't stopped her enjoying it. And she'd accused *him* of being the immature one! "Let's forget it," she added, hoping that she'd be able to do just that.

"You have an appointment with Dr. Williams this morning," she reminded him as he helped her carry the dishes to the kitchen.

"I'm not in the mood to talk to that shrink."

"Maybe not, but it was one of the conditions you agreed to, remember?"

"How can I forget?"

Hearing his lack of enthusiasm, Lynn said brightly, "I thought tomorrow we could take a trip on the bus. You'll need to do that a few times before you'll be ready to manage it on your own."

"Okay." He placed the dishes carefully on the counter. "What's the time? How long before we have to leave?"

Making a mental note to ask someone if there were special wristwatches for the blind, she glanced at the clock. "It's only eight-thirty. We don't have to be there until ten."

"Good. In that case I'm going for a walk."

Lynn picked up the dishes and put them in the sink. "I'll do these later, then," she said, reaching for a dishtowel. "I'll get my jacket."

"I want to go alone," Ward said, in a voice that warned her not to argue.

Acute disappointment robbed her of words for a moment. "Oh," she said finally, "in that case, I'll do the dishes now." She'd done her best to sound indifferent, but she knew she'd failed when she saw his mouth tighten.

"I've got to do it sometime," he said, "so I might as well start now."

"Of course. You're right. Do you want me to get your cane?"

His scowl deepened. "No, I'll get it. I won't be long."

"Sure. Take your time." Her cheerful tone sounded more genuine this time. Deliberately turning her back on him, she turned on the faucet and held a plate under the rushing water, making as much noise as she could manage.

She heard him leave and waited for the door to close before dropping the dish and turning off the water. Drying her hands on the towel, she rushed across the living room and peered out of the window.

Sunlight sparkled across the dew-covered grass as Ward made his way steadily down the path, his cane tapping with confidence along the edge of it.

Lynn shook her head as she watched him. With his head held high, shoulders back, he looked every inch a Navy man. Seeing him like that, she found it hard to believe he was blind. Pain knifed through her when she realized how far he'd come. He was so close to independence now. Once he mastered the bus, there wouldn't be much left for her to do.

Very soon now, maybe a matter of days, Dr. Harper would find no reason not to release him from the hospital's care. And what then? Lynn wondered, watching the tall, dark-haired figure striding along the path.

Would he stay in Seattle and begin a new life? Or would he go back to California and try to pick up remnants of the old one? What would he do if he couldn't fly again?

That question must be tormenting him, she thought with a sigh. And he would soon have to deal with that decision. She was about to turn away when a patch of canary yellow caught her eye.

Heart sinking, Lynn watched Jamie Morris tripping along the path toward Ward, her black leather jacket topping bright yellow pants.

Lynn held her breath as the blond woman halted right in front of Ward, forcing him to come to a stop. Lynn was too far away to read his expression, but she could guess what he was thinking.

Turning, she headed across the room to pick up her jacket. She had actually opened the door when she paused, Ward's voice haunting her. *You're suffocating me with your help.* Slowly, she dropped the jacket on a chair and walked back to the window.

He was still talking to Jamie. At least *she* talked to him, her plump hand inscribing invisible arcs in the air. As Lynn watched, Ward bent his head, said something, then side-stepped the woman blocking his path and brushed by her.

The last thing Lynn saw before she turned away was Ward striding with supreme assurance down the path, with Jamie Morris staring after him, her hands dug deep in the pockets of her jacket.

Lynn dashed away the tears on her cheeks. She didn't know why she was crying, she thought in self-disgust. It was obvious by now that Ward was fully capable of taking care of himself. She should be happy for him. He'd accepted his condition and was prepared to live with it.

She started to cross the room, then stopped. "Damn it," she yelled suddenly to empty air, "it isn't enough!" She grabbed a cushion from the couch and flung it across the room. He didn't deserve this...he needed his eyes. He needed to be back where he belonged, in the sky. She sank onto the couch, tears spilling down her cheeks.

She didn't know how long she sat there hugging her body, the violent sobs shuddering from her chest. She wasn't sure if she cried for him or for herself. All the pent-up emotion of the past weeks had finally burst through the dam, and she seemed helpless to stop it. She let them come—deep, ragged sobs that tore through her body in a savage storm of grief.

When it finally passed, she felt exhausted and thoroughly drained of sensation. She washed her face in cold water and dabbed it dry, thankful, for once, that he wouldn't be able to see her face. She still had a few days left with him, and she would make the most of them, she promised herself.

In the meantime she had the surprise she'd planned for him. If that went well, she would at least have the satisfaction of knowing she'd done something special for him before she left.

Ward seemed preoccupied when he returned from his walk, and he said little on his way to the hospital. Lynn had planned to do some shopping while he was there. She left him in the waiting room, where a nurse assured Lynn she would take care of him.

Taking advantage of the opportunity, Lynn phoned her parents. She'd been calling from the store at the park, but the lack of privacy had made conversation difficult. Now she was settled in a booth inside a large department store, enjoying the comparative isolation.

She was relieved when her mother announced she was alone. "Your father will be sorry he missed you," Ellen Barclay said. "He's been worried about you. We both have."

"I told you, Mother, everything is fine. I've been calling you practically every day, haven't I?"

"I know but you don't tell us anything. You used to tell us everything. That's why we can't help worrying about you, Lynn. This isn't like you."

Lynn curbed her rush of irritation. "Mother, you have to trust me to take care of my life. Sometimes you forget I'm an adult."

"I don't forget," her mother protested, sounding hurt. "It's not that I . . . we don't trust you. It's just that we want to share in your life. It hurts when you shut us out."

Lynn uttered a quiet groan. "I don't want to upset you and Dad," she said, wishing they'd understand for once, "but I need to live my own life without having to account for every single moment."

"Well, if you feel that way, I guess there's not much I can say. When are you coming home, anyway? Can you at least tell me that?"

Lynn unclenched her teeth with an effort. "Soon, Mother, I promise. Now I have to go do some shopping." She cut into her mother's protests by promising she would call again the next day. Then with a sigh of relief she hung up.

Couldn't they see that they were smothering her? Lynn pushed open the door to the booth. They still treated her like a child. . . .

She paused in front of the jewelry counter, staring blindly at the display of glittering diamond and sapphire rings. They were, she realized with a shock, doing exactly what she'd been doing to Ward. Refusing to let her do things her own way, without interference from anyone.

Now she knew how Ward felt. He'd been like a wounded bird, and she'd put him in a cage, refusing to let him out to learn to fly again. No wonder he'd been so irritated and frustrated.

She'd been so anxious to take care of him, to help him, she hadn't given him what he really needed—the encouragement and the freedom to find his own way, to make his own mistakes and learn from them.

But he'd learned in spite of her. He'd been so determined to be rid of her, he'd fought her every step of the way. And now she had to let go. He didn't need her anymore. And no matter how painful it was, she would have to face it with courage and never let him know how much it hurt.

His next appointment with Dr. Harper was in four days. She would tell the surgeon then, Lynn decided, that in her opinion, Ward could manage without her. As she wandered aimlessly around the store, one thought kept coming back to torment her. He could manage without her. But how, she asked herself in silent desperation, how in the world was she going to manage without him?

Ward sat in the waiting room when she got back to the hospital, his face set in a forbidding mask. "How was it?" Lynn asked, already knowing the answer.

"It was a complete and utter waste of time. I keep telling her that. I don't know why she can't get that through her dense little mind."

"Dr. Williams is only trying to help," Lynn said quietly. "We all are."

"I know that." He tilted his head to one side. "Did you get all your shopping done?"

She deliberately put a smile in her voice. "Not really, though I did pick up that tape you wanted. As for me, all the clothes I can afford, I hate, and the ones I love are too expensive. Just once I'd like to be able to splurge on something wildly extravagant." She let out an exaggerated sigh. "The trouble is, I have millionaire tastes and a pauper's bank account."

"I'd say that's a common complaint from women."

And that, Lynn thought wryly, was a typical remark from him. She forced a cheerful note in her voice. "Well, Commander, let's get out of this dreary place and get some sunshine."

She'd planned the day carefully and had no intention of letting him spoil the surprise. Even the weather had decided to cooperate, she thought, as she glanced at the fluffy white clouds chasing across a powder-blue sky. This late in September, the sunny days became more rare in the Northwest. Luckily the sun had cleared the skies this morning.

Long before she reached her destination, Ward apparently realized they were not headed for home. "Where are we going?" he asked, his forehead creased in concentration. "This isn't the way back to the park. We should have been there before now."

Lynn smiled. "We're going to another park. Discovery Park, in fact. I thought you'd like to walk along the beach."

His shoulders relaxed, though his expression remained unchanged.

She switched her gaze back to the road, unsettled by his lack of enthusiasm. "It's such a beautiful day, and there won't be many more of them before the winter..." Her voice trailed off as she realized how little time she had left with him.

She wouldn't be there to share the winter with him. Already the last days of summer had given way to fall, and the dying leaves had begun to paint the trees in yellow and gold. Soon, Lynn thought, as she turned into the park, the crimson and copper would add fire to the glorious blaze of color. And he wouldn't be able to see it.

But she would. And she would never again be able to see the colors of fall without visualizing him striding into the wind, looking so powerful and confident, even without his sight.

She let him climb out of the car, forcing herself not to offer help. He managed it without hesitation and reached back inside for his cane.

She guided him to the path, then let him go, knowing that he could navigate with his cane. He let her do most of the talking, apparently listening as she described the quietly lapping water and the slender firs that dotted the bluff.

He seemed to enjoy her account of the poodle who played around its young owner, tangling its lead around the boy's legs. Though she couldn't really tell, since his set expression gave nothing away.

The sun warmed her shoulders, and even the breeze that lifted strands of hair from her face still carried the faint memory of summer heat. The salty fragrance blended with the pungent smell of pine, cleansing the air of the sooty odors from the city.

A perfect day, Lynn thought, lifting her face to the sky as the hoarse cry of sea gulls joined the shouts of childish laughter. If only she knew what he was thinking, and if he was enjoying this change of environment. A prickle of apprehension disturbed her when she saw the vapor trail of a high-flying jet. The day was far from over. She just hoped she'd done the right thing.

Again the lilting echo of children's laughter drifted across the water as they rounded the curve of the bay. Ward turned his head toward the sound, and just for a second she saw a wistful shadow darken his face. Her heart ached for him. It must be so awful to hear familiar sounds and not be able to see where they came from.

"Are you hungry?" she asked him in an attempt to steer his thoughts to a more pleasant track. "I thought we could stop at a drive-in on the way back. It's been a long time since I ate a hamburger in the car."

"Sounds good."

Lynn frowned. He seemed even more preoccupied than usual. She wondered if it had something to do with his session with Dr. Williams. Really worried now, she was beginning to wish she'd never set up the surprise she had in store for him.

She glanced at her watch. This trip to the park had been a diversion, until it was time to take him back across town.

She still had an hour to kill, she realized. She would have to make the lunch last.

With that in mind she parked in the small parking lot behind the drive-in. The hamburgers smelled wonderful, and Ward even murmured his appreciation when she unwrapped one and placed it in his hands.

"It's been a while since I had one of these," he said, before sinking his teeth into it.

"Me, too. I try to stay away from junk food." She took a bite out of her own. "I have to admit, though," she added, "when you're really hungry a good hamburger can taste great."

"And this is a good one."

Lynn glanced at him out of the corner of her eye. He seemed more relaxed now—perhaps it was safe to ask him the question that had been on her mind so much lately. Taking a chance, she asked tentatively, "Have you decided what you're going to do, now that you're so much better? Are you going back to California?"

"No. There's nothing for me there anymore."

She hated the way his voice had hardened, but she'd started the conversation, she decided, so she might as well finish it. "So you're going to stay in Seattle?"

"I might as well. Thanks to you I have a home here now, and I'm beginning to find my way about. The dragon lady tells me I have a couple of options to choose from, as far as job choices go."

Lynn raised her eyebrows. "The dragon lady?"

"Dr. Williams. The shrink. From the way she takes such a macabre delight in probing into my personal life, I imagine her to have bloodred eyes and fangs."

Lynn's laugh rang out. "Well, you couldn't be more wrong. She's a very attractive woman. I'd give anything to have her dark curly hair."

"There's more to being an attractive woman than looks."

They were treading on dangerous ground, she knew, but she couldn't resist following up that evocative remark. "Like what?"

He finished the last of his hamburger and crushed the paper napkin in his fingers. "Like a sense of humor, compassion, understanding. A woman you can enjoy talking to, share all your thoughts with and just enjoy being with her."

Someone like Sarah? The question sprang unbidden into her mind, spreading a cloud over her momentary pleasure. Of course that's who he was thinking of—who else? He'd never married. He'd never forgotten her. He probably never would.

She packed up the remains of their meal and slipped out of the car to deposit the trash in the bin. The wind ruffled her hair as she dropped the lid, and she lifted an anxious face to the sky. Was it her imagination, or could she see more clouds than before?

Even the sun seemed to have lost its earlier radiance, and the breeze now held a definite chill. Lynn flipped up the collar of her jacket and shivered. Sarah. If it hadn't been for Sarah, she would never have met Ward. It was ironic that the person who had brought him into her life could be such a formidable obstacle between them.

But then, Lynn thought, as she began to walk back, if Sarah had lived, Lynn's own feelings for Ward would have been quite different. Even now she should never have let herself fall in love with him. For Ward still belonged to Sarah, as irrevocably as if the two of them had shared the past eighteen years.

Inside the car Ward tried to relax his tense shoulders. He had come very close to giving himself away. This couldn't go on. He couldn't go on. He had to talk to Harper the next time he saw him and demand his release as an out-patient.

Once Lynn had no valid reason to stay, she could go home and put this entire episode behind her.

He hunched his shoulders again, thinking about the session with Dr. Williams. The psychiatrist had implied that his troubles were almost over. He would have his pension from the Navy, of course, which would provide adequate, if limited, funds to live on. There were programs, she'd told him, which would accept him as a trainee, if he wanted to supplement his income.

She'd radiated enthusiastic optimism, and he'd gritted his teeth while he'd listened to her carefully worded spiel about the strides the government had made in placing the handicapped. The training programs, she'd explained, practically guaranteed him a job.

He'd wanted to yell at her and try to get it through her head that he wasn't ready to settle for half measures. That he couldn't stand the thought of being imprisoned in front of a computer, or behind a conveyor belt, when all he wanted was to be back in the air and free as a bird.

But he'd said nothing. It wasn't her fault. It wasn't anyone's fault. It was just one, big, fat, stupid, senseless act of fate that had sent him hurtling out of the sky and into this black, meaningless hell.

Ward lifted his head when he heard the car door open. No way was he going to let Lynn see him down. No one was going to see him down. Somehow he'd work this out.

He was going to have to let Lynn go. The one person who could have given his new world some sanity. The one person who could have put some meaning into his life. The one person who could have made it all tolerable.

He felt her slide in next to him and slam the door. She brought a flurry of cool breeze with her, mixed with the warm scent of meadow flowers. How he longed to reach out to her and touch her silky hair. He wanted to run his fingers over her face. He saw her so clearly in his dreams, yet

here in the car, she seemed no more than a shadow, a vague
memory in the mist of time.

He felt a moment's panic as he wondered if the day would
come when he could no longer recall her face. He remembered how he'd felt when he couldn't see Sarah clearly in his
mind anymore. At first he'd been devastated, then, as time
had drifted on, he'd stopped trying to visualize her. After
all, he'd had the ever-present pain to remind him of what
he'd lost.

He felt the car jerk, then begin to roll forward. The pain
was different now, though. Ever since he'd found out that
Sarah's death had been an accident, he'd begun to let go.
What had happened couldn't be changed, he'd told himself, and there was no point in fighting the past.

His blindness might have had something to do with that,
Ward thought, as the car gained speed. Maybe he'd considered the debt paid. Or maybe he'd simply wanted to be free
of the past at last. He had enough problems with his future.

"You're awfully quiet," Lynn said at his side. "Are you
feeling all right?"

"Just a little tired." He had to be, he thought. He didn't
even have the energy to resent her question. He slumped
back in his seat, trying not to think about his ambiguous
prospects.

A few minutes later he sat up. His ears had caught the
sound of a jet screaming overhead. And it wasn't a com-
mercial jet. "Where are we?" he asked sharply.

"Where do you think we are?" Lynn said, with an unmistakable note of excitement in her voice.

She must have rolled down the window, Ward thought, as
the sounds of aircraft rumbled in his ears. He waited, ears
straining, as the roar grew louder. Soon he detected a familiar smell, one that never failed to pump adrenalin
through his veins.

"We're at an airfield?" he asked, wondering why on earth she would bring him to this place of all places. Didn't she realize what these sounds and smells could do to him?

His hands clenched when she answered, "You've got it, Commander."

He said nothing while the car turned first one way then the other. He was too busy dealing with his seething array of emotions. How could she think that he would enjoy hearing those engines, the roar of freedom, knowing that he was imprisoned on the ground like some rat in a hole?

Another earth-shattering roar erupted, shaking the car as a jet thundered by on its way to the limitless sky. God, how he longed to be on board. He could almost feel the savage kick of the afterburner, the awesome thrust of the sleek machine as it defied the force of gravity.

He could feel it all—the force of seven Gs clawing at his belly, his hands firm and sure on the controls. The cold, clear, precise commands hovered in his brain, waiting for his lips to form the words. His fingers closed around an imagined throttle as he listened to the jet streak toward the heavens, and his heart went with it as the sound gradually faded into the distance.

The car jolted to a stop, and he felt the cool sheen of sweat breaking out on his forehead. No, he thought, with a sudden fierce explosion of resentment. Damn it, this time she'd gone too far. He fought to regain some semblance of control before he told her—ordered her—to get him out of there.

The door opened on his side, startling him. The breeze cooled his face as a man's voice said, "Commander Sullivan. It's a pleasure to meet you, sir."

Confused, trying to understand what was going on, he hadn't realized Lynn had left the car, until he felt her hand under his arm. "Come on," she said in his ear, "there's someone I want you to meet."

Still trying to make some sense of it all, he let her hold his arm as he climbed out. His stomach felt like scrambled eggs, and his throat ached with the force of his longing as his remaining senses absorbed the familiar surroundings.

He heard Lynn speak, and his stunned mind struggled to make sense of the words. "Ward, this is Major Brad Tinker, of the Washington National Guard. He's going to take you for a ride."

"That's right, sir. I have a Phantom standing by, ready to take off. Whenever you're ready, we'll take her up."

He stood very still, letting the reality of it sink in. He was going to fly again. Oh, maybe not under his control, but he was going up there, to soar into the piercing blue silence of the skies. For one more precious moment in time, he was going to be free . . . and she had understood after all.

For the second time since Charlie had come hustling back into his life, he felt the strange, unfamiliar prickle of tears.

Chapter 9

He thought his memories had been unaffected by his absence, but he was wrong. He'd forgotten the searing excitement of sitting in that cramped cockpit, feeling the shuddering vibrations of a powerful fighter jet preparing to take off.

He concentrated, intent on imprinting every last second of the experience on his mind. It all felt so familiar—the pressure of numerous buckles and straps snug against his body, the acrid smell of burning fuel and the reassuring presence of the ejection lever between his legs.

If he'd entertained any doubts about apprehension left over from his accident, they vanished like dust in the wind. His entire body quivered with anticipation.

As the F-4 rolled forward and gathered speed, pulling him back in his seat, he felt the ice-cool calm settle over him. He replayed the scene in his head as he'd seen it so many times. The thin white ribbon down the center of the runway streaming underneath the belly of the jet, while the land-scape rushed toward him.

He felt the nose lift and braced himself, counting off the seconds as he always did. In his mind he saw the sky tilting, until it replaced the browns and greens of the earth below. The raw pain in his belly as the jet screamed straight up filled him with an exhilaration he had never found any-where on earth.

He wanted to shout, to release the sheer euphoria of a hunger satisfied. It filled him, lifting him far above mortal man, freeing him once more to roam the skies at will.

He felt the aircraft shudder as it reached the apex of the climb, and braced himself for the heart-stopping dive. He was disoriented when the Phantom leveled out and angled into a tight turn instead.

Disappointment was like a crushing pain in his chest. It was different after all. He wasn't in control. Dammit, he wanted to be in control. No, not *wanted*. He *craved* it. His fingers ached to feel the pull of the throttle. He longed to see the land spiraling beneath him as he hurtled toward it, only to see it disappear in a blur of speed until once more he was looking into the sun.

The flight came to an end all too soon. He'd enjoyed the ride immensely, but as he felt the wheels touch down he couldn't prevent the dark cloak of depression that once more threatened to suffocate him. It was over.

The chances of him going up again were almost nonexistent. In any case he would never again feel the special thrill of holding a powerful, screaming, soaring machine in the control of his own hands. For him it was indeed over. And that realization alone, after everything that had happened to him, finally made him feel less a man.

Lynn watched the two men walk toward her, and knew by the slump of Ward's shoulders that his depression still plagued him. Her own spirits plummeted. She had banked so much on this trip.

She'd hoped he would realize that just because he couldn't fly a jet anymore, he could still experience the thrill of it. She knew how much that had meant to him. Again her good intentions seemed to have misfired.

She waited for him by the car while he climbed out of his flying gear. She watched him shake the hand of Major Brad Tinker and thank him for the ride. She added her own thanks and held the car door while Ward eased himself inside, all the time wondering if he was angry with her for once more interfering in his life.

To her relief he thanked her for arranging the trip. "I wasn't sure that you'd enjoyed it," she said, as she headed the car back to the mobile home park.

"I enjoyed it very much. And I appreciate the trouble you took to arrange it. That was very thoughtful of you."

The words were right, but she sensed the melancholy behind them. She would almost have preferred one of his irritated outbursts. He barely spoke again on the way home, and didn't even argue when she helped him from the car.

Worried, she watched him pick at the lasagna she'd cooked for him. Her apprehension intensified when he made no move to help her with the dishes, something he'd insisted on ever since that first night.

"Do you want some coffee?" she asked, expecting his offer to make it.

"No, I think I'll skip it. It's been a long day, I think I'll go to bed and listen to that new tape you bought this morning."

Disappointed, Lynn finished clearing the table. She heard him bumping around in the bathroom with more noise than usual, and wished with all her heart there was something she could do. Anything to give him some sense of motivation.

She spent the next two days in a blur of worry and heart-ache. Her last few hours with Ward seemed to be flying by, and all they had managed was an occasional halfhearted attempt at conversation.

As the third day after his flight brought another cool shower of rain, she thought gloomily that this was worse than anything she'd dealt with before. He'd opted out of all the routines they'd established. He'd flatly refused to go with her on the bus, saying he could get a cab if he wanted to go anywhere.

She served lunch later than usual, since he'd stayed in bed most of the morning—another indication of his mood. After yet another quiet meal, she cleared the plates away, leaving him alone.

As she washed the dishes in the kitchen, Lynn wondered if she should call Dr. Harper. In all the time she'd been by his side, Ward had never sunk this deep into depression. For the first time she was seriously worried about his emotional state.

Up until now she'd always considered him far too strong to give in to his problems, but now she wasn't so sure. If only she hadn't arranged for that flight, Lynn thought, slipping another plate into the dishwasher. It was her fault he'd started this downslide.

And now she had only one day left with him. Tomorrow he was due for his appointment with the surgeon. Tomorrow she'd planned on leaving. She hadn't said anything to Ward about that yet. After all, the final decision would be up to the doctor.

Lynn picked up a mug and rinsed it under the faucet. Up until now she'd been sure of that decision. But what was she going to do if Dr. Harper decided he wasn't ready for her to leave after all? She turned the mug upside down and stuck it in the top shelf of the dishwasher.

She wasn't at all sure she could go on like this. She ached with longing every time she looked at him. She'd stayed as far out of his reach as possible these past few days, knowing that if she so much as touched him, she wouldn't be able to let go.

Lynn closed the door of the dishwasher with a thud. She had to leave tomorrow. She wasn't helping him by being there. Maybe once he was alone he'd snap out of this dungeon he'd dug for himself. She couldn't go on being with him, letting him tear her apart like this. She just couldn't take it anymore. Dr. Harper would simply have to release him from the hospital.

Deciding she needed a change of scenery, she suggested a trip to the general store that afternoon. As she'd expected, Ward refused.

"There's something I want to listen to on the TV," he said, when she tried to pressure him. "You go ahead."

"I guess I'll have to," she answered, making no effort to hide her disapproval. "Someone has to do the shopping."

He lifted his head, turning it in her direction. "We can do it tomorrow."

"You have your hospital appointment tomorrow."

"Then we'll do it when we get back."

But she wouldn't be coming back. No longer than it took her to pick up her things, anyway. The reminder cut off whatever she might have said. Muttering that she'd be back soon, she left, digging her hands in her pockets of her jacket as the cool wind greeted her.

She spent more than an hour in the store. Her call to her parents had taken longer than usual, since her father had to repeat everything she said for her mother.

Deciding to burn her bridges, she told them she would be returning home the next day. After she'd hung up, she felt almost relieved that the decision was now out of her hands.

She loaded up the cart with groceries and supplies, knowing this was the last time she'd be shopping for Ward. She might as well stock up for him, she thought. After this, he would be on his own. Ignoring the ache that had become a constant presence, she promised the clerk she would bring back the cart and wheeled it out of the store.

Ward opened the door before she had the key in the lock, apparently having heard the cart wheels on the path. She let him help her unload the bags and put the items away in the cupboards. Then, determined that he would have some fresh air, she insisted that he take the cart back to the store. In spite of her good intentions, she paced back and forth in front of the window until he returned.

She waited until he'd settled himself in the chair in front of the television. The time had come, she decided. She had to let him know she was planning on leaving the next day.

"Ward, I need to talk to you," she began, unnerved when he jerked his head in her direction.

"What is it?"

"Well, it's your appointment tomorrow, and I think Dr. Harper will probably release you from the hospital's care." Her teeth worried at her bottom lip while she watched his face for a change of expression.

"I hope he does." Something about the stillness of his face disturbed her.

"So, how do you feel about that?"

"I'd say it's long overdue."

She struggled not to let his impervious attitude get to her. "Yes, well, in that case... I guess you won't be needing me around anymore."

For a moment she thought he was going to protest as conflicting expressions fled across his face. Then the indifference she had learned to hate masked everything else. "I guess not."

She didn't know why she should feel so hurt. This was what she wanted, wasn't it? And he'd made it so easy for her. Too easy. "So, you think you'll be okay on your own?"

"Yes, I'll be okay on my own." He tightened his mouth, as if regretting the mimicry. "I have to start sometime, Lynn. This is as good a time as any."

She stood for a moment longer, watching him, longing to say something and at a loss to know what it was. "All right, then," she said, as the ache in her heart spread through her body, "I guess I'll go and pack."

His mouth thinned to a straight line. He gave a curt nod of his head and turned his face away in dismissal.

Her throat tight, she spun around and headed for her bedroom, praying she wasn't going to cry. If only he'd said something, one word, to indicate that he'd be sorry to see her leave. She didn't expect an outpouring of gratitude or anything, but it would have been really nice to know she'd been a little bit appreciated.

She dragged out her suitcase and threw it on the bed. She was being an idiot again. It was the best thing she could do for both of them, to get out of his life and let him get on with it, on his own. She straightened and turned to open a dresser drawer, then froze. Ward stood in the doorway.

She couldn't tell much from his face. Except for the tiny muscle twitching furiously in his cheek, there was no other indication that he was holding intense emotion in check.

Her pulse jumped, then began to race. She took a half step toward him, then halted. "Is . . . something wrong?"

"I just wanted you to know that I will always be grateful for everything you've done for me."

He took a step into the room, and her heart stopped beating, then began again in a pounding rush of excitement. "Forget it, Ward. I was happy to do it."

"I'm sorry I've made it so hard for you. I hope we can part as friends?"

She stared at his outstretched hand and had an insane desire to laugh. Friends? He had no idea what he was asking. "Sure," she said, reaching for his hand. "Friends."

The touch of his warm palm against hers was her undoing. Furious with herself when she felt tears on her cheeks, she added tightly, "I hope things work out for you, Ward." To her dismay, her words ended on a sob.

His expression changed. She saw concern, then when a look of such torment flicked across his face she knew she must have imagined it. She stiffened when he reached for her, and held her breath as he stroked her cheek.

"Don't cry, Charlie," he whispered brokenly. "Please, don't cry."

She pulled back from his touch, muttering, "I'm not crying." A stifled sob contradicted her statement, and she uttered a low curse.

He moved swiftly, dragging her into his arms. "Oh, God, Charlie, I don't want you to go. I want you so damn much."

Stunned, she replayed his words in her head, unable to believe what she'd heard. Then, with a muffled cry she gave in to the compelling urge she couldn't deny. She lifted her hands and dragged his head down until she could fasten her mouth to his. His arms gathered around her, crushing her to his chest while his tongue sought hers in a fury of need.

She clung to him, her fingers kneading his shoulders, her mouth and tongue fighting him in a fiery duel of ignited passion. Her mind spun with fragmented thoughts. This was *his* mouth on hers, *his* body hot and heavy against her, *his* hands gripping her arms and roaming with a fierce possessiveness that sent thrills chasing down her spine.

The impossible had happened. It didn't matter how or why. All that mattered was the savage pressure of his mouth establishing his primitive message, and his hands squeezing her flesh as if he couldn't get close enough. Don't let him stop this time, she silently begged. She couldn't bear it if he stopped this time. . . .

"I thought I could let you go," he murmured, when he finally lifted his head. "But I want you, and it's killing me." He ran his hands down her back and pulled her hips hard against him.

The touch of his eager body drove all coherent thought from her mind. The air rushed from her lungs when he lifted his hand to stroke her breast. Then his fingers moved to the buttons of her shirt.

She couldn't seem to draw a full breath. "Ward—"

"Shh." He found her lips with the tips of his fingers. "Don't talk," he whispered. "Don't even think. Unless you want me to leave. Because if I stay, I'm going to make love to you."

She wanted him to stay. She'd wanted this from the moment she'd first seen him walk into the bar at the Royal King. She just hadn't realized how much until now.

She didn't expect the impossible from him. She knew this was simply a physical need, born of the long weeks of frustration and pain. It didn't seem to matter. Heaven help her, nothing seemed to matter but the fact that for now at least, he was hers.

Maybe she was a poor substitute for Sarah, but she was there and Sarah wasn't. Things like pride and self-respect seemed less important when she looked into his face and saw the hunger burning in his sightless eyes. She could satisfy that hunger and hers, too. And if he were hers only to borrow, then she would take these moments and make them last a lifetime.

Without hesitation she took his hands and guided them to the neck of her shirt. "You do it."

She shivered when his cool fingers brushed her burning skin as he released the buttons one by one. She knew he had to feel her heartbeat; the force of it seemed to shake her whole body. His hands slid across her shoulders and pushed her shirt down over her arms.

She shook it free, and caught her breath as he pulled her against him to unfasten her bra. He released her, just enough to give him room to cup her breasts. She let a small whimper escape when he moved his thumbs in an erotic quest.

He finished undressing her, using his fingers for eyes as he appraised her naked body. "You are beautiful," he whispered, drawing the flat of his hand across her belly in a feather-light touch that cut off her breath. He found her hands and pulled them to his chest. "Now you do it for me."

She had none of his patience. With trembling fingers she tugged his shirt open and dragged it from his shoulders. She managed to get his belt undone; then lost her nerve, watching helplessly as he finished the task for her.

Finally he faced her, his chest heaving with the force of his rasping breath, his body magnificent and ready for her. "Come here," he said hoarsely and held out his arms.

She stepped into them, fitting her body against the length of his. He uttered a low growl deep in his throat, once more dragging her hips against his to let her understand the full force of his burning need.

His mouth found hers with unerring ease. Expert at giving pleasure, his tongue probed, tasted and tormented, until she felt as if her legs would crumble beneath her. Shaken by the force of her passionate response to his touch, she sagged against him.

Holding her tight in his arms, he lifted a knee onto the bed and lowered her, his mouth still hard on hers, then settled himself alongside her.

He seemed to know her body better than she knew it herself. Better than any man had ever known it. She had no idea she could feel so alive—so intensely alive. No one had ever touched her that way before, and she had never experienced that much pleasure in exploring a man's body. It consumed her until she thought she would die from the sheer delight of each new discovery.

His skin was smooth beneath her touch. She traced the length of his back and gasped when he deliberately moved against her. She reached lower, her pulse leaping when she heard his muffled hiss of breath.

Lifting himself, he straddled her and lowered his body to rest on hers. His mouth found hers again as he began another slow journey over her skin with his sensitive fingers. Gently he edged his thigh between hers, his mouth trailing a hot, torturous path of fire over her sensitive flesh.

He touched her, and her back arched of its own accord as white hot shivers of intense pleasure shot up her body. Her gasp mingled with his when she closed her fingers around him, urging him to join her on her headlong rush to ecstasy.

"Oh, God, Charlie," he muttered, "I wish I could see you."

"Don't think about it," she said urgently. "I'll close my eyes and we'll do this together." She shut her eyes tight, striving to join their minds as well as their bodies. She felt him raise himself off her, gently parting her thighs with his knee.

Again he touched her, and she thought she would faint with the jolt of pleasure. "Now," she begged, her voice raw with mounting pressure. "Please, Ward, now." Her voice rose sharply upward when she felt him nudge against her.

He entered her carefully, inching forward as if afraid to hurt her. Impatient with him she lifted her ankles and clamped them over his hips.

His sharp breath pleased her, then she forgot everything as he thrust forward, filling her in one incredible, smooth motion. She was drowning in the spasms of pleasure, her nails digging into his flesh. Her body strained with his as together they clawed toward release of the exquisite tension.

She could hear his sharp groans with each thrust of his hips, his muscles taut beneath her hands. She had never needed so much, never cared so much. Even in her wildest dreams love had never been like this.

Her own cries mingled with his when he finally lost control and drove into her with a desperate urgency that captured her mind. She clung to him, molding with him, becoming part of him, until his body claimed hers in one last, glorious burst of energy. Then he shuddered and lay still, his chest and belly moving gently against hers in the aftermath of his exertion.

For a long time he lay there, still resting inside her, supporting most of his weight with his elbows and knees. She stroked his back with her fingers, enjoying the sensation of his muscular body against her as he breathed.

She still found it hard to comprehend what had just happened. It was unreal, a fantasy she had welcomed in her dreams and tried to banish from her waking mind. Yet he was here, his hard body resting on hers, naked flesh against naked flesh.

His warm breath whispered across her bare shoulders as he murmured, "Am I too heavy?"

"No," she whispered back. "You're wonderful."

His low chuckle sent her spirits soaring. "If I am, it's because of you. You make me feel like Superman, King Kong and Rambo all rolled into one."

"Really?" She drew her fingers across his shoulder, enjoying his shiver of pleasure. "No wonder I feel so pleasantly exhausted."

He lifted his head and placed a fiery kiss on her mouth. "Not too exhausted to eat, I hope? I'm starving. I could eat an entire cow."

"I'm not surprised. You've eaten hardly anything these last few days."

"Yeah." He ran his tongue with disturbing accuracy across the tip of her breast. "Now I know what to do to get a healthy appetite."

Conscious of him still inside her, she fought to keep her mind clear. Already she could feel her body tightening in response. "Well, if you let me up, I'll be happy to get you something to eat."

He moved his lips across her cheek until he found her mouth again. His kiss almost destroyed her, and she was quivering with a new insistent need when he rolled off her with a loud groan.

"I'd better get some food inside me, before I get carried away again."

"Wait here," she said, sliding her legs off the bed, "I'll get your robe."

He let her go, using the moments alone to try to collect his thoughts. He'd just made a colossal mistake. He never intended this to happen. He should have let her leave.

It had all happened so suddenly. He'd realized he couldn't let her leave without at least letting her know how grateful he was for everything. Then he'd had a moment's vision of what it would be like without her, and he hadn't had the strength to stop himself from hauling her into his arms. She'd kissed him, and everything exploded inside him.

The second her mouth touched his, he knew he'd reached the limits of his control. He'd given her the option, but he knew if she'd tried to leave then, he would have done everything in his power to stop her.

He'd never wanted a woman that badly before. The force of his need had shaken him. He wasn't sure what he would have done if she hadn't stayed. And now he wished she hadn't. He wished she'd had the good sense to get out while she could. Because nothing had changed.

He groaned quietly, covering his face with his hands. No, that was wrong. Things had become even more complicated. Because now that he knew how good it could be, how incredible they were together, it would be harder than ever to let her go. And let her go he must.

He shivered, feeling suddenly cold, and reached for the quilt to pull it over his naked body. He should put a stop to their relationship right now. Tell her he was tired, that he'd changed his mind about eating something. Because he knew, even now, that he wanted her again. And if he didn't stay away from her, there was no way, no way on earth, that he could stop himself from taking her again.

He tensed as he heard her enter the room. "Here's your robe," she said, and he felt it plop onto his stomach.

"Thanks." He reached for it, pulling himself upright as his fingers grasped the soft fabric.

"Are you all right?"

He silently cursed when he heard the note of doubt in her voice. Either she was remarkably receptive, or he was ridiculously transparent. Here was his chance, he thought, to tell her he'd changed his mind and was going to his own bed to sleep.

He wasn't really surprised when he heard himself say, "I've never felt better. Just wait until I get some solid food inside me and I'll prove it."

Her throaty laugh warmed his belly, reminding him how potently she affected him. "In that case I'm on my way to the kitchen right now."

She wanted this, he told himself as he thrust his arms into the sleeves. He wasn't doing any real harm. She was a big girl, she knew this wasn't forever. Besides, why would she want someone like him on a permanent basis? He'd be a stone around her neck, an obstacle to everything a woman like her would want out of life.

He tied the belt of his robe and moved toward the door. He would have only this one night, and he was going to make sure they both got everything possible out of it. As for afterward, it would have to be enough that they had apparently buried the hatchet as far as the past was concerned.

He felt good about that. At least they could part without that ghost lying between them. He opened the door, aware that for the first time in eighteen years, he had finally let go of Sarah. It seemed ironic that just when he'd solved the biggest problem of his life, he was faced with an even more formidable bridge to cross.

But then, he reminded himself as he walked down the hallway, without that bridge he would never have known Charlie as a woman. And that would have been the biggest loss of all.

He heard her slapping dishes around in the kitchen and winced. She always attacked everything with a ton of enthusiasm and not much finesse. It was one of the things he enjoyed about her. Nothing she did was ever halfhearted. When she went, she went all the way. His body quickened when he remembered her feverish lovemaking.

Some lucky stiff was going to have one hell of a woman one day. He wondered what had happened to her marriage and how any man could let a woman like her slip through his fingers.

Later, when they were eating the macaroni and cheese she'd fixed to go with the last of the salad, he asked her about her ex-husband. He heard her lay down her fork on her plate and wondered if he was treading on forbidden ground.

Then she answered. "We didn't split up over any one incident, I guess. It was a lot of things. I wanted more out of life than he did. He was in a dead-end job and seemed perfectly content to stay there. He was capable of so much more, but he didn't seem to care that he was wasting his life."

Ward heard the distress in her voice and lifted his hand. "Look, if you don't want to talk about it—"

"No, it's okay." Her sigh drifted across the table. "We argued. We fought about a lot of things. He didn't like me spending time with my parents—I think he resented the close relationship I had with them. Maybe he was jealous, I don't know. He had no time for his own family and couldn't understand why mine is so important to me. In the end we spent more time fighting than we did loving. If we ever did love each other."

Ward's throat constricted. If only he had the chance... "So, you divorced him," he said, wishing like hell he could see her face. His handicap had never seemed more cruel than now.

"Yes. I couldn't see the point in going on when we were both so unhappy. Larry tried to talk me out of it, but I think he was secretly relieved. He just didn't like the blow to his ego, that's all."

"So what is it you want out of life?"

"To see a little more of the world than the west coast of America. To have children someday and, I guess, just to be happy. It's not really a lot to ask, is it?"

The wistfulness in her voice cut straight to his heart. If she only knew how much he wished he could be the one to give her that happiness. "I don't know," he said carefully. "I wonder how many people are truly happy?"

"I believe you can do anything, if you really want it bad enough."

He smiled, thinking of a warm summer afternoon, her hand holding his, her earnest voice urging him not to lose hope. "I know," he murmured, his smile fading as the ache filled his soul, "I remember you telling me."

"Ward, I don't want you to give up. I want you to go on fighting and believing that one day you'll see again."

He groped for her hand and felt a surge of warm comfort when her fingers closed over his. "I'll fight, Charlie. If that's what you want, I'll fight. And I'll never forget what you've done for me. I'll never find the words to thank you."

Her fingers slipped from his grasp, and the cold ache spread throughout his body. "I don't need your thanks," she said crisply. "Just get well again. That's all I want."

No, he thought, she wanted a lot more. He could hear it in her voice, in the little gasp of pain she'd tried to muffle. He wanted it all too, dammit. He'd kill to have it all. But it was out of the question.

She'd admitted she wanted more from life than a meager existence in some dreary suburban neighborhood. Travel, she'd said. Children. The things he couldn't give her. Things he could never give her, no matter how badly he wanted them.

He could not give her less than a whole man. He would be cheating her, and he would be cheating himself. He wasn't the type of person who could settle for half measures. And he knew how much alike they were in that respect. She deserved more than he could give her. So much more.

But he couldn't tell her that. He thought his heart would break right then, when he realized that by this time tomorrow she would be gone. And he would be more alone than he'd ever been in his life.

He pushed back his chair and stood, feeling for the edge of the table. He walked around it until he knew he stood in front of her, then he held out his hand.

For a long moment his pulse fluttered in panic when she made no move to take it, then relief flooded him when he felt her soft fingers entwine with his. He was being selfish, he thought, but surely he deserved this one night. He would have to make it last one hell of a long time.

He tugged at her hand, and she came willingly, straight into his waiting arms. His body stirred as he ran his fingers up her arm and across her throat. He could feel her rapid pulse beneath his fingers, and he smiled. "I want you again," he said softly.

"I know." She brushed her hips against his. "I want you, too."

"Then what are we waiting for?"

She gave a breathless little laugh, the laugh he would hear in his mind for all eternity. "What about the dishes?"

"To hell with the dishes."

He slipped his arm around her and turned confidently toward the hallway. Sure of his steps, he drew her with him, past her door to his. This was his night, and he wanted her his way, in his room, in his bed.

He could make it last this time, he thought, as he drew her down on the bed. He wanted her just as much, if not more so, than he had earlier. But the urgency had been tempered, and he wanted to make it last. He wanted to remember every second, every touch, every breath that he drew, every sound that she made.

His throat ached with the knowledge that this would be the one and only night with her. He laid the back of his fingers against her throat and drew them down the velvet-soft valley between her breasts.

He felt her shudder as he parted her robe and spread his fingers over the soft mounds, and his breath quickened when she pushed his own robe from his shoulders. Make it last, he urged himself, as he tasted her warm skin, renewing his memory of every secret of her body.

Her fingers found him, and his breath hissed from his lungs. She knew how to please him, how to excite him and drive him out of his mind with wanting her.

He felt her move against him, her naked flesh sliding over his, torturing, tormenting him as his body throbbed with need. His fingers moved faster, he couldn't get enough of her—the smooth, flat planes of her stomach, the firm swell of her breasts, the brush of soft curls at the base of her belly....

He heard her gasp when he touched her, and her hips rose beneath him as she arched her back. He could hear her little cries now, the whisper of sound somewhere between pleasure and pleading. It seemed to echo in his belly, in his groin, until his whole body pounded with the urgency he could no longer control.

He found her hand and pulled it down, his spine arching when she closed her fingers around him again, guiding him until at last he could bury himself inside that exquisite warmth. He could hear his voice, deep and raw in his chest as the groans he couldn't suppress kept time with the thrusts of his hips.

Hold on, he thought fiercely, not yet. He felt her legs clamp around him, felt her nails digging into his back. She thrashed wildly, her cries like magnificent music to his ears, then her body tensed, shuddered and relaxed.

"God," she whispered. "No one ever told me it could be like that."

"Hold on, sweetheart," he muttered, "we've got a way to go yet." He thrust forward and heard her gasp as beads of sweat formed on his forehead. Her skin felt damp, heightening the intense excitement of her flesh against his. He could smell wildflowers again, and he knew that fragrance would haunt him the rest of his life.

Don't think about it, he warned himself. Not now. Not yet. She was making those sounds again, and his groans became more urgent, the impulsive rhythm of his hips more violent. He felt the muscles in his neck straining as he threw back his head in a primitive gesture of triumph.

She was his. For this moment in time she was his. In these few, mind-blowing seconds he owned her body as surely as she owned his. They were together, they were one, and he loved her. God, how he loved her. He took that thought with him as his body convulsed in his final drive toward release.

He thought about it a lot throughout that long night. He listened to the sound of her breathing and felt the soft whisper of its echo across his chest. Her hair brushed his chin, like the touch of a fragrant ghost.

That's what she was, really, he thought, a ghost. A beautiful, warm, generous, totally unattainable ghost. He wanted to give her the world, and he could give her only one thing. Her freedom. And in doing so, he would destroy himself.

Fate, he thought wryly, had the last laugh. He had destroyed Sarah, and fate had returned the favor in a way he could never have envisioned. To be granted a glimpse of paradise, of what could have been, and to have the door close on that tantalizing vision, had to be the most cruel retribution of all. Payment in full.

Lynn stirred at his side, snuggling closer in the curve of his arm. She stroked her hand across his chest, sending shivers of desire down his belly. He was hard again, and in the same moment he knew this would be the last time.

He woke her gently, with kisses placed strategically in the warm hollows of her neck. He'd discovered this source of her weakness earlier and was rewarded when she mumbled a low sound of pleasure that echoed in his own throat.

He reached for her, and once more she came alive in his arms, willing and more than ready to ride with him again to the heights of ecstasy.

Afterward, when she fell asleep, he tried to stay awake, reluctant to waste a single moment of these few precious hours. In spite of his best efforts, he felt his lids closing, and finally he gave in to the insistent demands of his brain.

He didn't know how long he'd slept. He'd been dreaming. Weird dreams about flying, or had he been swimming? He wasn't sure. He still had his sight in his dreams. Bright Technicolor dreams where everything seemed sparkling clear and vividly alive. This dream had been different.

His heart started pounding as a new fear gripped him. He'd relied on his dreams to keep his memories fresh. But the dream he'd just woken from had been nothing but swirling mists and indistinct shapes. Surely, he thought as rivulets of cold spread through his veins, surely he wasn't going blind in his dreams, too?

The horror of it was too much for him. Lynn still lay with her head on his chest; her steady breathing seeming loud in his ears as the adrenaline started pumping fast and furious into his bloodstream.

He struggled to control his breathing, to subdue the panic that seemed to grip him with merciless fingers. Slowly he opened his eyes. He blinked, his entire body jerking in disbelief. Instead of the dense blackness he had become so damnably accustomed to, he could see light gray shadows. Sunlight? he thought, then his heart nearly stopped. For God's sake. *He could see.*

Chapter 10

He lay still, frightened to move his head, terrified it was all in his imagination. Lynn must have sensed his tension. She stirred, murmuring words he couldn't identify while she snuggled into his side.

He blinked once...twice...and the shadows were still there. His heart began to pound, so hard it seemed to vibrate down to his feet. If he closed his eyes and the shadows remained, he'd know it was his imagination. He shut his lids, praying like mad. The darkness returned, as solid as ever.

Lynn moved away from his side. "Ward? Are you awake?"

He mumbled a reply, pretending to be just surfacing from sleep. He couldn't say anything. Not yet. Not until he was sure this was really happening.

"Ward," Lynn said sharply. "What's the matter?"

It was impossible not to hope. With a sudden movement he turned on his side and opened his eyes. Nothing. Only the same, familiar black wall in front of him. His disappointment crushed him so badly he actually felt a sensation of falling, as if he were tumbling down a bottomless well.

He reached for her, clutching at anything that would stop his headlong plunge into the nightmare. The moment he pulled her into his arms, his sanity returned. He *had* seen shadows. If only for a few seconds. But he had seen them.

He closed his arms around Lynn and hugged her so tight she muttered a quiet protest. "Nothing's the matter," he whispered, his lips trembling against her hair. "Just a nightmare, that's all."

He felt her relax against him. "Do you get them often?"

"No, not anymore."

She moved closer, fitting her body against his. "Do you want to talk about it?"

He was almost tempted to tell her about the glimpse of light. But he wasn't sure what it all meant. He wasn't even sure it meant anything at all. He had to keep this to himself, at least until he'd had the chance to talk to Harper.

"Not right now." Harper. Lynn was leaving today. He couldn't let her go. If the shadows meant his sight could be returning... He shut his mind against the hope. He was too damn scared to hope.

He traced the line of her cheek with his fingers. "I'd rather talk about you."

"What about me?"

"I want to know if you're still planning on going home today." He hadn't realized, until he'd asked the question, how important her answer would be.

"Do you want me to stay?"

He struggled with his conscience. He had no right to ask her to stay. Still he prayed that she would. "I want you to do whatever you want to do."

"In that case," Lynn murmured, "I'll stay. At least until my month's leave is up."

He jumped as her lips brushed his and the soft strands of her hair swept across his shoulder.

"Something *is* the matter," she said and moved away from him.

"No." He reached out to her, dragging her back into his arms. "I'm just happy that you're not leaving today."

He could hear the uncertainty in her voice when she said "Ward, if you have any regrets about . . . last night, I'd really like to know."

"Regrets? You must be kidding. Why would I regret being kept awake half the night, robbed of all my strength and vigor, trying to satisfy a greedy, voracious woman who won't leave me alone?" He found her mouth and put his soul into his kiss.

He could feel her heart pounding against his chest when he let her up for air. "Voracious?" Her lips brushed his in delicate torment. "I seem to remember you waking me out of my beauty sleep."

If he hadn't been so anxious to get to the hospital, he would have answered the erotic invitation of her body. But now he was desperate to talk to Harper, to find out if what he'd seen just now had any significance at all.

"Is that right?" He breathed a reluctant sigh that was all too genuine. "Well, much as I hate to admit it, voracious lady, I'm all out of energy. If we're going to make that appointment this morning, I'd better get some coffee and eggs down me."

He gave her his best smile and was rewarded when she murmured, "You smile at me like that, Commander Sullivan, and you might have to wait for your coffee and eggs."

He felt her rise from the bed, and without the comforting warmth of her body, the doubts came crashing in. He wasn't even sure now if he'd actually seen the shadows. Maybe he just wanted so much to see, he'd conjured up the vision in his imagination. Impatient with himself, he pushed the negative thoughts away. Until he talked to Harper, he would try not to think about it.

He lay for several minutes, listening to the rush of water from the shower next door. He tried not to visualize her naked body, shiny and slick with soap.

He would kill right then to go in there and join her. His palms tingled when he thought about smoothing them over her soft, wet skin. Impatient with himself, he threw back the covers and sat up.

God, if only he could get back his sight. He'd never ask for another thing. He padded across the room to the closet and began the task of selecting his clothes.

In the kitchen Lynn filled the coffeepot, trying to come to grips with the fast-moving events of the past hours. He'd made love to her as though he'd really meant it. As though it meant a lot more than just a matter of satisfying needs. He'd said a lot of things, but he hadn't said he loved her. In all that long night together, he'd never once said he loved her.

She opened the door of the refrigerator and took out the tray of eggs. She was opening herself up to all kinds of heartbreak. Yet she didn't have the strength to leave.

"Fool," she muttered out loud. "You're an idiotic, love-sick, chicken-brained fool."

Later, on the ride to the hospital, Ward did his best to hide his anxiety. He listened to Lynn's chatter about the traffic and the gray skies that threatened rain, trying to answer with some measure of interest.

Privately he was churning, wondering what Harper would have to say about the shadows. If only he could see them again, just once more, he thought, to be sure he hadn't imagined them. He jumped guiltily when Lynn said sharply, "Ward? Are you sure you're feeling okay?"

"Sorry." He made an effort to smile. "I guess I'm tired. It's been a long time since I lost a night's sleep."

She sounded worried when she said, "I'm sorry."

"Hey." He stretched out his hand and gave her arm a squeeze. "It was most definitely worth it." To his relief he felt the car slow for the sharp turn into the parking lot.

The walk to the waiting room seemed interminable. Once there, he sat next to Lynn, wishing he could feel the comforting pressure of her arm. The space she'd put between them told him there had to be other people in the room.

Now that he concentrated, he could hear the rustle of papers, the slight cough from someone opposite him, and the nervous scrape of someone's foot on the vinyl floor.

By the time he heard his name called, his stomach muscles ached with tension. He got to his feet and felt Lynn's hand on his arm. For once he was grateful for her guidance. His mind was so chaotic he felt disoriented.

He let out a sigh of relief when he finally sat down in the doctor's office.

"Ward," Dr. Harper's voice said. "How're you doing?"

"I'm hoping you'll be able to tell me." That statement had more meaning than the surgeon could possibly realize.

"You're looking good. Any problems?"

Ward shook his head. "None that I can think of."

"Good. Well, let's take a look at you."

The physical examination took less than ten minutes, but he endured it with mounting impatience. He wanted that part of it over with before mentioning the shadows. If it meant bad news he wanted to get out of there fast afterward.

"Well, you're looking good," the surgeon announced when he was finished. "Everything is healing up nicely, you'll have hardly any scarring. Your body must have been in excellent shape to have come through this ordeal so well."

"Yeah, I guess so." Ward sat up and buttoned his shirt. "But there is something else I want to talk to you about. I think I saw some light when I woke up this morning."

The doctor paused long enough to scare him. Then he asked quietly, "You think?"

Ward made up his mind. "No. I *know* I saw shadows. It was like seeing ghosts in a dark mist, but I definitely saw something." He slid his hips off the table, and the surgeon grasped his arm.

"Come and sit down," he said, "and let's talk about this."

He made Ward go over and over again exactly what he'd seen, how long it had lasted, if he'd noticed any changes since then, until Ward finally lost patience. "So what does it mean?" he demanded. "Is there a chance my sight is coming back?"

His heart sank when Dr. Harper said slowly, "I don't know, Ward. I wish I could tell you. One thing we can be sure of now is that your problem is not a physical one. I think you should see Dr. Williams again."

At Ward's groan the doctor added, "I know how you feel about her, but she could be the answer to your problems, if you'd just give her a chance."

"I don't believe in all that stuff," Ward said wearily.

"I know you don't. But then I didn't believe they could put a man on the moon until they did it." Ward heard the chair creak as the surgeon stood up. "Give it a chance, Ward. It might be the only chance you've got."

He passed an impatient hand across his forehead. "All right. When can I see her?"

"Let me give her a call."

Ward listened to the surgeon make the appointment for that afternoon. He'd have to come up with some excuse for Lynn, he thought. He wasn't going to tell her anything until he knew more himself.

Dr. Harper led him to the door and gave him a reassuring pat on the shoulder. "Hang in there, Ward. Any improvement is better than none. And it could be the beginning of a full recovery."

"I wish I could believe that," Ward muttered, obeying the pressure of the doctor's hand to pass through the door.

Lynn had called her parents while Ward was in the doctor's office. It hadn't been easy trying to explain why she'd changed her mind again about coming home, and she was still smarting from her father's brusque comments when Ward appeared in the doorway.

The thrill of excitement that surged through her when she saw him banished her resentment. In spite of everything that had happened to him, he still stood straight and tall, with that proud set of his shoulders that set him apart from any man she'd ever met. Even in jeans and a sweater, his dark hair long on his neck, he bore the stamp of a military man.

She felt a rush of tingling warmth when she remembered his hands on her body and his soft groans that had quickly turned guttural and urgent when she'd touched him.

She would never forget, she thought, with a pang of biting agony. All the rest of her life she would remember how good they were together.

Hurrying over to him, she took his arm. "So how'd it go?" she asked, as she led him down the hallway. "Did he release you from the hospital?"

"Not quite. I have to come back this afternoon."

She looked up at him, aware at once of his change of mood. "Is something wrong?"

"No. Harper wants me to see the shrink again."

"I thought you were finished with her."

"I was. At least, I told them I was. I guess Harper figures I need one more session before he's satisfied. I decided not to argue if it means leaving this place for good."

He gave her hand a reassuring squeeze against his side, but she couldn't help feeling he was keeping something from her. "What time?" she asked, keeping her voice deliberately casual. He would tell her when he was ready to tell her. She hoped.

"Fourteen hundred." He smiled down at her. "That's two o'clock to civilians."

"I know. Some of us civilians are capable of working things out for ourselves."

"Just testing. I wanted to know if you were awake after last night."

She wondered if she'd ever be immune to that grin. "Barely. But you should know all about that."

"Yeah," he said softly, making her skin tingle. "I know all about that."

They reached the car, and she pulled open the door. "There's not much point in going home," she said, glancing at her watch. "Fancy another hamburger?"

"That's a great idea."

Climbing in beside him, she started the engine. "All right. Next stop, the drive-in."

Huge drops of rain splattered the windshield as she drove into the parking lot. She gave the order into the speaker, then joined the line at the window. "You want to eat in the car, or shall we go inside?" she asked, as she inched the car forward.

"The car. It's more private."

She could understand how he felt. He had turned down all her suggestions to eat in a restaurant. He still had trouble cutting up his food and stubbornly refused to let her do it anymore.

She wished he would get over his self-consciousness. He'd have so many things to deal with after she'd gone. The thought depressed her, and after she'd parked in the corner of the parking lot she looked at her hamburger without much appetite.

"So," she said, when she'd finally chewed her way through it, "you get to see the dragon lady again, huh?"

Ward crumpled the wrapper into a ball. If she didn't know him so well she might have imagined the subtle stillness of his body. "Yeah," he said lightly. "We get to have another heart-to-heart."

"Nice," Lynn said dryly, wondering what it was he didn't want to tell her.

He turned his face and aimed a grin at her that stopped her breath. "If I didn't know you better, Ms. Barclay, I'd say you were jealous."

Maybe she was, she thought ruefully. She'd give anything to know what they talked about. "Not really," she murmured out loud. "I lied about her. She does have red eyes and fangs."

"I'll be sure to tell her you said that when I see her."

"Do that." She reached for her napkin. "Come here, you have ketchup on your chin."

Obediently he leaned toward her and she caught his jaw with one hand and dabbed at his chin with the other. "There," she murmured, "you're handsome again."

He caught her hand and turned it over, pressing his lips to her palm. "And you're as beautiful as ever."

Her pulse leapt. "Now how do you know that, flatterer?"

He let go of her hand and touched her face, his strong fingers stroking her cheek. "I told you, beauty has nothing to do with looks, not that there's anything wrong with yours."

She wanted to speak and couldn't. She remembered his words. *A woman you can enjoy talking to, share all your thoughts with, and just enjoy being with.* She'd thought at the time he was talking about Sarah. Could he possibly have been talking about *her?* Careful, she reminded herself. That kind of thinking was dangerous. Only fools put their hopes in dreams.

She pulled away from him. "We'd better get back to the hospital if you want to make your appointment." She turned the key in the ignition, then drove out of the parking lot without looking at him again. But she couldn't fail to notice the way he drummed his fingers on the armrest between them and his lack of conversation on the way back to the hospital.

Once again Ward found himself sitting in the waiting room, his hands jammed between his knees to keep them still. God, he'd be glad to get out of this place for good, he thought. He wished now he hadn't agreed to talk to the shrink. The woman asked him far too many questions. Questions that he wasn't prepared to answer. This whole thing was going to be another waste of time.

He felt himself jerk as Lynn nudged his arm. "Wake up," she said, sounding a little edgy.

He felt her hand under his arm and stood, then followed the pressure of her hand until the soft voice of Dr. Williams said, "Hello, Ward. I'll take him from here."

This last must have been to Lynn, since she dropped her hand from his arm. He missed the warm pressure of her fingers. He was almost tempted to ask if she could come in with him, except he knew the dragon lady would never allow it.

What are you afraid of? he asked himself irritably, as he allowed the psychiatrist to lead him down the hallway to her office. For someone who was supposed to have nerves of steel, someone who could turn a plane on its nose and hurtle toward the earth at the speed of sound, he was being ridiculous.

For a moment he experienced such a sharp sense of longing to be back in a plane, it cut off his breath. He broke his
stride and felt the tug on his arm as Dr. Williams pulled him
along.

"I'm all right," he muttered, before she could say anything.

"Well, we're here now."

He heard the faint squeak of hinges as the door swung
open, then the psychiatrist drew him into the carpeted room
that smelled of polish and the subtle scent of leather. He was
beginning to hate that smell, he thought, lowering himself
into the chair.

"I'm glad you changed your mind about talking to me
again," Dr. Williams said, as the faint scuffling sound told
him she'd sat down opposite him.

"It was Dr. Harper's idea, not mine."

"Yes. He tells me you've been seeing some form of
light?"

"Shadows. I saw shadows."

He felt warm and wished he'd taken off his sweater. The
room was too stuffy—

"Shadows?"

"Yes." He repeated what he'd told Harper. "It looked
like ghosts in a dark mist."

"Did the shapes change when you moved your head?"

"I don't know... I don't remember." He heard the scratch
of a pen on paper and sat forward. "I did see them," he said
clearly.

"I'm sure you did, Commander. Now we have to find out
why."

He sat back, surprised to feel his heart pounding furiously against his chest. "I don't know why."

"Yes, you do. Deep in your subconscious mind you do."

He hardened his mouth. There she went again.

"Ward, you told me that the only time you are truly happy is when you're flying. That without flying, your life might as well be over. Is that right?"

He didn't remember telling her that. Yet he must have, since it was true. "I guess so."

"When I asked you why, you refused to answer. I'd like you to think about that now, and try to give me an answer this time. Why is flying so desperately important to you?"

"I don't know why."

"Try, Ward. It could be vitally important."

He closed his eyes. He wasn't sure why, but shutting his eyes made him feel more secure. Which was crazy, really, since he couldn't see either way. "I feel free up there," he said abruptly.

"And you don't on the ground? Why not?"

He began to squirm. "I have no idea."

"Tell me, Ward. Tell me what it is you're trying to run away from. What is it that you can't face?"

He opened his mouth for his usual denial, but the words wouldn't come. He saw Lynn's face, tears clinging to her long lashes, her mouth trembling. He heard his own voice, harsh with pain. *Sarah is dead and we can't bring her back. Talking isn't going to change that.* "Sarah," he muttered, without realizing he'd spoken out loud.

"Who is Sarah?"

The question shocked him, especially since it came from a stranger. He struggled for words to tell this phony physician that it was none of her business. And instead, to his intense embarrassment, he heard himself say, "She was Charlie's sister. She died eighteen years ago...and it was my fault."

"Your fault? In what way?"

He struggled with the words, trying to force them out. "She ... died trying to get rid of my baby."

He could hear the force of his heartbeat in his ears as he waited for her reaction.

"Why was it your fault? Did you tell her to do it?"

He shook his head in a violent denial. "I...didn't know...she was pregnant." He wondered why his voice sounded strange, then realized he'd spoken through clenched teeth.

"I see...And who is Charlie?"

"Lynn Barclay. She's...the woman who is staying with me right now."

"Ah, yes. I remember. Tell me about Charlie."

"I...can't." He could feel the sweat breaking out on his brow. He wiped it away with the back of his hand. "I..." He lifted his hands in a helpless gesture. He wanted to talk. He needed to get it all out. He knew that now. But something held him back, as surely as if he had a gag in his mouth.

"All right, Ward. Take it easy. Why do you think Lynn Barclay is taking care of you? She wouldn't do that if she thought you were responsible for her sister's death, would she?"

He couldn't take any more. He was going to explode if this damn shrink kept probing like this. "Look," he said, pushing himself out of the chair, "I know you're trying to help but I just can't talk about it. I'd like to go now."

He heard the steady scratch of the psychiatrist's pen and clenched his fingers. If only he could see, he'd walk out of there now.

"All right, I'll take you back."

He heard the chair legs scuff across the carpet and tried to relax. Even so, he jumped when he felt her firm fingers grasp his arm.

"You have to forgive yourself, Ward," Dr. Williams said quietly. "You have to understand why you're blaming yourself for something over which you had no control. Until you do that, you will never be completely whole."

How? Ward questioned silently. How do you forgive yourself for the loss of a life?

"Have you talked about this with . . . Charlie?"

Ward shook his head.

"That's what I thought. I think you should. There is so much still to be resolved. Maybe if you do that, you'll see things a little more clearly. You might even find your sight returning."

He held his breath, denial blocking his thoughts, making him afraid even to so much as think about the doctor's suggestion.

"Think about it, Ward," Dr. Williams urged gently. "It could be the answer to your problem."

He wondered if Lynn would see the distress when he followed the doctor into the waiting room. He waited, stiff-backed and uncomfortable, while the two women exchanged pleasantries. Then Dr. Williams left and once more he felt Lynn's warm fingers on his arm.

"You okay?" she asked softly.

He nodded. He couldn't have spoken if he'd wanted to, and right now he could think of nothing to say.

He sat in silence throughout the ride back to the mobile-home park, his thoughts in turmoil. Could it be possible that simply by talking things out, he could actually see again?

It was all too incredible to believe, yet by the time he felt the car pull to a stop, he knew that if there was the slightest chance of recovering his sight, he had to grab it.

He had no idea what it would do to his relationship with Lynn. To bring Sarah's death up again would certainly be painful and could put an end to the delicate, wonderful intimacy that was growing between them. By gaining one thing back, he could lose another.

The decision was agonizing, but he knew he had no real choice. Without his sight he had nothing to give her, anyway. He had to take the chance, however slim it was, and pray that whatever it was they'd found in each other would be strong enough to withstand the test.

It could all be for nothing. He might never regain his sight and might never have the chance for the kind of happiness he'd only glimpsed in his dreams. But he had to give it a try. He couldn't live with himself if he didn't.

He accepted Lynn's offer of coffee and waited until she'd joined him in the living room. While he was still trying to figure out a way to begin, she did it for him.

"So what did the dragon lady have to say?"

He smiled. "I wondered when you were going to ask that question."

"I asked you in the car. You were too deep in thought to answer me."

"You did?" He shook his head. "I'm sorry. I guess I must have been thinking about something else."

"Want to tell me about it?"

He took a deep breath. "All right. I was thinking it was about time we talked about Sarah."

He could almost touch the silence that followed. Silently he cursed the wall of darkness that prevented him from seeing her face.

Finally he heard her quavering sigh. "You loved her very much."

"Yes." The pain that accompanied his answer seemed no more than the ache of nostalgia. "And so did you."

"We all did. I guess that's why my parents reacted the way they did. They were looking for someone to blame, and you were there."

"And what about you?"

Seconds ticked by in the quiet room, then Lynn said quietly, "I felt you'd betrayed me. I was very young and naive. I'd been protected all my life—I'd never known real pain before. I didn't know how to handle it. I only knew that my whole world had crashed and nothing would ever be the same again. For some reason I believed it was all your fault."

"It was my fault."

"No, Ward. It wasn't. If anyone could be held to blame for what happened, it was all of us. Me, my parents, we all could share the blame. If my parents had accepted you, instead of trying to protect Sarah from someone they were afraid might end up hurting her, she might have felt able to confide in them."

He felt a flash of resentment and fought it down. "I would never have intentionally hurt her. They should have known that. They would have, if they'd taken the time to get to know me."

"Ward, try to look at it from their viewpoint. You were ... different from anyone Sarah had met before. Your clothes, your hair, the kind of music you liked—it all added up to someone they didn't understand, someone a little wild ... a little dangerous, maybe."

He frowned. "All right. I get your point. But that's your parents. I don't understand why you should feel part of the blame for what happened."

He heard the scuff of her feet crossing the room and knew she'd sat down in the corner armchair. "Sarah and I used to talk all the time," she said quietly. "About everything and everyone. There were never any secrets between us until she met you."

His frown deepened. "I still don't understand."

Again she sighed. "I refused to talk to Sarah about you. Every time she tried, I made some excuse and left, until she finally got the message and didn't mention you anymore."

He could feel his face stiffening. "You disliked me that much?"

"No," Lynn said quietly. "In my shy, gawky, adolescent way, I worshiped and adored you. I was feeling all these strange emotions I didn't understand. I couldn't bear to think of you and Sarah together, and when I saw you with her I hated her, without knowing why. And then she died. I felt so awful for the things I felt. But most of all I couldn't understand how you, my wonderful, strong, perfect hero, could have let it happen."

His throat felt so tight he could hardly swallow. Before he could think of something to say, Lynn spoke again.

"When I read the diary I understood, for the first time, what had really happened. I realized then that if I had let Sarah talk to me, she might have told me about the baby. I might have been able to stop her from doing what she did."

"God." He buried his face in his hands. "I caused so much pain. So much heartache."

He didn't hear her moving across the room. He didn't know she was there until he felt her hands on his knees. When she spoke, he knew she was kneeling on the floor at his feet.

"Ward, don't you see? We can all find reasons to blame ourselves for what happened. But Sarah was the one who did this to herself. And who knows? If we could have done things differently, we still might not have stopped her." She closed her fingers around his, holding them tight.

"I could have told my parents when I found the diary, and they could have located you and saved you years of guilt and pain. But I didn't. Ward, we're only human. None of us is perfect, and we make mistakes. But this was Sarah's mistake, not ours. And I truly believe that she wouldn't want us to go on torturing ourselves for things that can't be changed. She has forgiven us, Ward. It's time we did the same and forgave each other."

"I loved her." The words came out in a husky whisper, and he cleared his throat. "If I had known, if she had told me about the baby, I would have married her. I swear I would have married her.''

"I know.''

He heard Lynn's sob catch in her throat, and drew her fingers to his mouth. He tasted the salt of her tears, and suddenly the hard shell of guilt began to crumble.

Slowly, painfully, he found the words he wanted. "Sarah was the one good thing in my life,'' he said, holding tightly to Lynn's hands. "After she...died, I began running. I tried to leave it all behind, all the memories, the guilt, the bitter accusations, everything. Only I couldn't shake them off. They kept coming back to haunt me...in my dreams, in my thoughts...they were everywhere.''

He drew a painful breath. "Except in the sky. Up there I could finally break free, where I was all alone and no one could touch me. Up there my mind was clear, empty of everything except that incredible feeling of power and speed...and the ultimate control.''

He pressed his lips to Lynn's trembling fingers again. "That was it,'' he said slowly. "Up there I was in control. While down here the past controlled me.'' He let go of her hands and leaned back in the chair, feeling light-headed from the intense emotions.

"I was reasonably content with my life,'' he went on, "and then out of the blue there you were, and you sent everything crashing down around me again.''

She started to speak, but he stopped her with an uplifted hand. "No, wait. I resented you because you'd stirred up everything I'd tried to forget. You made me take another hard look at myself, and I hated what I saw.''

"I'm sorry. I should never have come to see you that day.''

He frowned. "Why did you? Was it simply for the chance of a story?''

"Partly." She paused, and he waited anxiously for her next words. "I wanted to see you again, to reassure myself that in spite of what my family had done to you, it hadn't affected your life. I was pretty upset when I found out you were still so bitter about it all."

"And—" he waved a hand around the room "—all this?"

She hesitated just a little too long. "I thought I could make up for all the terrible things we'd said to you. I didn't realize at the time just how badly we'd hurt you."

"Nor I you." He leaned forward to reach for her hands again. "After all this, it seems a little inadequate to tell you I'm sorry."

"There's no need." He heard her rise, and she tugged on his hands. "My parents and I are the ones who should apologize."

He stood and pulled her into his arms. "Not you," he whispered against her hair. "You never did anything except waste your admiration on someone who didn't deserve it."

"I said some terrible things to you."

"You were twelve years old, Charlie. How could you be expected to understand?"

He traced her mouth with his fingers, then bent his head, kissing away the tears he tasted there. When she trembled against him, he knew it was going to be all right after all. They had survived the past. Now all he could do was pin his hopes on an uncertain future.

All through dinner that evening he listened to her voice, imprisoning each and every memory of her, in case it was all he'd ever have.

He helped her with the dishes and made the coffee for her. He sat through a movie on television, listening to her describing the action without really hearing it. He had only one thing on his mind, and he couldn't wait until it was time

At long last the movie ended, and he heard Lynn yawn. "I'm ready for bed," she said, just a little too casually.

He pushed himself up from the chair, his body already stirring with anticipation. "So am I." He held out his arms toward her. "Do I get a good-night kiss?"

"I thought you'd never ask."

He grinned, then the fire ignited in his groin as she walked into his arms, her mouth eager under his, and her body giving him the message he'd been waiting for.

He took her slowly, building the fire in leisurely stages until it consumed them both. He fell asleep holding her in his arms, and when he awoke in the morning the shadows were back. And this time they didn't go away.

Chapter 11

He waited for long, agonizing minutes before he dared move his head. He opened and closed his eyes until his lids ached, and still the shadows remained. At last he found the courage to turn, an inch at a time, onto his side.

At first the disappointment crushed him. Lynn had to be right on top of him, yet he couldn't see her. Then he saw her move her head. It was no more than a vague shape moving through a dark gray mist. But it was movement.

It was true. He could see. Dammit, *he could see!*

He closed his eyes, reaching for her. She mumbled something, and excitement made his voice hoarse when he answered, "Good morning, beautiful."

He could almost make our her features when she lifted up to look at him. "You all right?"

He grinned. "You bet I'm all right. I'm downright wonderful."

"Wa'al them's my sentiments too, pilgrim."

Her attempt at a John Wayne impersonation made him laugh. The laugh welled up in his throat, and he rolled onto his back, releasing the sound in a joyful shout of celebration.

"It wasn't that funny," Lynn said, shifting herself to lie on his chest.

The touch of her soft warm body sobered him instantly. He had to think. He wanted to tell her. He wanted to shout it from the rooftops, but he'd been disappointed before. He couldn't afford to take anything for granted.

"You seem a little preoccupied," Lynn murmured.

"Do I?" At this close range he could see the outline of her hair and the sweep of her jaw. He wrapped his arms around her, careful not to squeeze her too tightly in his exuberance. "I was just thinking about last night and wondering if I had the energy for a repeat performance."

"Mmm." She nuzzled his nose with hers. "Want me to find out?" She moved her hand down and nearly sent him through the ceiling. "Yep," she announced smugly. "I'd say you have the energy."

"Witch." A thought formed in his mind, so incredibly intoxicating it took his breath away. He drew her face back down to his and found her mouth. Locking her in his arms, he rolled her over until his body covered hers. It was fitting, he thought, as he pressed his mouth into the warm hollow of her throat, that one of the first things he should be able to see was her naked body.

Later, as he lay spent and hurting for breath, he knew he couldn't wait to find out for sure. He fought his impatience for another half hour, losing himself in the murmured love talk that was so much a part of the whole, incredible experience.

Finally, when he could contain himself no longer, he said as casually as he could manage, "I forgot to tell you, I have another appointment at the hospital."

He sensed her tension at once. "I thought you were all through with them."

"No, I have one final appointment and it's this morning." He prayed that Harper would be able to see him.

"What time?" Lynn asked, moving her arm.

Guessing that she was reaching for the clock, he said vaguely, "I think it was around eleven. I'll have to call and ask them."

"I'll do it." She moved away from him, and he grabbed at her arm.

"No, I'll do it while you take a shower. I need more practice using the phone."

"Okay, but I wish you'd told me. Who's the appointment with?"

"Harper." He could hardly speak. He could see her figure as she reached for her robe, and his throat closed. Quickly he closed his eyes, before he gave himself away.

"I'd better get my shower right away then. It's almost nine-thirty."

He heard the door shut and let out his breath in a rush. If he was having this much trouble now, he thought, just wait until he could really see her.

He sat up and combed his hair back with his fingers. *If* he would be able to see her, he reminded himself grimly. He could be setting himself up for another shattering blow.

In spite of his caution, he couldn't resist punching the air with his fist in silent triumph. Excitement, chilling in its intensity, raced through his body. He was going to see again. Somehow, deep down, he just knew it. The dragon lady had been right. He'd finally rid himself of the poison in his system, and he was going to see again.

He flung back the covers and swung his legs over the side of the bed. Almost afraid to breathe, he stood, half-expecting the darkness to close in on him again. The light remained, and he closed his eyes in gratitude. If only he could recover his sight, he promised silently, he would spend the rest of his life making up for all the years he'd wasted. And he'd find some way to help those people who might never know the miracle of vision.

Soft, fuzzy shapes seemed to loom up and fade away as he moved around the room. He could barely distinguish colors, but he could detect the different shades on the bed covers and the carpet, when he bent down to find his slippers.

As he watched the pale shadow of his hand move over the buttons on the phone, he actually shook. His fingers hurt as they clamped around the receiver. He could hear the rush of water from the bathroom and knew Lynn wouldn't be able to hear him. Even so, he kept his voice down when he spoke.

"Dr. Harper, please."

"One moment." There was an agonizing pause, then the surgeon's voice said calmly, "This is Dr. Harper."

"Sullivan." He took a shaky breath. "I can see."

"That's wonderful." The doctor actually sounded excited as he added, "How well?"

"Not too well at the moment. It's all kind of fuzzy, keeps fading and coming back."

"I'll set you up for an appointment with an eye specialist." Again a long pause. "How about Friday?"

"How about this morning?"

"Ward, I know how you feel—"

"Doc." He gripped the phone, closed his eyes and prayed. "I've waited a long time," he said quietly.

The pause was even longer this time. "All right," Dr. Harper said at last. "I'll see what I can do. Be at my office at noon, I'll try to catch Foster before he goes to lunch."

"Thanks." Aware that he was grinning as he laid down the receiver, Ward composed his face. He was going to find a special way to tell her, he promised himself. And a special place. Until then, and until he knew for certain that he would recover completely, he would have to be very careful not to give himself away.

He did his best to hide his excitement on the drive to the hospital later. He had to force himself not to try to focus on anything, since Lynn would pick up on it right away. But his spirits soared when he could distinguish the sun overhead and the fast-moving shadows rushing past the windows of the car.

In his haste to get out, he almost tripped when he opened the car door in the parking lot. Lynn was at his side in an instant. Although she didn't touch him, he could hear the puzzled note in her voice when she said, "Take it easy. We've got plenty of time."

Silently cursing himself for his impatience, he aimed a wild grin at her. "Sorry. Got my feet tangled up." He stuck out an elbow and waited for her to take it.

"Aren't you going to take your cane?" she asked, slipping her hand under his arm.

"No, I'll let you lead me this morning." And hopefully she might never have to do it again, he added silently.

The building appeared out of the mist as he walked toward it, solid and reassuring. The edges were fuzzy, and he could barely see the doorway until he was up to it. Again his heart pounded as he managed the stairs, fighting the urge to look down.

He allowed Lynn to lead him down the long hallway while subtle shapes slid by him with soft rustles and tapping footsteps. He sat in a fever of impatience in the waiting room until he heard his name called, then shot off the seat like a greyhound out of a trap. He saw a shape move toward him, and Lynn said, "Good morning, Dr. Harper."

"Morning, Lynn. Ward, how're you doing?"

He almost knocked the surgeon over in his haste to get him back in the office before he could say anything to Lynn.

Once inside he sent the fuzzy outline of the doctor a wide grin of sheer joy. "It's coming back," he said, his voice cracking with elation.

"I can't tell you how happy I am to hear that." The doctor guided him to a chair. "I talked to Dr. Williams—she wants to be here when Foster gets here. I hope that's all right with you?"

"I don't care if the entire staff comes in, I just want this to be official so I can start believing it."

A sharp rap on the door made his pulse skip. He watched the shadows of the surgeon and the two other doctors as they converged in front of him.

The short, squat shape introduced himself as Jim Foster and then leaned down to peer at him. "Can you see my face?" he asked.

Ward nodded with intense satisfaction. "You're wearing glasses and you have a good-looking mustache."

"Thanks." Foster sounded amused. His hand, holding a light, appeared in front of Ward's eyes. "Just look straight ahead," he murmured, then zoomed in on Ward's face until their noses were touching.

Trying to curb his impatience, Ward answered all the questions, then finally it was over. "Well," the specialist said, "physically, your eyes are perfectly normal. I'll need you to come in for a complete examination in a week or two, but as far as any damage is concerned, my initial conclusions remain unchanged."

"Dr. Foster examined your eyes when you were first admitted," Dr. Harper explained.

"Yes, you were in a lot worse shape than, I can tell you." Foster tapped Ward on the shoulder. "Why don't you stand, and we'll find out how much you can see."

Several minutes later the specialist was satisfied. "Well, you won't be driving a car just yet," he said, shaking Ward's hand, "and I wouldn't try crossing a street unless you're at

a crosswalk, but otherwise, I'd say you're well on the way
to recovery."

"Can you say how long before my sight is back to normal?" Ward asked, waiting anxiously for the answer.

"It's hard to say. Could be as little as hours, or overnight, could be a week or two. Just try not to strain your
eyesight, okay? Wear sunglasses when you're outside."

"I will," Ward promised. "And thanks."

"Don't thank me." The specialist moved to the door. "I'd
say it's my two colleagues here who deserve the credit for
your recovery. Good luck, Commander Sullivan."

The door closed with a quiet thud, and Dr. Williams said
with a smile in her voice, "Congratulations, Ward, I'm
happy for you."

He looked at the petite, narrow outline in front of him
and held out his hand. "I took your advice and I guess it
worked," he said, wishing he didn't feel so awkward with
her. "I want to thank you for your patience."

Her slim fingers grasped his. "You're entirely welcome.
I'm glad things worked out so well for you." Dr. Williams
withdrew her hand, and a moment later Ward heard the
door close behind her.

"I guess you can find your own way out," Dr. Harper
said, moving over to the door.

"I'd rather you took me." The sheer pleasure of actually
seeing the door brought a lump to his throat. He swallowed
hard. "I don't want Lynn to know yet, I'd like to surprise
her."

"Of course." The surgeon opened the door and took hold
of his arm. "Let's go then."

Ward had a hard time keeping his eyes unfocused as he
walked into the waiting room and saw Lynn, wearing a red
sweater, coming toward him. It might be his imagination, he
thought, but it seemed as if his sight had improved since
he'd left home.

"Well, he's all yours," the surgeon said cheerfully. "And I don't want to see you in here again, Ward." He slapped Ward on the shoulder.

"Don't worry, Doc. I'll do my best to stay away." Ward felt Lynn's fingers close around his arm and covered them with his hand. "Thanks for everything, Dr. Harper."

"You're very welcome, Commander Sullivan." The doctor raised his hand in salute, then turned and strode away into the fuzzy background.

"Is this really the end of it?" Lynn asked, as they emerged into the brilliant sunshine.

"You bet." He didn't mention the specialist's appointment yet to come. That could wait until he'd told her the big news. It took all his willpower not to reach for the door handle and open it for her. Not much longer now, he promised himself, and he'd be able to do all those things again— and more. So much more.

He waited until Lynn was seated next to him in the car before saying, "Would you take me to do some shopping?"

She started the engine, and the car rolled forward. "Sure. What kind of shopping?"

"I'd like to buy you a gift . . . for everything you've done for me."

She sounded edgy when she answered. "You don't have to do that, Ward."

"I know I don't have to, but I want to. I remember when you said that just once you'd like to buy something extravagant. Well, I'd like to buy you a dress, a special dress."

"Ward, it really isn't necessary . . ."

He could hear the protest in her voice now, but ignored it. He wanted to do this right. "I want to buy you a dress, and then I want to take you to the best restaurant in town so that you can show it off."

He didn't dare turn his head, but he knew she was shocked when she said, "A restaurant? But you hate the idea of eating out."

"That just goes to show how much I want to do this for you."

"Ward—"

"Please, Charlie," he said softly, "it would mean a lot to me."

After a long while, she sighed. "In that case, I can hardly refuse. But I insist on buying my own dress."

"Not on your life. You get to choose it of course, but I get to pay. It's part of the deal."

"Has anyone ever told you that you're a remarkably stubborn man?"

He laughed. "If anyone has, it's probably you. You've called me just about everything else."

"That's because you've been just about everything else."

She braked, and he almost shouted in pleasure when he saw the red stoplight gleaming at him out of the misty sunshine. "So, do we have a deal?" he asked, avidly watching people cross in front of the car like ghosts in the early dawn.

"All right, Commander, but it's going to cost you. There's a little black number I have my eye on that's wickedly expensive."

"Is it wicked looking, too?"

He felt her start of surprise. "It could be," she said warily.

Hastily he amended his slip. "I'm not sure I want every male in the place ogling my date."

"Don't worry. I won't tell you if they are." She pulled forward again, and he had to hide his grin. He couldn't wait to see her face when he told her. He settled back, thinking that there couldn't be a more wonderful word in the world than that little word *see*.

Lynn felt self-conscious at first as she tried on the dress that had caught her attention when she'd shopped a few days earlier. She felt differently about it now, knowing that Ward intended to pay for it.

She knew he meant well, but she couldn't help feeling that the dress was a payoff, especially since it seemed as if her time with him was rapidly coming to an end.

She had four days left before she would have to go back to Portland. Four days. She knew she was being a fool, but she couldn't help hoping that he'd offer some kind of commitment.

Surely, she thought, it couldn't end just like that? Surely those hours they'd spent together had meant something more to him than just a night of pleasure? When she was in his arms, he swept away all her doubts in the fever of his passion, but now, in the cold light of day, the misgivings returned to plague her.

She couldn't believe he was simply using her, yet he'd said nothing about a permanent relationship. He didn't seem concerned about managing without her, once she'd gone, and when she mentioned going back to Portland, he'd raised no objections other than to ask her to stay until the end of her leave.

Standing in the tiny dressing room, Lynn surveyed herself in the long mirror. Black had always suited her, and the dress looked as good as she had known it would. She pulled her hair back from her face with both hands. A sophisticated chignon would complement the deeply cut neckline, she decided.

So what if he couldn't see her, it would make her feel good to know she looked her best. Sighing, she slipped out of the dress. If only she knew for sure how he really felt about her. She could have truly looked forward to this dinner date.

Was it possible, she wondered, that he was afraid his blindness would be a burden to her? It could be that he didn't want to saddle her with the responsibility of caring for a handicapped person.

Pausing in the act of pulling on her jeans, she wondered why that hadn't occurred to her before. It would be so like him to consider her happiness and well-being above his own.

She dragged the jeans over her hips and fastened them, her pulse suddenly racing with excitement. There was one way to find out. Tonight at dinner. She'd have to find some way to let him know how she felt about him, without putting him on the spot. She'd have to let him know that she'd be willing to spend the rest of her life with him, no matter what faculties he might lack.

Picking up the dress, she grimaced at herself in the mirror. So she was building castles in the air again, putting her hopes in dreams. But as long as she had an atom of hope, she would cling to it. And if Ward Sullivan was too stubborn to take a chance on the happiness they both deserved, then she would just have to find a way to break him down.

Smiling, she emerged from the dressing room to find Ward waiting where she'd left him. "This is the one I'd like," she told him as he turned his head at her approach. "I don't suppose you'd reconsider letting me pay for it?"

"Not a chance. This is my treat, and you're not going to spoil it for me." He pulled his wallet from his jacket pocket and gave it to her. "My credit card is in the front, there."

She pulled it out and gave it to the clerk, then took the slip and guided his hand to the place for him to sign. He was getting very good at signing his name, she thought, as she watched the flowing signature appear. Hooking her finger through the handle of the shopping bag, she grasped Ward's arm. "You can at least let me buy you lunch," she said as he stood.

"As long as it's only a hamburger at the drive-in. I don't want to spoil my appetite for tonight."

It was a poor substitute for a new dress and dinner, Lynn thought as she led him back out to the car. But it would have to do. And now she was really looking forward to her dinner date after all.

As soon as they arrived back at the mobile home, Ward insisted that she call and make reservations for dinner that evening. "Where do you want to go?" she asked him as she hauled out the phone book that held the restaurant numbers.

After much discussion they decided on a small French restaurant in the suburbs. Lynn was relieved he'd agreed, since the atmosphere of a small room would be less daunting for him. She dialed the number and made the reservation.

"All set," she announced as she put down the phone. "Eight o'clock it is."

"Great. I'm going to need you to help me pick out what to wear tonight."

She frowned at him. There was something different about him today. He seemed really excited about the prospect of dinner.

She felt a flicker of excitement as she watched his face. Maybe he was beginning to realize how much she meant to him. Was that what this dinner was all about? Was he going to ask her to stay, after all?

Her heart skipped as she began to think about the practicalities. She'd have to give up her job in Portland, of course, and move up to Seattle. Unless she could talk him into moving down there.

Hold it, she warned herself. She should know better than to count on daydreams. That's what heartaches were made of, and no one knew it better than she did. However, she could see no harm in good old-fashioned hope.

"Just tell me what you want to wear and I'll find it," she said, picking up the bag with her dress in it. "I'm going to hang this up before it gets full of creases."

He was in the kitchen when she came back, making a pot of coffee. He was so sure of himself, she thought, watching him from the doorway. It was almost uncanny the way he laid his hands so confidently on everything.

"I have to take some clothes to the laundry," she said after they'd finished the coffee. "Do you want to go with me?"

"No, I think I'll catch up on my sleep and take a nap." He grinned, straight at her face. "I'll need my energy for tonight."

She wasn't sure if he meant the dinner or afterward. He was taking a hell of a lot for granted, she thought as she walked up the pathway to the laundromat. It would serve him right if she made him sleep alone tonight.

Who are you kidding? she asked herself as she pushed open the door. One word from him, one brush of his lips, and she was putty in his hands. She had to be the biggest idiot in the world to go on hoping, yet something kept urging her on.

After washing the clothes, she dumped them in a vacant dryer, then decided to call her parents. They had been so upset with her the last time she'd spoken to them, she thought as she crossed over to the general store, she hoped she could smooth things over this time.

To her dismay she saw Jamie Morris leaning against the counter, deep in conversation with the manager. The last person she felt like dealing with just then was Jamie. Twisting around, she walked back to the laundromat.

It wouldn't hurt to call her parents from the mobile home for once, she decided. Now that she and Ward had resolved all that mess of the past, she didn't need to worry so much about him being there. She collected the clothes, then hurried back down the path, anxious to be back with Ward.

He wasn't in the living room when she opened the door. Deciding he must still be asleep, she dumped the clothes on the couch and crossed to the phone.

Her mother answered, sounding anxious, as usual. "Have you decided when you're coming home?" she asked as soon as Lynn had greeted her.

"I'm not sure. Probably in a few days. I'll let you know." Lynn's heart skipped. How would they take the news, she wondered, if Ward did ask her to stay? How long could she keep them from finding out who he really was?

"So is your friend coming with you?"

The abrupt question took her by surprise. "No, of course not," she said quickly. "He has his work up here."

"You never told us what he does. And when are we going to meet him? Anyone would think you're ashamed of us or something."

"I'm not ashamed of you, Mother," Lynn protested. "It's just that he's . . . pretty tied up most of the time, and it isn't easy to get away."

"We know nothing about him. We don't even know his name."

"I haven't told you his name because I'm not sure how things will work out between us."

"What difference does that make? Supposing we had to get in touch with you. How would we find you if we don't know where you're staying?"

Lynn closed her eyes. "I gave you a number where you could reach me."

"A convenience store way out in the wilds? What good would that be?"

"It's not out in the wilds, Mother. It's a couple of hundred yards away. I explained to you that there's no phone where I'm staying. Besides, I'll probably be home soon."

"Well, I certainly hope so," Ellen Barclay said, blowing a loud sigh down the phone. "I'll be glad when you're here and I can get to the bottom of this. I can't help feeling that there's something going on you're not telling us about."

"Nothing is going on," Lynn said firmly. "I am fine, and I will be home in a few days. I'll call you again as soon as I know exactly when, okay?"

She hung up, shaking her head. Sooner or later she would have to tell them. But it wasn't going to be on the phone. This was something she would have to do face-to-face.

She began sorting and folding clothes and had almost finished the task when she heard Ward speak behind her.

"I'm glad you're back. I've decided to go for a walk."

She looked up, and the expression on his face gave her a flutter of apprehension. It was the same closed look he'd worn so many times in the early days of his recovery. "Ward?" She moved toward him, her eyes searching his face. What had happened to give him that look? Had he had one of his nightmares again?

She reached him and put a hand on his arm as she usually did. "What is it, Ward? Is something wrong?"

He shook his head and gently pulled away from her grasp. "Nothing's wrong. I just need some fresh air. I'm going for a walk."

"Do you want me to come?"

"No, I won't be long."

He strode toward the door and she snatched up his cane from its spot in the corner. "Here, you'll need your cane."

He paused, his back toward her, then held out his hand. She put the cane in it.

"Ward, don't go without telling me what's wrong."

"I told you, nothing's wrong. You've got to stop worrying about me." The door slammed behind him, leaving her staring after him in hurt bewilderment.

For almost an hour she paced the floor, trying to figure out what could have gone wrong. He'd been fine when she left. She went over everything she'd said again and again, but could come up with no sound reason for his attitude.

The longer she waited, the more worried she got. He was so damned unpredictable, she thought, moving back to the window for the tenth time. She couldn't keep up with his change of moods. She pulled back the drapes, then froze.

Ward was walking back along the path, striding confidently at a fast pace with his cane tucked underneath his arm. She didn't realize the significance of that—until she saw Jamie Morris skip up to him.

Without hesitation, he sidestepped off the path as she reached him, lifted his hand in greeting, then stepped back on the path after he'd passed her. A few steps farther on, he turned his head and looked over his shoulder at Jamie's retreating figure.

He looked back. Numb with shock, Lynn let the curtain drop back in place. He could see. As unbelievable as it seemed, she couldn't mistake the confident gestures and the sure step.

A torrent of mixed emotions tore through her. He could see. He could live a normal life again. He could fly again. Happiness for him made her giddy, until the questions brought her back to earth with a jolt.

When had he recovered his sight? And why hadn't he told her? She stood rooted in the middle of the living room, feeling as if the earth had just split in two.

The door opened and he walked through, coming to an abrupt halt when he saw her face. Her heart turned over. His eyes were focused directly on her.

"How long have you been able to see?" She felt faintly surprised that her voice could be so calm.

He raised his chin in a defensive gesture that chilled her. "Since this morning. That's why I went to the hospital. I wasn't sure at first, things were pretty fuzzy, but it's getting clearer all the time.''

"I see. And you didn't think it was important enough to tell me?'' She watched him cross the floor and sit down. How could she not have noticed? she wondered. She'd known there was something different about him—but this? It was so incredible it was almost laughable—except that she felt as if she were breaking apart inside.

"I was going to tell you tonight,'' Ward said quietly. "That's why I wanted to go out to dinner. To celebrate.'' He shrugged. "I figured you'd be happy for me and that you'd be able to go home without worrying about me anymore.''

Stunned, she could only stare at him. She couldn't believe what he was trying to tell her.

"You kept your part of the deal,'' Ward said, dropping his gaze to his hands, "and I'm grateful for that. I appreciate all the time you've spent with me and all the help you've given me.''

He hesitated for an instant, then looked up, and the chill that had begun in her heart spread through her body. She could see nothing but a faint apology in his eyes. "Now that I can see again,'' he added, "my problems are finally over. I'll be going back to California, back to the base.''

She wanted to hit him. She wanted to throw something. Anything to hurt him the way he was hurting her now. Her throat ached, but she was damned if she was going to cry. Why was she hurting like this? she thought. Wasn't this what she'd expected all along?

But not this way, her heart cried. *Not this way.*

Until that moment she had no idea how much she'd hoped he could love her. Her silent laughter burned with bitterness. What a fool she'd been. He could see now. He didn't need her anymore. He'd been using her, after all.

In spite of her best efforts, in spite of the certainty that she was about to make a colossal fool of herself, she said tightly,

"A dinner and a dress. Payments for services rendered, is that it?"

He stared at her across the room, his gray eyes glinting steel. He held the gaze for a long moment, while her heart pounded and her throat ached. "If that's the way you want to look at it," he said finally.

"Oh, that's the way I look at it, all right."

"Charlie..." He held up his hands in a gesture of apology. "I'm sorry, but I never made any promises."

"No," she said more calmly. "You didn't. And I'm very happy that you've recovered your sight. I'm sure the Navy will be delighted to have you back as good as new."

He nodded. "Thanks."

She couldn't go on with this any longer, she thought. She had to get out now, before she broke down completely. "Under the circumstances, since you don't need me around anymore, I think I'll go and pack. If I leave now I can get out of town before the rush hour."

She saw his mouth tighten and thought she saw a brief flash of pain cross his face, then it was gone.

"I guess that would be the best thing," he said gravely.

Alone in her room, she dragged out the suitcase and flung it on the bed. The last time she'd done this, he'd come to the door and... Stop it, she told herself fiercely. He'd still been blind then, and still needed her. Now everything had changed.

She opened the drawers and dragged out clothes, flinging them into the suitcase without caring if they creased or not. She was glad that he could see again. Of course she was glad. Now she wouldn't have to spend the rest of her life worrying about him, wondering how he was managing all the little things she'd done for him the past few weeks.

She opened the closet and dragged out the rest of her clothes. Everything except the black dress. She left it hanging there and shut the door. She wouldn't give him another thought, she promised herself, as she closed the lid of her suitcase.

Lugging it off the bed, she prayed that he wouldn't still be in the living room. She was going to leave with her dignity intact, she vowed, if it killed her.

Her heart sank when she saw him standing by the front door, his face once more an impassive mask. "Lynn," he said, as she crossed the room toward him, "I want you to know I'll always be grateful for everything you've done. I'll never forget what you did for me."

The hot memory of her abandoned response to his love-making made her cheeks burn. "Think nothing of it, Commander," she said crisply. "It was all part of the service."

"It wasn't like that." For a moment his silver gaze faltered. "You know it wasn't like that."

"Do I?" She reached the door and grasped the handle. Looking straight into his eyes she said quietly, "I hope you consider the debt paid, Ward."

"That goes both ways."

She smiled—a grim smile full of bitterness. "Oh, I do, Commander Sullivan—I do. Paid in full." She jerked open the door, stepped through and closed it gently behind her.

Chapter 12

"Are you going to tell me what's been happening?" Marjorie asked as Lynn sat down in her office less than a week later. "I expected you to come back and tell me you were quitting your job."

The remark cut a little too deep, and Lynn winced. "No such luck. You'll have to put up with me for a while longer, I guess." She'd hoped to pass the question off, but Marjorie knew her too well.

The editor's shrewd gaze sharpened. "Want to tell me about it?"

Lynn began to shake her head, then slumped in her chair. She needed to talk, and Marjorie was the only person she could confide in. "Do I have your promise that this is off the record?"

"Of course." Marjorie put down her pencil and leaned back. "You don't have to ask, you know. This is personal, I can see that."

"Yes," Lynn said. "This is very personal."

She left nothing out. She told it all, including her own idiotic belief that Ward could actually be falling in love with her. "I should have expected it," she said, after she'd recounted her last hours with him. "I knew he'd never forgotten Sarah. He'll never love anyone the way he loved her."

"The man's an arrogant fool, and he doesn't deserve a woman like you." Marjorie leaned forward, her eyes gleaming behind her glasses. "So, how about doing the whole story for me? You don't have to make it a personal issue, just the facts. The fact that he was blind because he couldn't face his past, and how finally coming to terms with it all gave him back his sight."

"No!" Lynn looked in alarm at her friend. "I don't want the story published. Not by me, not by anyone."

"But look what it might do for your career. It would make a super story, it might even get picked up by—"

"Marjorie!" Lynn pushed back her chair and jumped to her feet. "You're not listening to me. I said no story, and you gave me your word."

"Okay, okay." Marjorie flapped her bright red fingernails in the air. "Don't get your hormones in an uproar. I promised, and I'll keep it under wraps. But if you're doing this out of some cockeyed loyalty to a no-good bum who doesn't know a good thing when it's thrust under his nose, you're wasting a great opportunity."

"I'm doing this because a lot of people could get hurt if I went public with it. Not just Commander Ward Sullivan."

"If you say so." Marjorie peered over the top of her glasses. "You going to be okay?"

"I'm going to be fine. Which reminds me . . . I have work to do." Lynn reached the door and looked back at the woman behind the desk. "Thanks for listening."

Marjorie smiled. "Hey, what are friends for?"

Lynn closed the door and leaned against it for a moment, more upset by her confession than she'd been willing to admit. She had promised herself she wouldn't think about Ward Sullivan again, but after telling the whole story to Marjorie she could see things a lot more clearly.

She couldn't blame Ward, she thought, as she walked back to her office. As he'd said, he'd never made her any promises. He'd given her a choice that first night together, and she'd made her decision...willingly and knowing what she was getting into. It wasn't his fault if he hadn't been able to love her. It wasn't anyone's fault that after eighteen years, Sarah still had possession of his heart.

She had to let go, she told herself, as she walked slowly back to her office. She had to let go of a lot of things. She had to put the past behind her—all of it, not just Ward— and start over again.

She opened the door of the office and walked inside. Maybe a new job, a new town. But first she would have to deal with her parents. All her life she'd been protected and dictated to by them. It was that same tight control over Sarah that had destroyed her.

She had to break free. And that meant confronting her parents about Ward. She'd been making the same mistakes they had. She'd protected her parents and in doing so, perpetuated an injustice that should have been put right a long time ago. They had to know the truth. She had to clear Ward's name, even if he never knew about it. It was the least she could do for him now.

Her parents were surprised to see her, since she'd already turned down an earlier invitation to dinner. "I rearranged my schedule," she told them when her father reminded her of that fact. "I had something important to talk to you about, and it couldn't wait."

"You're not getting married, are you?" her mother exclaimed, wide-eyed with concern.

"No, I'm not getting married." Though she wished with all her heart that she could have made that announcement. "Actually this concerns someone else."

She sat on the armchair that had been reupholstered twice since she'd curled up in it as a child to read her books. It was almost as familiar to her body as her own skin yet at that moment she felt like a stranger in the room she'd known all her life.

She faced her parents, who sat side by side on the couch, and tried to think where to begin. There didn't seem to be any right place, and in the end, she came right to the point.

"Do you remember," she said to her father, "the diary you gave me after Sarah died?"

She heard her mother's gasp of pain, and it became hers. But she had to go on now. It was already too late to go back.

Her father looked at her with eyes that had lost their customary warmth. "Vaguely. What about it?" His tone clearly said, *And why are you bringing this up now?*

"You never read it, did you?"

She waited for the brief shake of his head before saying, "Well, I did. Sarah wrote in it—that last day. She never meant to kill herself. She took the pills and alcohol because someone had told her it would abort the baby."

Her mother's strangled cry unnerved her, but she pushed relentlessly on. "It's also clear, from what Sarah wrote, that Ward Sullivan never knew about the baby until after Sarah died. He was telling the truth. She never told him."

Lynn watched her father's face turn from white to red. She could feel her heart banging wildly against her ribs and wished she were anywhere else but in this room, breaking the hearts of the people she loved most.

"Your mother and I don't want to talk about this," George Barclay said, his voice tight with pain. "I have no idea why you feel it necessary to bring all this up now, but—"

"The friend I've been staying with in Seattle," Lynn said deliberately, "is Ward Sullivan."

She listened to her father's harsh breathing as she watched shock, disbelief and bewilderment cross her mother's face in quick succession. Lynn felt a moment's apprehension as the color faded from her mother's fragile features. She would never forgive herself, Lynn thought, if her mother got sick because of this confrontation.

Then Ellen Barclay leaned forward, anger bringing a flush back to her cheeks. "I never thought a daughter of mine would stoop so low."

Lynn winced. "He needed help, Mother. He was blinded in an accident. After everything we'd done to him, after all the terrible things we said, I felt I owed him. I needed to help him, so that I could feel better about what we did."

"What we did? What about what he did? It was his baby. If he hadn't made...my daughter pregnant, she'd be alive today. He killed your sister. He deserves everything that happens to him."

Lynn jumped to her feet. "Haven't you heard anything I've said? Hasn't it occurred to you to wonder why Sarah never told you about the baby?"

"Lynn—" her father began, but she whirled on him. "Sarah was scared of you both. She was ashamed of what she'd done and frightened you'd break up her relationship with Ward. You were always telling her what to do, trying to run her life, just like you've both tried to run mine."

"Wait a minute," George Barclay put in harshly. "That's not fair. We've always done our best for you, and for Sarah. Darn it, Lynn, we loved you both. No one could have loved you more."

"I know." Lynn's voice cracked, and she took a moment to compose herself. "But sometimes, you can go too far. It's very hard to step back and watch someone you love make their own mistakes. I know that. But sometimes, you have to love enough to let go."

"We only wanted you to be happy," her father said, looking confused. "We wanted Sarah to be happy. Ward Sullivan was a street bum, she deserved better than that. She could have done so much better than that."

"Wasn't that her decision to make?"

"She was seventeen. What did she know about life?" He shook his head. "Anyway, we never said she couldn't see him."

Lynn uttered a mirthless laugh. "No, you just made it obvious he wasn't welcome. You even made me feel uncomfortable the way you treated him."

"Are you saying that it was our fault Sarah killed herself?"

For a moment Lynn had forgotten her mother, and the frail voice shook her. Anxious to reassure her, she said gently, "It wasn't anyone's fault, Mother. It was an accident. A tragic accident. It wasn't your fault, or mine and it certainly wasn't Ward's."

Her mother looked at her reproachfully. "I can't believe you spent all that time with that . . . man and didn't tell us. You've never lied to us before, Lynn. I knew you'd changed, and he's the one to blame for it."

Lynn looked at her father, holding her hands out to him in appeal. "Can't either of you understand that Ward is the victim in all this? Do you have any idea what his life has been like all these years? If it's any consolation to either of you, he's never forgotten Sarah. He's never stopped loving her. And it's ruining his life." *And mine,* she added silently.

"I'm tired," Ellen Barclay said, getting to her feet. "I'm going to bed."

Lynn watched her cross the room, waiting for a word that never came. Her mother walked out the door without a backward glance. Trying to calm the tremble in her voice, Lynn muttered, "I'd better go home."

Her father followed her to the front door. As she pulled it open, he said awkwardly, "Give us time, kitten. This has all been a shock to us."

Lynn glanced back and gave him a wistful smile. "I know. I'm sorry. But I felt you should know."

"What about... this guy? Is he all right now?"

She nodded, catching her lower lip between her teeth. "I love him, Daddy. But he doesn't love me. He'll never love anyone but Sarah. Tell Mother that, when she's ready to listen."

He shrugged, looking embarrassed. "I don't know if we'll ever be able to talk about it again."

"That's sad." Lynn stepped out into the night and turned to look at her father. "You won't learn to live with it unless you do." She heard the door close behind her as she walked down the path, and the sound filled her with pain.

She cried herself to sleep that night, wondering how Ward was doing and if he was back in California. She also wondered if she would ever be able to forget the passion she had known in his arms and the intense emotions only he had been able to arouse.

Several hundred miles away Ward lay in his bed, staring at the ceiling. He'd been in California for two days, and still he couldn't put her out of his mind. He'd thought that once he got back to the base and immersed himself in the military life again, he'd be too busy to dwell on memories he'd sooner forget.

He'd known before he arrived that his stint with the Angels was over. Although he'd recovered his sight, his vision was still unpredictable, and he hadn't really been surprised when he'd learned he'd been replaced permanently by the pilot who'd filled in for him while he'd recuperated.

He'd received his new orders that morning and would be shipping out for Honolulu at the end of the week. In five days, he told himself, he could put three thousand miles and an ocean between him and the memory of an experience that shouldn't have happened.

He turned on his side and closed his eyes. Who was he trying to kid? He could put himself on Mars and it wouldn't help. Every time he shut his eyes he could hear her voice, as warm as a caress, encouraging, gently scolding and, most disturbing of all, murmuring soft sounds of pleasure.

He would wake up still tingling from the remembered touch of sensitive fingers that could drive him wild. She invaded his dreams and tormented his days, until he could hardly think straight anymore.

He kept seeing her direct blue gaze clouded with pain, and his answering agony was almost unbearable. How was he going to survive the rest of his life without her?

He asked himself that question once before. After Sarah had died. At the time it had seemed impossible that he would ever find happiness with a woman again. But he had. And it was far more intense this time than the way he'd felt with Sarah.

He sat up and peered at his alarm clock . . . 3:00 a.m. He didn't even feel sleepy. What was she doing right now? he wondered. Was she sleeping, or was she, like him, wide awake and hurting with the hunger that wouldn't go away?

Cursing, he threw back the covers and wandered over to the window. He could see the lights of the base clearly from his bedroom. Once, the sight had filled him with a warm sense of belonging every time he'd looked at them.

For a long time, when he thought he'd never see them again, he thought he'd die for one more glimpse of those twinkling lights. Now he would die for a glimpse of something else. A beautiful woman who should have known better than to get tangled up with someone like him.

Sighing, he reached for his jeans and pulled them on. He needed some fresh air, he decided. Maybe then he could sleep. He found his shoes in the dark and slipped them on. Tugging a sweater over his head, he headed for the door.

Outside, the night sky was shrouded by mist, masking the stars. In the distance he could see the faint glow of the city, and from the sea the cool night wind carried the muffled moan of a foghorn. It seemed to echo the ache of misery in his heart.

He had done the right thing, he told himself, as he began walking toward the airfield. He had hurt her, he knew, but it was better this way.

He heard the whine of the jet engine as a plane rolled out of the hanger. Someone was getting in some night practice. He would fly again, he'd been told. As soon as his vision stabilized. He could hardly wait until that day.

The whine accelerated to a roar, vibrating along the ground beneath his feet. He watched the wing lights stream past him as the jet raced down the runway, then lifted off like a hungry eagle for the sky.

Ward watched the tiny pinpoints of light until they faded from view. Soon he'd be able to soar like that again. And once more he'd be free.

He stood for a long time, staring into the starless sky until his neck ached and his body chilled in the damp, misty air. Then he turned and strode purposefully back to his quarters.

The dry leaves crackled under Lynn's feet as she strolled across the damp grass of the park. Sunlight, pale and without warmth, penetrated with ease through the bared branches of the cottonwoods that lined the path.

She paused to let a jogger pound by, his breath misting the cool air in front of him. A crimson leaf drifted down in his wake, and Lynn watched it settle on the ground.

Was everything she saw going to remind her of Ward forever? she wondered. It didn't matter if she was in the park or in her office, awake or tormented by dreams, his face haunted her.

Every time she saw a certain walk, a pair of broad shoulders, a dark head, her heart seemed to stop. Like right now, she thought, as she watched a tall, straight-backed figure marching down the path toward her. He even looked Navy, she realized in disgust, with those dark blue pants and a bomber jacket over his blue shirt.

She raised her gaze to his face as he came closer, and her heart stilled. The face she had seen so many times in her dreams, the face she had thought she would never see again, the wonderful, handsome face she would never stop loving, halted right in front of her.

"Hello, Charlie," Ward said quietly.

A hundred questions burst through her mind. Questions she was afraid to ask. Questions she desperately wanted answered. She settled on one, knowing it was the only safe one. "How did you know where to find me?"

"Your father told me you would be here."

Of all the answers she'd expected, that was the last one. She stared at him, her heart overflowing with all the things she couldn't say, and felt a tiny flicker of hope.

She dismissed it almost at once. She'd hoped before. She didn't have the capacity for any more. She'd used it all up. Whatever he wanted to say to her, it couldn't possibly be what she wanted to hear.

"What were you doing talking to my father?" She felt a sudden stab of anxiety. "He's all right, isn't he? I mean, nothing's wrong?"

She saw his face change instantly and knew how that must have sounded. She steeled herself against the pain she saw there.

"Of course he's all right. What do you take me for?"

She shook her head. "I don't know. I thought he might...I don't know what I thought." She looked up at him, trying to hide the misery that almost overwhelmed her. "What do you want, Ward?"

"I want to talk to you. Let's find somewhere to sit down."

She wanted to run, as fast and as far as she could. She didn't want to hear any more of his excuses, his reasons for hurting her. She knew now why he'd gone to see her father. He'd been angry that she wouldn't tell her parents the truth, so he'd decided to do it himself.

He'd probably found out that she'd already told them and, in his usual noble way, wanted to thank her. Well, she didn't want his thanks. She didn't want anything from him—

"Don't look at me like that, Charlie. I don't want to hurt you."

She lowered her face, aware of what must be in her eyes. "So what do you want?"

He took her arm, and she had to summon all her willpower not to snatch it away. His fingers burned through her jacket, warming her in spite of herself.

"I want to sit down," he said firmly, "so that I can talk to you without worrying that you're going to take to your heels any second."

She didn't answer, though the questions buzzed so loud in her mind she felt dizzy. She let him lead her toward a park bench, sheltered beneath an aging sycamore. She no longer felt chilled. His body blocked the cool draught of wind that swept down from the mountains to play with the dying leaves.

"Is your sight fully recovered?" she asked, more for something to say than anything. She could tell he had no trouble seeing.

"Yes. Though it will take a while longer for it to stabilize."

"So you'll be flying again?"

"Not for a while. And not for the Angels. I'm shipping out to Honolulu in a few days."

She tried not to show the dismay his words had caused. "A ground post?"

"Yeah."

"I hope it won't be for too long. I know how much you love flying."

He shifted his body to face her. "Lynn—"

"Did you see my mother?" she asked abruptly, afraid to look at him now.

"I talked to both your parents, yes."

Lynn watched a squirrel race across the path. It paused and sat up to turn its head around at them before darting off again. "I told them," she said, a trace of defiance in her voice.

"I know. I was...surprised you'd told them...everything."

"So were they."

With a hint of dry humor he murmured, "I can imagine."

"I felt they should know. They blamed you for something that wasn't your fault. They wouldn't listen to you all those years ago—I had to make them listen to me now."

"That must have been difficult for you. I'm grateful for what you did, I know what it must have cost you."

There is was—gratitude. It was the last thing she wanted from him. "I did it for me, as well," she said stiffly. "I'd tried to protect them all these years, at your expense. That was wrong. I knew that I would never be able to break free and be my own person if I didn't make a stand." She sighed. "I'm afraid I hurt them, but I hope they'll soon come around and try to understand."

"I'm sure they will...eventually."

Something in his voice alerted her. "Did they give you a hard time?"

His elbow bumped hers as he flicked at a leaf that had landed on his knee. She shifted away from him and watched the leaf spin like a tiny propeller blade to the ground.

"They weren't too anxious to talk to me at first," Ward admitted. "But when I told them why I was there, they finally agreed to listen."

Lynn lifted her head, her pulse skipping as she met his intense gray gaze. "But they already knew everything about Sarah."

"I know. That made it easier, but that wasn't the main reason I went to see them."

Something in his face started her heart pounding again. Her voice sounded a little too high when she asked, "So what was the main reason?"

He lifted his face to the sky for a moment, and she studied his profile, trying desperately to see what was in his mind. "I did a lot of thinking after you'd left," he said, lowering his chin to look at her. "I know I hurt you, and I wanted you to know why I sent you away."

She tore her gaze away, back to the pile of leaves swirling in the wind. She didn't want him to see the hope that had to be burning in her eyes. "You already told me why you did that. You were going back to your job. You didn't need me anymore."

She couldn't help the bitterness that had crept into her voice. She knew he'd heard it when he said, "I'm sorry, Charlie. But I knew if I told you the truth, you would've given me an argument about leaving."

Still she couldn't look at him. "The truth?"

"Yeah." Ward sighed, and she knew how hard this was for him. But she couldn't help him this time. Now he was on his own.

"I heard you talking to your mother that last day," Ward said, "and I realized you hadn't told them about me. I also realized why. You couldn't. They would never accept me, and you couldn't hurt them all over again. You would have to make a choice, and I couldn't ask you to make a choice like that."

She was surprised by her anger. "Why not, Ward? Did you think I'd choose them? Did you really think I'd turn my back on you because my parents didn't think you were good enough for me?"

"I was afraid that you would choose me and then regret it. I know your last marriage broke up because of your loyalty to your parents. After all, blood is thicker than water. I could see that happening again. I know how much they mean to you, and I guess I didn't want to face the possibility of losing you. I know how that feels. I didn't want to go through that kind of pain again. I figured it was easier to break it off now, before I got in too deep."

"I don't—"

He held up his hand. "Wait, let me finish. I couldn't sleep the other night, so I got up and went for a walk. I watched a jet taking off, and I thought about how I'd soon be flying again. And how I'd soon be free again. And the longer I thought about it, the more I realized that even in the sky I wouldn't be free, because my heart didn't belong up there anymore. It belonged to a certain beautiful, kind, caring woman right here on the ground, and that was something I could never escape."

She could hardly breathe, the hope was so suffocating.

"I realized I was still running," Ward went on. "I didn't want to run anymore. I had to take a chance if I was going to be happy again. I knew I had to go and see your parents. I had to tell them that I loved their daughter and intended to ask her to marry me. I had to tell them that in spite of any objections they might have, if their daughter would have me, for her sake I hoped they would accept me.''

For some ridiculous reason she was crying again. He was the only person in the world who could make her cry like an idiot. ''What did they say?''

''They weren't too happy. They're afraid I'll hurt you again. I swore I'd take care of you to the best of my ability as long as I drew breath, but I'm not sure they're convinced.''

He shrugged. ''Maybe your father is, but your mother's going to take some working on. She still thinks of me as a no-good kid from the wrong side of the tracks.''

Her breath came out in a sob and she choked it back. She looked up, meeting his gaze, and in that moment knew that she could finally believe the hope filling her heart.

It was the same look that had haunted her dreams since she was twelve years old. The look he used to give to Sarah, the look she'd envied so much. Yet now it was even more special, because it was directed at her. At her!

''I think the important question here,'' Ward said softly, ''is what does their daughter say about all this? Could you possibly love this Navy man enough to live in Honolulu, or anywhere else in the world I happen to be?''

''I already love this Navy man enough to go to the moon if he asked me.''

He smiled, carving the dimple in his cheek once more. ''Then come here, Charlie, and convince me.'' He pulled her into his arms, and she lifted her chin for his kiss. Mindless of anyone who could see them, she answered the questioning passion of his mouth. Pouring all her heart and soul into the healing warmth of his arms, she gave herself up to the sheer joy of showing him how very much she loved him.

When he finally lifted his head, his breathing was ragged. "Do you think your parents would fly out to Hawaii for a wedding?" he asked unsteadily.

She shrugged. "If they want to stay in contact with their daughter they will. And if they want to see their grandchildren."

"Grandchildren?" His eyes lit up, capturing her breath. "How many?"

"How many Navy brats can we afford?"

He grinned. "I think four's a nice round figure. As long as they're not all boys. I don't think I could stand four Navy pilots trying to outdo me in the skies."

She poked a finger at his chest. "Hey, sailor, aren't you forgetting women's lib? Women fly jets now, you know."

"I know." He covered her mouth again with his until she pulled away for breath. "But if you think any daughter of mine is going to take one of those machines up," he added, "you've got another think coming."

"Any daughter of yours, Commander Sullivan, would have a mind of her own. You wouldn't be able to stop her."

He looked at her for a long moment, then threw back his head and laughed. The joyful sound rose through the branches of the sycamore, disturbing an indignant blue jay. The bird rose with an angry flutter of wings and flew across the grass, squawking its outrage.

Lynn watched it go, then looked back at the man she loved. She had waited a long time, and they had been through a lot of pain together, but it was worth every single minute of it.

She listened to Ward's laughter and hoped that Sarah would approve. Then, as he turned to her once more and gathered her into his arms, the last of the late-autumn sun fell across her face, warming her skin.

She smiled. She knew, without a doubt, that Sarah approved. She had just sent her blessing. *I love you, Ward,* Lynn thought, sending the message in her heart, then repeating it aloud to the man she loved more than life itself. "I love you, Ward."

"I love you too, Charlie. More than you'll ever know." And with his kiss, he finally convinced her.

*   *   *   *   *

From the popular author of the bestselling title
DUNCAN'S BRIDE (Intimate Moments #349)
comes the

LINDA HOWARD

COLLECTION

Two exquisite collector's editions that contain four of
Linda Howard's early passionate love stories. To add
these special volumes to your own library, be sure
to look for:

VOLUME ONE: *Midnight Rainbow*
                  Diamond Bay
                  (Available in March)

VOLUME TWO: *Heartbreaker*
                  White Lies
                  (Available in April)

 *Silhouette Books*®

SLH92

Silhouette Special Edition

salutes

MOMENTS OF GLORY

from Lindsay McKenna

In a country torn with conflict, in a time of bitter passions, these brave men and women wage a war against all odds... and a timeless battle for honor, for fleeting moments of glory, for the promise of enduring love.

February: RIDE THE TIGER (#721) Survivor Dany Villard is wise to the love-'em-and-leave-'em ways of war, but wounded hero Gib Ramsey swears she's captured his heart...forever.

March: ONE MAN'S WAR (#727) The war raging inside brash and bold Captain Pete Mallory threatens to destroy him, until Tess Ramsey's tender love guides him toward peace.

April: OFF LIMITS (#733) Soft-spoken Marine Jim McKenzie saved Alexandra Vance's life in Vietnam; now he needs her love to save his honor....

SILHOUETTE® Desire™

The Case of the Mesmerizing Boss
DIANA PALMER

Diana Palmer's exciting new series,
MOST WANTED, begins in March with
THE CASE OF THE MESMERIZING BOSS....

Dane Lassiter—one-time Texas Ranger
extraordinaire—now heads his own group of
crack private detectives. Soul-scarred by
women, this heart-stopping private eyeful
exists only for his work—until the night his
secretary, Tess Meriwether, becomes the target
of drug dealers. Dane wants to keep her safe.
But their stormy past makes him the one man
Tess *doesn't* want protecting her....

Don't miss THE CASE OF THE MESMERIZING
BOSS by Diana Palmer, first in a lineup of
heroes MOST WANTED! In June, watch for THE
CASE OF THE CONFIRMED BACHELOR... only
from Silhouette Desire!

SDDP-1

MOST WANTED

NORA ROBERTS

Love has a language all its own, and for centuries, flowers have symbolized love's finest expression. Discover the language of flowers—and love—in this romantic collection of 48 favorite books by bestselling author Nora Roberts.

Starting in February, two titles will be available each month at your favorite retail outlet.

In March, look for:

Irish Rose, Volume #3
Storm Warning, Volume #4

In April, look for:

First Impressions, Volume #5
Reflections, Volume #6

Collect all 48 titles and become fluent in

THE LANGUAGE of LOVE